PAINT IT BLACK

Mark Timlin's Nick Sharman thrillers have established him as Britain's leading writer of hardboiled detective fiction. Born in south London, where he still lives, he worked for many years in the rock'n'roll business but is now a full-time writer. Carlton TV is currently producing a TV series, following a successful pilot in 1995, starring Clive Owen as Sharman and due for transmission in autumn 1996. Mark Timlin has written twelve Sharman novels. *Find My Way Home*, the latest in the series, is published in Gollancz hardcover.

markTimlin
PAINT IT BLACK

VISTA

author's note:

I have had to take some liberties with the
timings of various festivals up and down
the country. My apologies to all concerned.

First published in Great Britain 1995
by Victor Gollancz

This Vista edition published 1996
Vista is an imprint of the Cassell Group
Wellington House, 125 Strand, London WC2R 0BB

© Mark Timlin 1995

The right of Mark Timlin to be identified as author of
this work has been asserted by him in accordance with
the Copyright, Designs and Patents Act, 1988.

A catalogue record for this book is
available from the British Library.

ISBN 0 575 60014 4

Printed and bound in Great Britain by
Cox & Wyman Ltd, Reading, Berkshire.

96 97 98 99 10 9 8 7 6 5 4 3 2 1

For Robyn

1947–1995

I woke last night and spoke to you
not thinking you were gone.

part one

east of eden's gate

The modern ecstasy; A dead man's knell.
Macbeth

1

Dawn and I were living the straight life when it started. As straight as we could, anyway. With our history.

We'd been married just over a year, and after Dawn had helped me on a case involving a dead rock star who wasn't. Dead, I mean. We were just kicking back and letting the dust settle.

There was nothing stronger in the house than a bottle or two of German beer and some vodka. We had plenty of money and we spent it on eating out, going to the movies and generally having a good time. Don't knock it till you've tried it.

Then one Sunday evening my ex-wife called me up.

There were no preliminaries. 'Are they there?' she demanded.

'Who?' I recognized Laura's voice straight away and I didn't expect any endearments. But I thought a 'hello' would have been nice.

'Judith and her little friend. Who else?'

'Why should Judith be here?' I asked. Bit slow on the uptake there, I give in. 'And what friend? I don't know who you're talking about.'

'Because they're gone. Both of them.'

'What? What do you mean?'

'Aren't I making myself clear? Judith has decided to take a little trip. God knows where. She left me a note. And I'm phoning you to find out if you've heard from her.'

'No, I haven't,' I said.

Dawn looked up from the book she was reading. I told you we were living the straight life. We'd already finished the

9

Sunday papers and completed the *Observer* crossword. She gave me a quizzical look.

I covered the mouthpiece of the receiver with one hand and said, 'Judith's done a runner. Laura's checking to see if she's ended up here.'

'I thought she was just punishing me. I thought she'd be back by now,' Laura went on, and her voice broke. I hadn't heard that in a long time.

'Slow down, Laura,' I said. 'Just tell me what's happened.'

So she told me.

'Judith's got a new best friend,' she said. 'I don't like her. I told Judith not to see her any more. She disobeyed me as she does constantly. Judith told me she had a rehearsal for the school play. She lied. She was off with her friend. Now they've both gone.'

'Gone where?'

'If I knew that I wouldn't be telephoning you.'

Fair comment.

'When?'

'Friday night.'

'*Friday!*' I exploded. 'Two days ago. And you're only phoning me now.'

'Don't take that attitude, Nick,' said Laura. 'Don't come on all aggrieved like some kind of perfect father. It won't wash.'

'OK, Laura,' I said tiredly. 'Have you informed the police?'

'Of course.'

'And you told them about me.'

'Yes.'

'They haven't been here.'

'I only told them this afternoon.'

'Bit late.'

'I told you, Nick. Don't start all that. You don't know what Judith's been like lately.'

10

'What has she been like lately?'

'A little bitch. Fourteen going on forty-five.' She paused. 'You should hear the way she speaks to Louis and me.'

Louis is Laura's husband.

Laura paused again. 'She's rude. Aggressive. Sarcastic. Just awful.'

A bit like me, I thought.

'A bit like you, in fact,' Laura went on, as if reading my mind. 'Mixing with the wrong people.'

Again, a bit like me.

'What kind of people?' I asked.

'Girls from the council estate. That's who she's gone missing with. One of them.'

'Who?'

'A girl called Paula. Paula McGann. A little cow. Older than Judith. A foul-mouthed little slut.'

'I can see you welcomed her into your house with open arms.'

'I did, too. Then she went into my purse and stole ten pounds.'

'Big time.'

'Don't make fun of me, Nick. It wasn't amusing.'

'Sorry. You're right. Have you checked the local hospitals?'

'Of course. They're not in hospital. They've run away. I told you she left me a note. They've probably gone to London. I imagined they'd call in on you while they were there.'

'Why?'

'Because *Judith loves her daddy*.' Her voice rose. Then dropped again. 'That's why. You can do no wrong. And I can do no right.'

'Don't get bitter, Laura,' I said.

'Bitter . . . Me bitter.' She laughed with no amusement. 'What do you know?'

11

I didn't reply. Exactly. What did I know? 'Have you got the note there?' I asked.

'Of course.'

'Read it to me, will you?'

'It doesn't say much.'

'That doesn't matter. I'd still like to hear it.'

There was a pause, and I heard the rustle of paper being unfolded.

'"Mum,"' read Laura. '"I'm going away for a bit. With Paula. Down south probably. I've got some money. Don't worry. I'll be in touch. Judith."'

'That's it?'

'That's it.'

'What about the other girl? Paula. Did she leave a note too?'

'I don't think they're very big on leaving notes where she lives. I doubt whether many of her family can read.'

'*Laura.*'

'I'm sorry. I'm just so worried. I phoned her mother. She didn't seem very concerned. Probably glad to see the back of her. And you're sure Judith hasn't been in touch with you?'

'Of course I'm sure. It's hardly something I'd forget,' I said.

There was a long pause. Laura had a strange note of sadness in her voice when she spoke again. 'You're not lying to me are you, Nick? I can imagine what they'd say about me. The Wicked Witch of the West's got nothing on me, according to Judith. If they *are* there and they've convinced you not to tell me . . .' She paused. 'Just tell me. I'm so worried.'

'I'm not lying, Laura,' I said. 'I wouldn't do that.'

'Wouldn't you?'

Of course that brought it all back. All the bad things. All the things that split us up. 'Who the hell do you think I am, Laura?' I demanded. 'If Judith was here I'd tell you. I'd've phoned the minute she showed up. I'm not into scoring points. I'm as worried as you are.'

Dawn got up from where she was sitting in one graceful move and took the phone out of my hand like a relay runner taking the baton. 'Laura,' she said. 'It's Dawn. He's telling the truth. Judith isn't here. And she hasn't been in touch.'

She paused and listened.

'I'll get him on to it right away.' She gave me a sideways look. 'If we hear anything I'll make sure he phones you.'

Another pause.

'All right, Laura. Goodbye.' And she put down the phone. 'Come on then, Nick,' she said. 'You know everyone who's worth knowing. Get on it. Your ex is climbing the walls.'

2

Before I could reply, the flat doorbell rang.

'Cops,' I said. 'Pound to a peanut.'

'Or maybe your wayward daughter and her friend.'

I looked through the window. Outside was a police panda. 'Cops,' I said, and went to answer the front door.

Standing inside the porch were two uniformed constables, a male and a female. They were both young and earnest looking.

'Mr Sharman,' said the male officer.

'That's me.'

'I wonder if we could come inside. It's about your daughter.'

'Sure,' I replied. 'I just had my ex on the phone. Have you heard anything yet?'

'No. We wondered if you had.'

'No,' I said. 'Come on up.'

13

They followed me up the stairs, and I introduced them to Dawn, and the male officer told us that his name was Blair and the female officer was PC Hawkins.

'Sandra,' she said after I'd got them sat somewhere and Dawn had got the kettle on.

'So,' I said, lighting a cigarette and noticing a slight tremble in my fingers as I did so. 'What's the state of play?'

'The usual,' said Blair. 'We've put Judith and Paula McGann on the computer. We've notified the officers who cover the railway stations and coach stations to look out for them. Your wife—'

'Ex-wife,' I corrected him.

He reddened. 'Sorry. Your ex-wife, Mrs . . .' He consulted his notebook. 'Rudnick. Has supplied us with an up-to-date photograph of your daughter. We have photos of the other girl too. Copies are being made. We're checking hospitals, hostels, shelters. Anywhere where two girls who've run away might end up. But there's a lot of places between Aberdeen and here that they might go. If indeed they have come to London. The note she left mentioned "down south", I believe.'

I nodded.

'Like I say. That covers a lot of ground.'

I nodded again.

'But your *ex*-wife thought they might turn up here.'

'They might. But they haven't yet.'

'If they do, you'll be sure to inform us.'

'You'll be the first to hear.'

'I hope that we are.'

At that, I knew that he knew who I was and wasn't very happy about it. Tough shit. I wasn't best pleased myself, but I had to live with it.

There was a moment's strained silence as the copper and I looked at each other.

14

'Jack Robber sends his regards,' said Sandra Hawkins to relieve the tension.

I looked at her. 'Inspector Robber?' I said. 'You must be from Gipsy Hill.'

She nodded.

Inspector Jack Robber was the closest thing I had left to a friend on the force. Christ knows why. We'd been webbed up in a couple of cases together. I hadn't heard from him for a while, and the last time we'd spoken he'd told me he was jacking the job in and going to live by the sea with his sister.

'I thought he'd retired,' I said.

'He decided to spend a few more months in harness,' said Sandra.

'Couldn't face moving to the seaside,' I said. 'Under his sister's thumb.'

The policewoman smiled. 'Something like that,' she said.

'Send him my best back.'

'He said that he'd do anything he could to help,' she went on.

'Tell him thanks. I need someone like him on my side.' And I blimped her colleague again. 'I just hope the pair of them will turn up soon.' And for the first time since Laura had phoned I felt the full significance of what was happening and what the consequences could be for two young girls on their own, out there somewhere, unprotected from the loonies who stalked this once benign country of ours. 'What the hell does Judith think she's doing?' I said.

Neither of the uniformed police answered. It was an impossible question.

Dawn brought the tea. When she gave me mine, she put her hand on my shoulder for comfort. It wasn't much help, but it was something. We all drank in silence.

'You're a private detective,' said Blair, after a moment.

'That's right.'

15

'You've been in some trouble.'

'I attract it.'

'I hope you'll keep out of this.'

'No chance. If there's been no news by tomorrow, first thing, I intend to get very involved.'

'We're the professionals, Mr Sharman.'

'And she's my daughter.'

There wasn't much they could say to that, and the two police officers finished their tea and left. I sat on the sofa, picked up the phone and made a few calls.

3

First of all I called Laura back. She picked up the phone before I heard a ringing tone my end. 'Any news?' I asked.

'No.'

'I just had the boys and girls in blue here. They seemed to think I had Judith and her mate hidden away somewhere.'

'I think I over-reacted when I spoke to the inspector here.'

'You must have. Did you really think I'd have them here for more than a minute without letting you know?'

'I didn't know what to think. I'm sorry, Nick. I was frantic.'

'It's OK. I don't blame you. I know how you feel.' I lit another cigarette. 'Anything could happen to them . . .' I didn't finish the sentence. She didn't need it and nor did I.

'They'll be all right, won't they?' Her voice was little more than a whisper.

'Christ, I hope so, Laura.'

'Can you do anything?'

Things had to be bad if she was asking for my help.

'I can try. I'm going to make some calls. Get a few things

rolling this end. Call me any time tonight if you hear anything at all. I'll do the same to you.'

'I don't want to wake you—'

'I'm not going to get much sleep, Laura. If I had any idea where they were I'd be out now looking. But we mustn't panic. We need to conserve all the energy we've got . . .' I hesitated. Once again I knew she didn't need it, but it had to be said. 'I dealt with a few of these sorts of cases when I was in the job . . .' I hesitated again. 'It could take time.'

I heard Laura sob at the other end of the line and for the first time in years I wanted to hold her.

'Laura. I didn't mean to upset you. We've just got to take it an hour at a time.' Jesus. Me and my big mouth. 'Is Louis there?' I asked after a moment.

'Yes.'

'Can I have a word?'

'Hold on,' she said.

I heard the phone go down with a bang and voices in the background. Then the receiver was picked up again and a male voice said, 'Hello.'

'Louis. Nick.'

'How are you?' As if he could give a shit.

'Could be better,' I said. 'This is a bad do.'

'You don't need to tell me that.'

I knew that I didn't. But I still felt a tinge of resentment towards old Louis. He was the one who ended up with my wife and daughter, and now one had vanished and the other sounded like she was on the verge of a nervous breakdown.

'Yeah. I know,' I said.

There was a long pause.

'I'm sorry,' he said finally.

'You don't have to be. These things happen. I just wish I'd known that things had got so bad.'

'What would you have done?'

'Probably nothing. I'm not pointing fingers, Louis. I'm not apportioning blame. I don't have that right. I'm as much to blame as anyone. Probably more so. All that matters is that we find Judith and her friend safe and well. We can do any sorting out that needs to be done after that. I'm only sorry that Laura thought that I might know where they were and not tell her.'

'She was upset.'

'I know. Listen. If you hear anything overnight, let me know, it doesn't matter what time it is. I probably won't get much sleep anyway. If I don't hear from you by morning, I'll call again. And naturally if *I* hear anything I'll get right on to you.'

'OK, Nick,' said Louis. 'I'll put you back to Laura.'

There was another pause, then Laura spoke again. 'Nick,' she said. 'She will be all right, won't she?'

'Course she will,' I said reassuringly, or at least I hoped it was reassuringly.

Laura wasn't convinced. 'You just read such dreadful things . . .'

'Don't worry. She'll be fine. She's probably hanging out at a mate's.' But even as I said them, I knew how empty those words were.

'No,' said Laura. 'She's gone.'

'Then we'll get her back.'

'I hope so.'

'Count on it. Call me if you hear anything and I'll do the same.'

'All right, Nick.'

'And don't worry.'

More empty words.

'Goodbye,' said Laura, and she put down the phone.

I stood holding the receiver until Dawn took it out of my hand and put it back on the cradle.

She gave me a drink and I got back on the dog. Next I called Gipsy Hill police station. Jack Robber was in, as he always seemed to be. I don't think he's got a home to go to. He answered the phone on the first ring.

'Robber,' he said.

'Nick Sharman,' I said back.

'Sharman. I've been expecting a call from you. I'm sorry to hear about your trouble.'

'Thanks. I've just had a pair of your officers here.'

'It's usual in cases like this.'

'I don't think PC Blair was too enamoured with me.'

'Did you expect him to be?'

'It's not me I care about. It's Judith. And her friend. And their safety.'

'Meaning?'

'Meaning, I hope that the way you lot feel about me won't affect the way you look for them.'

'Don't be stupid. It's not your girl's fault who she's got for a father. We'll look for her the same way we'd look for any missing kid.'

'Jesus, I'm sorry,' I said. 'This is starting to get to me. There's no news, I suppose.'

'Not so far. And I'm keeping an eye out for anything that comes in.'

'I appreciate it. Will you call me if you hear anything? Anything at all, and any time.'

'I will.'

'Thanks, Mr Robber.'

'Don't bother . . . And Sharman . . .'

'What?'

'Don't go going off half cocked. Keep out of this. Leave it to us.'

'That's what Blair said.'

'And what did you say?'

'That if I don't hear anything by tomorrow, I'm going to start looking for her myself.'

'You'll be wasting your time. If we can't find her . . .' He didn't finish the sentence.

'I can't just sit here doing nothing.'

'I know, son,' he said. He'd certainly never called me that before.

'I thought you were up for retirement.' I changed the subject.

'Still am. I'm just hanging on as long as possible.'

'Frightened of your sister?'

'You've never met her. If you had you'd be frightened of her too.'

'And you a big strong copper.'

'She'd frighten the Marine Corps.'

'Listen,' I said, 'I'd better get off now. Just in case . . .'

'Sure. And try not to worry.'

I knew he meant well but they were just more empty words.

'I'll try,' I said, and put down the phone.

Finally, I called my old mate Chas, a journalist who now works for a big Sunday tabloid out of Wapping and who was best man at Dawn's and my wedding. He's helped me out on a couple of cases in the past and is about as close to a real friend as I've got. He was at home. I explained what had happened.

'Sorry, mate. That's a bastard,' he said. 'What can I do?'

'Anything.'

'I'll see if I can get something into the daily paper about it.'

'That's what I'm scared of. I'm worried that they'll dig up my past again.'

'It goes with the territory.'

'It might make things worse.'

20

'If it does, it will anyway. At least I might be able to do a damage limitation.'

'Yeah.' I wasn't totally convinced.

'Look. It's my day off tomorrow, but I'll shoot into the office and see what I can see. I'll get back to you. But if you hear anything first, let me know.'

'I might not be around tomorrow. If nothing turns up tonight I'll probably fly up to Aberdeen in the morning.'

I saw Dawn raise her eyebrows.

'Will Dawn be around?' asked Chas.

'Yeah.'

'Then I'll check in with her.'

'Do that, Chas. And thanks.'

'Don't thank me. I haven't done anything yet.'

'Even so. Thanks.'

'OK, Nick. And take it easy.'

'When don't I?'

'You want a list?'

'No.'

'Right. See you soon.'

'You will.'

And we both hung up.

'Will you go to Aberdeen?' asked Dawn when I'd put the phone down.

'If there's no news by tomorrow. It's a place to start. Don't mind, do you?'

'Course not. Don't be silly. I'd do the same in your shoes.'

'And you don't mind staying down here and holding the fort?'

She shook her head.

'Thanks, love,' I said. She came over and sat next to me on the sofa and put her arm round my shoulder. 'Are you going to get some sleep?'

'I'll stay here,' I said. 'Try and take a nap. I need to be close to the phone.'

'Then I'll stay too.'

And she did.

4

I didn't get much sleep. I was too edgy. And by seven I was up, showered, shaved, dressed and drinking my first cup of coffee. At three minutes past I called Laura. She answered on the second ring, so I assumed there was no news and that she hadn't slept much either, but I asked anyway.

'Nothing,' she said.

'Right. I'm coming up.'

'There's no need . . .'

'Isn't there? I think there is.'

'She's probably closer to you than to here.'

'But at least I can get a better idea of what happened. It's a start.'

'The police —' Once again I didn't let her finish her sentence.

'Sod the police,' I said. 'I'm coming. I'll see you later this morning.'

Then I phoned London airport. BA did a walk on, walk off shuttle service and I could buy a ticket at the airport. Dawn drove me straight over. By nine-fifteen I was on a plane and just before eleven I walked through the main entrance of Aberdeen airport and grabbed a cab.

I'd never been to Laura and Louis's place before and I was impressed. It was a big, ranch-style house in its own grounds just outside of town. There were three cars parked on the

U-shaped drive. A Volvo estate, a Golf GTI and an official-looking dark blue Ford Sierra bristling with aerials that just screamed Old Bill.

I let the car go and walked up the wide, grey stone steps to the front door that looked like it had been pinched from the House of Usher. I rang the bell and Louis opened the door. I hadn't seen him for a couple of years and he wasn't weathering early middle age well. Too much money and booze in general and too little sleep over the weekend in particular, I guessed. He was dressed in baggy jeans, a white polo shirt and a navy blue cardigan. He was putting on weight, especially in the face, and his hair was grey and thin-looking. It made me feel loads better.

'Hello, Nick,' he said. 'Long time.' He didn't offer to shake hands and nor did I.

'Louis,' I said.

'You'd better come in.' As if I'd travelled all that way to stand in the porch and communicate by semaphore.

He stood back and I entered the wide hall, moodily decorated in muted colours. 'Laura's in the lounge,' he said. 'That way.'

He pointed to the left and I walked through another wide door into a room that resembled a set decoration for a BBC production of *Vanity Fair*. All regency stripes and uncomfortable straight-backed armchairs. Not much like the place Laura and I had shared during our marriage, or where I lived now for that matter. No wonder Judith had done a runner. Louis didn't come into the room. Maybe his and Laura's marriage was in a particularly bad shape, or maybe it was just a bad time. Or maybe it was me.

Laura was sitting on the arm of a sofa smoking a cigarette. That was new. A big, burly geezer in a black Burberry was sitting in an armchair balancing a cup on his knee. Laura stood up as I went in.

'Nick,' she said, and came over and embraced me briefly. I hadn't seen her for over a year either, but she looked pretty good, although the cigarette and the tremor in her voice as she'd spoken weren't good signs. But then maybe that was me again.

'Any news?' I asked.

'No. This is Inspector Todd. He's from the local station. Inspector, this is Nick Sharman. My ex-husband. Judith's father.'

The geezer in the mac nodded, but that was all.

I directed my next question to him. 'You've heard nothing at all?'

'No. But we're working on it.'

'Do you want a coffee, Nick?' asked Laura.

'Please. Then I'd like to see Paula McGann's parents if that's possible.' I looked at Todd as I spoke.

'Why?' he asked.

'Because they might know something.'

He shrugged. 'And it's parent by the way. Her mother, Margaret. The old man left about a year ago. We're trying to trace him, but no luck. She thinks he might be on a rig. But we've drawn a blank so far.'

'Bloody people,' said Laura, and left the room.

'She's not taking this too well,' I said.

Todd put his cup on a spindly-looking table and got up. He was about my height, but much bigger built, and the raincoat he was wearing added to his bulk. As I looked at him, I thought that I wouldn't like to meet him in a detention cell on a dark night. Or at high noon for that matter.

'No,' he said. 'But you must have seen that kind of reaction before. You were in the Met, weren't you?'

'That's right.'

'I spoke to a couple of people who knew you. Know you.'

'And?'

'And this is my ground. I don't want you trampling all over it.'

'I've come up here to find out what happened to my daughter, Inspector,' I said. 'That's all that matters to me. Your sensibilities don't have anything to do with it.' It was a stupid thing to say and I regretted the words as soon as I'd uttered them.

'You're not in London now, Sharman,' he said. 'My sensibilities have everything to do with it. I sympathize with what's happened, but don't mess me around or you'll be in trouble.'

'OK, Inspector,' I said. 'Fair enough. This whole deal is doing me in. I'm sorry. I'll try and keep my mouth shut from now on.'

He nodded, and seemed to relax a little. I didn't know who he'd spoken to or what he expected. Me to draw a revolver and shoot out the china figures on the sideboard, maybe. Or challenge him to an arm wrestle to see which of us was toughest. Whatever it was, he was going to be disappointed.

'So what can you tell me about Paula McGann?' I asked instead.

He walked over to the window. 'See those?' he asked, and pointed his finger.

I followed him to where he was standing and looked in the direction that he was pointing. Over the roofs of the houses across the wide road opposite, the top stories of a couple of tower blocks could just be seen in the distance.

'Yeah.'

'The Grace Darling Estate. That's where the McGanns live. It's about as different from here as could be. The people who live in those blocks may look down on these houses, but the people who live here look down on them more.'

I knew the deal. It was the same in Dulwich.

5

Laura came back with my coffee. I drank it and smoked a cigarette. In the time it took me to smoke that one, she lit four and stubbed them out again. I felt sorry for her, but I knew I wouldn't be able to communicate that, so I just shut up.

When my coffee was done, Todd offered me a lift to the McGann residence. I accepted.

All three of us walked out to the blue Sierra. I told Laura I'd be back soon. Todd told her he'd be in touch if he heard anything, but that she could call him at any time. I thought that was decent of him. He and I got into the motor. He started it and we pulled away leaving Laura standing in the driveway looking like a little girl whose puppy just died. I knew how she felt.

Todd steered the car down some increasingly mean streets until he pulled up outside a semi-detached house in a row of identical semis with that certain air of neglect that tells you they're council houses where the tenants haven't taken up the right-to-buy option.

'Twenty-two,' he said nodding in the direction of the most dilapidated house in the street. 'That's Maggie's place.'

The front fence, this side of the square of mud that an optimist might call a front garden, was bowed with the weight of the three young children leaning against it. The front gate was missing, and a rusty tricycle sat on the narrow concrete path that led to the front door.

'Want me to come in?' asked Todd.

'No,' I replied.

'Probably best,' he said. 'We've never been popular in that house. Shall I wait?'

'No thanks. I'll find my own way back. It's not far.'

'Good luck then.'

'Cheers,' I said. 'I expect we'll talk again.'

'Expect so,' he replied, and I got out of the car and waited as he put it into gear and drove off.

The three kids looked at me and I looked back.

'You live here?' I asked.

No response.

I shrugged, and walked through the gap where the gate should have been and up the path, avoiding the tricycle, and on to the porch.

There was no bell, so I knocked hard on the paint-stained translucent square of glass set into the door.

A dog barked somewhere in the house.

I looked back at the kids who had turned and were regarding me steadily, as you might someone who's just stepped out of an alien spaceship.

I turned round and knocked again. The dog barked once more and I heard a woman call out to it, then a figure appeared behind the glass and the door opened.

The woman who answered my knock was small, barely five foot tall I guessed, and pretty much the same wide. She was about thirty-five with long brown hair, and she wore a tight jumper and jeans that didn't suit her figure. Her face was bare of make-up and showed signs of recent tears. In one hand she held a cigarette, in the other a chocolate biscuit.

'Mrs McGann,' I said.

'Aye.'

'My name's Sharman, Nick Sharman. I'm—'

'Judith's daddy,' she said, and her face split into a grin, which lit it from within, and for a moment I saw the attractive young girl she must once have been. 'I've heard all about you. Come on in.'

She held open the door and I walked into the hall. If I'd expected the interior of the house to match the exterior, I was wrong. It was spotless. And although the carpet may have been a bit thin in parts, it was obviously regularly Hoovered.

'Come on through, we're in the kitchen,' she said.

I followed her down the corridor into a fair-sized kitchen which was as clean as the hall. In one corner was a dog basket filled with a pooch who was as fat as his mistress. He looked up at me through the one eye that wasn't hidden by a greying fringe, growled softly, then decided I wasn't worth worrying about, closed the eye, yawned and went to sleep. At the huge kitchen table that dominated the centre of the room sat a girl of about fifteen, with a cup of tea in front of her and a chocolate biscuit of her own, which she popped into her mouth as I entered.

'This is Clare,' introduced Margaret McGann. 'One of Paula's pals. She's come round to keep me company. This is Mr Sharman, Judith's daddy.'

'Nick,' I said.

'Nick,' echoed Paula's mother. 'Sit down, will you.'

I did as she said and she sat opposite me. 'Are you all right, Mrs McGann?' I asked.

'Call me Margaret,' she said.

I nodded. 'Margaret,' I said.

'As well as I can be with what's happened. When I get hold of Paula I'll tan her backside, big as she is.'

I turned to Clare. 'Do you know Judith well?'

She shrugged. 'Fairly.'

'Do you know where they are?'

She shook her head, then said, 'I'd better be off, Mrs McGann, I should be at school as it is. But I was worried about you.'

28

'You're a good girl, Clare,' said Margaret. 'Better than my own. Be off with you now, you don't want to be getting into trouble with the headmaster.'

Clare smiled at her, then me, got up and went through the kitchen door into the back garden and round the side of the house.

'School,' said Margaret McGann bitterly. 'What a waste of time.'

'I don't think Judith's mother would agree with you on that.'

Margaret McGann looked up at me through the fall of her hair. 'Oh, your Judith's different. She goes to a good school. The girls round here go to a dump of a comprehensive that's rotten with asbestos and should have been pulled down years ago. The teachers haven't got a clue and hardly ever last longer than a term. There's drugs sold like sweeties, and if the girls get to be sixteen without getting pregnant it's a miracle.'

And I thought I was cynical.

Margaret McGann offered me a cup of tea from the huge enamel pot that sat on the top of the stove. I accepted gratefully. It was strong and sweet, just the way I like it.

'So where do you think they are, Margaret?' I asked, when she placed the thick, white china mug in front of me and accepted a cigarette from my packet. 'Our daughters.'

'God knows, Nick,' she said. 'If I had a clue I'd tell you. Judith's always on about her daddy the private detective. She's got a scrap book full of clippings about you.'

I didn't know that.

'I thought it wouldn't be long before you turned up to try and find her,' she went on.

'That's why I'm here,' I said. 'I thought I might be able to help.'

'You trust the coppers about as much as I do, is that what you mean?'

I pulled a wry face. This woman was no fool. 'That's about

it,' I agreed. 'But I could use some help myself. I don't really know where to start. Not up here.'

She stubbed out her cigarette in a 'Glasgow Smiles Better' ashtray. 'I don't know where they are, Nick, as God is my judge. If I did, do you think I'd be sitting here greetin' into my tea?'

I think she meant crying.

'I didn't even know what to tell the police. They must think I'm a shocking mother. Not that they think much of any of us round here. And my Gordon – my husband. If you could call him that. He was always in and out of the station. Drunk. Not that the kids have ever been in trouble. Not up until now that is.' And her face dissolved into tears again. 'What kind of mother doesn't know where her daughter is?' she said through sobs.

I left my chair, went to where she was sitting, knelt down and put my arms round her shoulders.

'Exactly the same as Judith's mother. She's as much in the dark as you are. She thought Judith might be with me.'

'In London?'

'That's right. My wife's down there at home now, just in case Judith gets in touch.'

She dried her eyes on the tea towel I handed her and I went and sat back down again.

'I heard all about your wedding. Judith was *so* excited,' said Margaret McGann.

'I know. So was I.'

'That's good.'

All this was very nice, but it wasn't going to get baby a new bonnet.

'Does Paula have a boyfriend?' I asked.

'No one special. She knocks about with the lads from the estate, but she wants someone better. Not that I blame her, mind. If I'd've had any sense I would have got someone better

30

myself, and not ended up here bringing up four bairns on my own.'

Then I asked the question that I didn't want to ask. 'What about Judith?'

Margaret McGann looked at me and laughed. 'Lord no. Judith was an innocent, Nick. Compared with my girl anyway. No. She has more sense. She wants a career. To move south and catch a boy with some brains himself. The lot round here are as thick as planks. The ones from the estate *and* the ones from the posh end.'

I had to smile at the way she described Laura and Louis's neck of the woods.

'Do you mind if I have a look at Paula's room?' I asked.

'Paula's and young Maggie's you mean,' she said. 'They share.'

'Whatever.'

'Course you can. It's upstairs. I'll show you.'

Which she did. It seemed to be a typical teenager's bedroom. Untidy. With clothes, tapes, magazines and school books everywhere. And posters of current pop stars on the walls.

'The police have been through the place twice already,' said Margaret McGann. 'They found nothing.'

Nor did I.

We went back downstairs and Margaret McGann made me another cup of tea, we smoked two cigarettes each and I left. I walked back past the three kids who were still leaning against the fence, who studied me again like the strange species I must have appeared to them, and in the direction that I thought Laura and Louis's place was. When I was half a street away from the McGann house I heard someone call my name and I looked round.

6

It was Clare and a couple of her pals. Girls of about the same age, all dressed in similar, baggy, brightly coloured clothes, where a big feature was a baseball cap worn backwards.

I waited until they caught up with me.

'How ya doin'?' said Clare.

I shrugged.

'This is Dottie. This is Maria,' she said, introducing her pals, but not indicating which was which.

I nodded at them.

'We wanted a wee chat.'

'I'm listening,' I said. There was something up, and I wanted them to tell me what, without any prompting.

'It's about Judith and Paula.'

I said nothing. I gathered it was. I just looked from one of them to the other and finally back to Clare.

'We . . . er . . .' she said.

Fuck this, I thought. It was like drawing teeth. 'You know something,' I said. A statement, not a question.

'Mebbe.'

'Like what? And if you do, why haven't you told the police, or Mrs McGann? You saw the state of her in there just now.'

'We daren't. If Paula found out . . .' She didn't finish the sentence.

'She's tough, is she?' I asked.

'You can say that again, Mister,' said one of the other girls. Dottie, I think. I wasn't sure.

'A nutter,' said the other one, who must have been Maria.

'And she's with my daughter.' I was beginning to get angry. Angry and scared for Judith's safety.

'You don't have to worry about her,' said Clare. 'Paula wouldn't let anything happen to Judith.'

'They're best mates,' said the one I thought was Dottie.

'She looks after her,' said the other one.

'And besides,' said Clare, 'the coppers and Mrs McGann won't pay.'

'And I will.'

All three smiled. Little bitches. I clenched my fists until the nails bit into my palms. I felt like clouting all of them. But what would have been the point? I unclenched my fists and spoke softly. 'And what's to stop me going off and telling the coppers what you tell me? And who told it to me? And telling Paula later on, when they find them?'

If they find them, I thought, and my blood ran cold.

'Because your Judith says you'll never break a promise. Never,' said Clare.

'I haven't made any promises.'

She shrugged and said, 'OK, girls, let's go. *Neighbours* is on soon.'

'Wait a minute,' I said.

She smiled at me, like an angler getting a bite.

'How much?' I asked.

'Promise first.'

I felt stupid.

'Go on,' she insisted. 'Promise.'

'What?' I asked.

'That you won't tell anyone what we tell you, or who told you it.'

I hesitated. It was a hell of a promise. But one I had to make to find out what they knew. 'OK,' I said. 'I promise. Now will you tell me?'

Clare held out her hand.

33

'How much?' I said.

She shrugged.

I reached into my back pocket and took out some notes. I offered her a tenner.

She gave me a look of pure contempt. 'Between three of us,' she said.

I added another ten.

The look she gave me then was only slightly less contemptuous.

I separated a fifty-pound note from the rest and said, 'That's it. I don't even know if what you're going to tell me is the truth.'

'We wouldn't lie,' said Clare. She sounded offended at the very idea. I've found that the younger generation do, even when they're extorting money from you.

'Course not,' I said.

She reached out for the fifty and I pulled it back. 'Tell me first.'

'You might diddle us.'

I shook my head. 'No I won't,' I said. 'I promise.'

'OK,' said Clare.

'So?' I said.

'There were these people. Hippies. Ravers.'

'New agers.' Dottie.

'Travellers.' Maria.

'They came up from Glastonbury, stopping at festivals on the way. There's this sacred mound just outside of town by the sea. They said they wanted to commune with nature.'

'They had an old coach with a rainbow painted on the side, a little bus, and some cars.' Dottie.

'They were real grungey.' Maria.

Clare shot her friends a look. 'They camped out for a couple of nights just up the road. There's an old sports ground there. It was the only place where people didn't chase them off. Paula met them at the post office when they were cashing their giros. They invited her to visit. We all went. For a laugh.'

'Including Judith?'

Clare nodded.

'Paula thought they were great.'

'Free spirits.' Dottie.

'And they invited us all to go with them when they left.' Maria.

'And Paula and Judith went?' I asked.

'That's right,' said Clare. 'Judith wouldn't let Paula go on her own.'

'Jesus Christ.'

The three girls looked at me.

'They could be anywhere,' I said.

'No,' said Clare. 'They told us where they were going. The hippies.'

'Where?'

'Banbury.'

'Why Banbury?'

'There's another festival there next weekend. Some old band from the sixties. Fairport something.'

'Convention?' I asked.

'That's right. They reckoned they'd be there today or tomorrow. Wednesday at the latest. There's a campsite, but the travellers aren't welcome, so they said they'd camp close by and bunk in for the music.'

'You should have told the police,' I said. 'You've caused a lot of upset by keeping quiet. A lot of time and money's been wasted.'

'We're telling you now,' said Clare.

'And if they've come to harm?'

She shook her head. 'It'd take more than that lot to hurt Paula. They're just people. Families. Wee children.'

'They were nice,' said the one I think was Dottie. 'Kind,

gentle. They didn't mean anyone harm. They didn't have much, but what they did have they shared with us. Food, cigarettes.'

'Drugs?' I said.

The three girls didn't answer, just kicked the toes of their oversized trainers on the kerb.

'They were OK,' said Maria hotly.

'But not everyone they meet will be like that,' I said.

'That's why we're telling you now,' said Clare. 'We got a bit worried. With Mrs McGann so upset and you coming all the way up here.'

'Well I'm glad of that at least,' I said.

'But we know they're OK,' said Maria.

Clare shot her another look.

'How?' I asked.

Clare's tongue flicked over her lips.

'Clare,' I said.

'I got a telephone call this morning, after me mam went shopping.'

'From Paula?'

She nodded.

'Where is she?'

'On the road.'

'Whereabouts?'

'She didn't say exactly. Somewhere down south.'

'Is she all right?'

Clare nodded.

'And Judith?'

'She's fine too.'

'Thank God for that.' I wanted to say more. To give the three of them a bawling out for not speaking up before. But once again, what would have been the point? These kids were at an age when responsibility is just a word in the dictionary, and loyalty to your friends and not grassing them up is much more important than what your parents or the police think. What could I say? I'm not the most responsible person in the world myself. But Judith is my daughter.

'Have they got any names, these hippies?' I asked.

'Eno was the boss,' said Clare. 'He's a ginger nut with dreads.'

'And there was Spider. She's his girlfriend,' said Dottie.

'Anyone else?'

'Max, Mechanic and Noddy,' said Clare.

'Charming,' I said. 'Is that the lot?'

'There was a few more,' said Clare. 'But we never knew their names.'

I nodded.

'So what will you do now?' she asked.

I looked at my watch. 'I'll go back to London, then go to Banbury and meet these travellers. I want to see the people who took Judith away from her mother. And meet Paula while I'm at it. She sounds like quite a character.'

'Aren't you going to tell the coppers?' asked Clare.

'No,' I said. 'I've promised, haven't I?'

The three girls grinned in unison. 'Can we have the money now?' said Clare.

I nodded, and passed over the Nelson, which Clare had the cheek to put up to the light to see if it was genuine. Then the three girls ran off in the direction they'd come from and I resumed my walk back to Louis and Laura's place with a lot on my mind.

7

I found the house easily enough and Laura opened the door at my ring. She was smoking again and led me into the lounge, as Louis had called it, once more. He was nowhere to be seen. I sat on one of the armchairs and she sat on another. She looked just as stressed out as when I'd left.

'Did you see Mrs McGann?' she asked.

'Yes.'

'What did you think?'

'I think she's very upset.'

Laura made a hissing sound between her teeth as she blew out smoke. 'Upset,' she said. '*She's* upset.'

I could see that she was close to tears again and I knew I couldn't not tell her what Clare and her mates had told me before I went back to London. It would have been too cruel. But on the other hand I didn't want her blabbing to Old Bill. I had an appointment with the new age hippies, or whatever the fuck they called themselves, and it was a date I wanted to keep without the company of any coppers.

'Laura,' I said, then noticed that Louis was standing in the doorway, staring at me.

Laura looked up when I said her name, then noticed Louis too.

'What?' she said.

I imagine she meant me, but she might have been talking to Louis. Anyway, he ignored her and continued screwing me hard.

'Am I in your chair?' I asked him.

'They're all my chairs,' he replied.

So that was the way it was.

I looked back at Laura. 'Can we go for a drive?' I asked.

'What?'

'A drive.'

'Where?'

'Just around,' I said. 'I want to see the area.' It was a lie. I had a destination in mind, but I didn't want Louis to hear.

'I suppose,' said Laura. 'Where are my car keys, Louis?'

'Usual place,' he said. 'On the hook in the kitchen.' And he turned and walked off.

Laura looked at me and shrugged, got up and left the room. She returned a minute or so later pulling a hip-length jacket over the sweater and skirt she was wearing and said, 'Ready?'

I nodded. Stood up and followed her out to the front of the house, where she unlocked the doors of the Golf GTI with a little electronic gizmo.

I got into the passenger seat and fastened my seat belt and she got in behind the wheel and did the same.

'So where to?' she asked, as she fired up the car and the engine caught with a throaty roar.

'Is there an old sports ground round here somewhere?'

She looked at me in amazement. 'How do you know about that place?'

So it existed. That much was true anyway. I wasn't sure if Clare and the girls hadn't been winding me up for the fifty quid.

'I heard about it,' I said.

'It's horrible. It's where the courting couples go to park.'

'So that lets us out,' I remarked. 'Can we go there?'

She shrugged, stuck the VW into gear and took off with a rattle of gravel on the undercarriage of the motor.

The sports ground was about three miles up the road, where the houses thinned out and the country began to encroach. Laura turned off the main road at an unmarked track and the

Golf lurched up the rutted lane with branches rubbing the flanks of the car. After a couple of minutes she turned through a gateless gateway and we were there.

The sports ground was overgrown and surrounded by unhappy-looking trees. In one corner was a once white, half-collapsed, graffiti-scarred pavilion. Laura drove to the centre of the field and stopped.

'Why are we here, of all places?' she asked.

I took out my cigarettes and offered her one. She accepted, and I took one myself and lit them both with a cheap Clipper lighter I had in my pocket. I slid down the electric window of the Golf my side to let in some warm air and I told her what Clare, Dottie and Maria had told me.

She listened, holding the cigarette between her fingers, not smoking it, until there was an inch of ash at the end that fell on to the floor without her noticing.

'Why the hell did they tell you,' she asked when I'd finished, 'and not me?'

'I paid.'

'So would I have done.'

'Maybe they were frightened to tell you. They knew you'd go straight to the police.'

'The Wicked Witch of the West,' she said. 'That's what they think I am. I told you that.' And she started to cry again.

I took the cigarette from her and threw it and mine out of the car and held her for a moment. It was strange. I hadn't held her for years. In fact I bet you could count the times we'd actually touched on the fingers of one hand, since she'd slung me out of the house all those years ago.

'Jesus, Nick,' she said into my shoulder. 'How did it all end like this?'

'I don't know,' I said. 'It just did.'

Then she realized what I'd said, pulled away and looked at

40

me. 'Aren't *you* going to tell the police what they told you?' she said.

'The police,' I said back. 'What's the bloody point? They're useless. Talk about lions without teeth. We know that the girls are OK, and where they'll be tomorrow or the next day at the latest. I'm going to meet them. I'll teach those travellers not to take my daughter away.'

'You're crazy. How do you expect to find them?'

'The same way the police would, but easier. Those people don't get on with the law.'

'But what happens if something happens to the girls between now and then?'

'Why should it?'

'Why shouldn't it?'

'Because it won't.'

'I wish I could be as sure as you are.'

So did I. 'I'm sure that Paula will take care of that,' I said. And from what I'd heard, I was. Although I wasn't best pleased about her taking Judith with her on her adventures. Far from it.

'You have more faith in her than I do,' said Laura.

'Obviously. So are *you* going to tell the police, or let me handle this my way?'

'I don't know.'

'Make up your mind. I'm going to have a look round while you do it.'

'I'll come with you.'

'I don't think you're dressed for it.'

She was wearing her usual, thin, high-heeled shoes and the ground outside was muddy and wet.

'I don't care. I'll come anyway.'

I shrugged. She had plenty of money for new shoes. Or Louis did.

We got out of the car and walked over to the pavilion. On

the way we saw plenty of evidence that someone had recently camped on the site. There were the ashes of fires, discarded but still fresh cigarette packets and soup and baked bean cans, with the labels still bright and readable and not dulled by time, like some we saw.

As we went towards the half-demolished building Laura stumbled several times on the uneven surface of the ground and I reached out for her, and she took my arm for support.

The pavilion was a tip. More fires had been lit inside and the grey walls were black with smoke. As I kicked through the detritus that coated the floor I saw several used condoms, and thought that maybe I should tell Old Bill rather than search for Judith and Paula by myself.

'This place is horrible,' said Laura. 'Let's go back to the car.'

When we were sitting in it again she said, 'So? What did coming here prove?'

'It proved that the place existed and that someone has been camping here recently. Those three girls could have been lying about the whole deal just to rip me off. But I reckon that if they were telling the truth about these people, they're probably telling the truth about the rest.'

'They were here all right,' said Laura. 'It was the talk of the shopping precinct. They were collecting their dole from the post office, much to the disgust of the little old lady that runs the place. You only had to ask me.'

'I wanted to see for myself,' I said. 'And I wanted to get out of the house. I don't think old Louis is too crazy about me being there.'

'He's not too crazy about much these days,' she said sadly. Then changed the subject abruptly. 'Look at the state of my shoes.'

She reached down to remove the offending articles, their uppers and heels caked with mud, and as she did so her skirt worked its way up her thighs, which I noticed were still as good as I remembered.

She saw me look, but didn't pull her skirt down, and I felt a strange tension inside the car.

'Our relationship hasn't been up to much for ages. Not since the baby was born,' she went on.

'Where is Joseph?' I asked. Joseph is Louis's and Laura's son.

'Louis's mother came and collected him on Saturday. She doesn't live far away. She moved up here soon after we did. We thought it was better that he stayed with her until all this is over.'

'How old is he now?' I asked.

'Three.'

I nodded.

Laura put her hand on my knee. Things must've been really bad for her to do that. She looked into the back seat of the car. 'Do you remember what we used to do in the back of your old Cortina?'

'Course I do.' My voice sounded thick in my ears.

'This car is a bit smaller, but do you think we . . . ?' Her skirt rode another inch or two up her thighs, and her hand mimicked its move on mine.

I took hold of it and lifted it off my leg. 'No, Laura,' I said. 'That's not the bloody answer. We're finished. I'm married again and so are you. It wouldn't work. Christ. Can't you see that?'

She pulled down her skirt and nodded. 'Yes, Nick. Course I can. Sorry. I'm just being stupid. Middle age marches on.'

'Leave it out, Laurie.' Jesus, I hadn't called her that for years either. This was getting like old home week. 'You're just a kid.'

She looked at me through red-rimmed eyes. 'Thanks for that at least, Nick.'

I smiled at her and she smiled back.

'So?' I said.

'So what?'

'So what are we going to do about our wayward daughter?'

'Whatever you think is right, I suppose.'

'So I go and meet the travellers and we leave the cops out of it.'

She nodded. 'But I'm coming with you.'

'Do what?'

'You heard.'

'You're coming to a rock festival to meet a convoy of new age hippies?'

'That's right.'

'Christ, Laura,' I said. 'Wonders will never cease.'

8

I got Laura to stop at Margaret McGann's on the return trip. I felt I had to tell *her* what was going on too. I owed it to her. The three little kids were still leaning against the fence when the Golf drew up in front of the house. It seemed that schooling was a forgotten concept in this part of the world.

Laura stayed in the car, and once again the kids blimped me as I walked up the path and knocked on the door. Margaret McGann answered after a moment, looked past me at the VW and shrugged. 'Too grand, is she?' she asked, as she stepped aside to let me in.

'No,' I said. 'Just too messed up.'

We went into the kitchen once more, and the dog gave me his once over before going back to sleep and I sat at the kitchen table again.

I told Margaret McGann what I'd told Laura, only this time I didn't let on who'd told *me*. Then I told her what I intended to do.

'Thank God they're all right,' said Paula's mother.

'Do you want me to tell the police or handle it my way?' I asked.

'You know how I feel about the cops,' she said. 'You do it. From what I hear you'll have a better chance of finding them.'

'Not necessarily,' I said. 'But I do have a vested interest.'

'You'll find them,' she said. 'And when you do, you've got my permission to give Paula a good clout.'

'I'll remember that, Margaret,' I said as I rose to leave. 'I'd better get off now. I want to get back to London as soon as possible.'

'And Madam's going with you?'

'She insisted.'

'Well, I hope she comes back with a little more understanding of people.'

'I hope so too,' I said, and Margaret McGann walked me to the door.

'Just get them back safely,' she said.

'I will.' And I went back to the car and gave her a wave as I got in.

'What did she say?' asked Laura as she put the car into gear and pulled it away from the kerb.

'She said she trusted me,' I replied.

'Good,' said Laura. 'So do I.'

Which once again made a change.

We went back to her and Louis's place, and Laura went off to find him, tell him what she was doing and pack a few things. I told her to dress for bad weather. We didn't know where we'd be ending up. When she came back she was wearing a sheepskin-lined leather jacket that couldn't have cost less than five hundred smackers, tight jeans and desert boots, and carried a crammed holdall.

'What did Louis say?' I asked.

'Not a lot. Are you ready?'

'Are we going to call a cab?'

'No. I'll take the car. Leave it in the parking garage.'

'Suits me,' I said, and we split.

Louis didn't come and wave us off.

On the way to the airport, I said, 'You're going to need somewhere to stay tonight. There's no room at my place.'

'I don't know why you keep that poky little flat,' said Laura. 'Now you're married again you should buy Dawn somewhere with some space.'

'It's OK,' I said defensively. 'We'll get a bigger place soon.'

'When?'

'When I can afford it. Now, about a hotel for you tonight.'

'Is there somewhere local?'

'Course there is, but I thought you always stayed in the Connaught when you were in town.'

'I'll make an exception this time,' she said coldly.

'There's a couple of places on Crown Point that don't look too bad,' I said. 'It's only for one night after all. I'll phone Dawn from the airport, get her to meet us and she can reserve a room for you.'

We got to the airport in time for the three-fifteen flight to Heathrow, and Laura went off to get the tickets whilst I called Dawn.

'Anything?' I said.

'No. You?'

'Yeah. I think I know where they'll be tomorrow or Wednesday.'

'How come?'

46

'Long story. I'll tell you later. We're on the three-fifteen flight, getting in at four-forty-five. Will you meet us?'

'We, Whiteman? Us?'

I knew this was going to be difficult. 'Yeah. Long story again, but Laura's coming down with me.'

'Why?'

'Because I haven't told Old Bill what I've found out and she wants to be there when we find the girls. Otherwise she blows the whistle and spoils the fun.'

'Oh.'

'Don't say it like that, Dawn. It wasn't my idea. She'll need somewhere to stay local. Can you find out if the Christopher at Crown Point's got a room for tonight. We'll be off tomorrow to Banbury.'

'*Where?*'

'I'll explain everything when I see you. Just get her a room. If the Christopher's full, try and find somewhere else local. And make it decent, or else she'll moan like hell.'

'And we couldn't have that, could we? Am I coming to Banbury, or is this a private excursion?'

'Course you are.'

'Right.'

I saw Laura waving at me from the concourse, tickets in hand.

'Look, I'll have to go. I'll see you in a bit. Bye now.'

'Bye,' she said and hung up in my ear hard. I knew that taking Laura back to London with me was going to cause problems, but that's what you get with extended families.

I went and collected my ex-wife, and at four-forty-five we were back at Heathrow where Dawn was waiting in the Chevy wagon in a no waiting zone outside the terminal.

'You remember Laura,' I said as we got into the car.

'Of course I do,' said Dawn politely, pulling away under the eyes of a traffic warden in a turban. 'Nice to see you again, Laura.'

'And you, Dawn,' said Laura from the back seat. 'Though it could be under better circumstances.'

On the way back home I filled Dawn in on what had happened in Scotland. By the time I'd finished we were just coming up to Battersea Bridge and she said, 'So it's Banbury tomorrow?'

'That's right,' I replied. 'And I need to make some calls before we go. Did you get Laura a room?'

'A single at the Christopher. I believe it's very nice, Laura,' she said glancing round. 'It caters especially for salesmen.' And I saw Laura wince.

We got back to the flat around five-thirty, and I called up my old rock and roll chum, Christopher Kennedy-Sloane, on his mobile number.

He answered on the third ring. 'Nick,' he said when I'd identified myself. 'How's the boy?'

I told him about Judith and Paula's disappearance, then asked him if he knew about the Banbury festival.

'Know about it?' he said. 'One of my clients is making a guest appearance this year. The organizers like to dig out the odd famous, geriatric pop star, to bring tears of nostalgia to the punters' eyes,' and he mentioned the lead singer of one of the most famous blues-cum-heavy-metal bands of the seventies.

'So are you going?' I asked.

'Catch me standing in a bloody freezing field all weekend contracting the flu just to see some old duffer reprising his greatest hit? No chance, love. But I do happen to have a handful of artists' passes sitting on my desk. They'll get you on to the site, and backstage if needs be.'

'You're a diamond, Chris,' I said.

'Anything for a friend in need. I'm truly sorry to hear about Judith. I hope you find her.'

'So do I.'

'Will you be staying over?' he asked.

'Probably.'

'Well there's a halfway decent hotel in the town I believe, where most of the bands stay. You'd better phone them tonight before the rush starts. They might have some rooms this early in the week, but later they'll almost certainly be chokka.'

'You think of everything, mate.'

'I have to.' And he told me the name of the hotel, which I wrote down on a pad.

'When can I get the passes?' I asked. 'I want to be off pretty early tomorrow. I just need to sort out some transport.'

'I'll bike them over to you first thing. You've caught me on the way to a bit of a do for the next big thing.'

'Who no doubt you represent.'

'No doubt at all. I'll be in the office by nine in the morning and I'll make it my first task.'

'Get the geezer to put them through the letter box if there's no one home, all right? I'll probably need to pop out tomorrow, first thing.'

'All right, Nick, and good luck.'

'Cheers,' I said and hung up.

Next on my list of calls was my pal in the motor trade, Charlie. I caught him on his mobile too, heading home after a hard day ripping off people who knew nothing about cars.

'Got any four-wheel drives in stock?' I asked.

'A couple. A Discovery and a Vogue.'

'Is the Vogue automatic?'

'Sure. Power everything, mag wheels and leather up-holstery. To you, nineteen grand. Eighteen, and that hunk of Detroit garbage you're driving now.'

I ignored the insult to the Chevy. 'I don't want to buy it, Charlie,' I said. 'I want to borrow it.'

'*Borrow* it,' he bellowed. 'I should bleedin' cocoa.'

So I told him the story too, and at the end I heard him sigh and he said, 'When do you want it?'

'Tomorrow morning, first thing.'

'Just bring it back in one piece, and Judith too,' he said, and hung up in my ear.

Then I phoned directory, got the number of the hotel in Banbury and called it up. They did indeed have a double and a single room for the next night and Wednesday, and I booked them. When I enquired about later in the week, they told me that was when the bands came in for the festival and they were full. But I hoped that we'd be back in London by then with Judith and Paula in tow.

Finally I got back to Chas. He was at home. He'd been into the offices of the sister daily to the Sunday he worked for. He'd asked around discreetly, but nothing had been known about Judith and Paula's disappearance. I told him I hoped it stayed like that.

When I put down the phone after the fourth call, I told Laura and Dawn what had occurred, then we drove Laura up to her hotel where she insisted that we stayed for dinner, which wasn't half bad. She had no complaints about the room, which was a miracle, and as the evening wore on she and Dawn seemed to be getting on better, which suited me down to the ground. The last thing I wanted on our little excursion was a pair of feuding women.

Around about ten Dawn drove me home in the wagon and we went to bed.

It looked like tomorrow was going to be a long day.

9

I was up early and woke Dawn with a cuppa after I was dressed. 'Come on, girl,' I said, 'shake a leg.'

She rolled out of bed and went to the bathroom, whilst I knocked up a couple of bacon sandwiches.

After we'd eaten, we packed a bag and went out to the Chevy and drove it to Charlie's. He'd just arrived, and his boy was making tea. We sat in his office and I had to tell him the whole story over mugs of Co-Op 99.

'So that's why we need a four-wheel drive,' I said. 'God knows where we're going to end up.'

I saw his look.

'Don't worry, Charlie,' I assured him. 'I'll put it through the car wash before I bring it back.'

'Cheers,' he said drily, but nevertheless hunted through his desk drawers until he came up with an ignition key on a leather fob attached to a yellow cardboard label. 'Here you go,' he said. 'It's on the front. The boy's taking the price stickers off.'

'Cheers, mate,' I said. 'I'll take care of it.'

'Make sure that you do.'

'Can I leave the Chevy here?'

'If you want, but put it round the back. I don't want to get a bad name having something like that where my customers can see it.'

'What customers?' I asked. 'I thought you were a victim of the recession.'

'I do all right.'

We went out on to the lot where a dark green Range Rover sat tall on its huge town and country tyres. I gave the keys of

51

the wagon to the boy, who expertly steered it round the back out of sight, and I opened up the Vogue. 'Want to drive?' I asked Dawn.

'No. I'd hate to deprive a boy of his new toy.'

I hoped she'd say that. But I knew if I'd got straight behind the wheel I'd never hear the last of it. Still a bit of a libber at heart, our Dawn.

'Right,' I said. 'Hop in then.' I turned to Charlie and said, 'I appreciate this, mate. I owe you one.'

'One? As I remember we've still got the matter of a small outstanding bill from about eighteen months ago.'

'Didn't I settle up?' I said. 'I'll have to have a word with my accountant.'

'Make sure you do,' said Charlie. We shook hands and Dawn and I climbed into the leather interior of the motor.

It was a real classy set of wheels and the engine started with no more than a hum. I put the gear stick into 'Drive' and bounced the Rover over the kerb and on to the road, pointed in the direction of Crown Point.

We arrived at Laura's hotel and found her in the restaurant finishing her breakfast. We ordered more coffee and discussed our plan of attack.

It sounded simple. Go to Banbury, find the hotel, check in, go to the festival site and ask around about any groups of travellers who'd been spotted in the area. It sounded simple, but I had the feeling it wasn't going to be as simple as that. And of course I was right.

Dawn and I waited in reception whilst Laura settled her bill and got her stuff together. Then we went back to the Range Rover. Laura was well impressed with the wheels and we headed back to the flat.

Whilst we'd been out a messenger had called and I found an envelope addressed to me propped up on the radiator in the hall. I opened it to find three artists' passes and a car park sticker for the festival, plus a short note from Chris Kennedy-Sloane wishing us luck in our endeavours. Endeavours. I ask you.

I collected our bag, stowed it in the back of the Vogue with Laura's and we took the South Circular to Shepherd's Bush, joined the A40, then the motorway, and we were in Banbury before lunch.

The hotel was close to the town centre and we checked in quickly, grabbed a drink and a sandwich in the bar, got directions to the festival site and set off. It was about a fifteen-minute drive away and we found it easily. There were already quite a number of people around. A motley collection of old and new hippies, skinheads, grungers, folkies and straight-looking ex-grammar school boys and girls. The site was a hive of activity, with riggers putting the finishing touches to a large, enclosed stage, technicians setting up a massive PA, concessionaires getting their stalls set up and about forty people from a northern brewery organizing a massive open air bar down one side of the field. I stuck the car park pass on the inside of the windscreen of the Rover and we were waved through an open five-barred gate by a couple of security guys under the watchful eye of two uniformed coppers. More security stopped us inside at the gate of a storm fence around the festival site, and we were sent over to a Portakabin to exchange our artists' passes for plastic bracelets that allowed us access to all areas. It was all very efficient, and when I mentioned the name of Chris Kennedy-Sloane's management company we were made very welcome.

I drove the Range Rover through the inner security gates and bumped it down the long, sloping field, through more gates and into the backstage car park, where we abandoned the motor and went exploring.

Next to the field where the festival was held was another larger field that had been turned into a temporary tent city for people who wanted to camp at the site, and that was where we started our search for the travellers that Paula and Judith had left Scotland with. There was no sign on the campsite of the convoy that Clare had told me about, but we found half a dozen bikers gathered around a campfire and I collared one of them. At first he regarded me with the suspicion I expected, but when I explained why Dawn, Laura and I were there, his attitude changed. 'I've got three girls of my own at home,' he said tiredly. 'What with them and the wife I can never get into the bleedin' bathroom. This is luxury compared.' He threw his arm out to encompass the site. 'If it wasn't for me bike and weekends away with the boys I think I'd go barmy. The people who run this thing won't let new agers on the site,' he went on. 'They cause trouble and never want to leave. You can't blame the organizers I suppose. Not them or the hippies. It's hard enough for 'em to find anywhere to stay at the best of times. They hang out wherever they can find a spot with no hassle. And they're few and far between. Your best bet is to go round the local boozers. Some of the landlords won't let hippies within a mile of the place, others will. Just depends on their attitude. But you won't have much trouble spotting the ones that will.' He grinned. 'Loads of dogs on bits of string tied up out front. Then you'll just have to buy a few drinks and you'll be top man. Anyhow, we'll be about tonight ourselves getting a few pints. I'll ask around meself. If you have no joy come round again tomorrow. My name's Ace. Just ask for me. Everyone knows me.'

I took out a twenty-pound note. 'Have a drink on me tonight, Ace,' I said.

'You're all right, mate.'

'No. I insist.'

He shrugged. 'If you like,' he said. 'I never say no to a freebie.' And he took the note with his oil-stained fingers and tucked it away in one of the zippered pockets of his leather jacket. Then he opened another and pulled out a fingernail-sized piece of black. 'If I have a drink on you, you have a smoke on me. It'll 'elp you relax if you get stressed out.'

'Cheers, mate,' I said, and took the proffered dope and put it into my shirt pocket.

'Be lucky,' he said. 'I hope you find your girl.'

'So do I,' I replied, and went back to Dawn and Laura and told them what Ace had told me.

So we started our pub crawl search. Ace had been correct. It wasn't hard to spot which pubs welcomed the hippies and which didn't. And there were lots of pubs available, dotted around those lazy, twisting Oxfordshire highways and byways. That afternoon I think we hit about twenty. Ace had been right on his other point too. Where we did find gatherings of the new age, a few quid spent on beer soon found us many friends willing to listen to our story. So willing, in fact, I felt we were being wound up a lot of the time, and as the wad of notes in my pocket rapidly diminished I began to realize how my clients must have felt when I presented them with the bill for expenses on cases I'd worked for them.

By six that evening, Dawn, Laura and I were tired and dispirited. We'd spoken to a hundred or more people but no one recognized our description of the convoy that we were searching for, or admitted any knowledge of Eno, Spider, Max, Mechanic or Noddy. Or if they did, they weren't telling.

Just past the hour, after another fruitless interrogation, I turned the car in the direction of Banbury again and said, 'I could do with something to eat.'

'We should tell the police,' said Laura from the back seat. 'This is pointless.'

'We'll eat and try again later. People are still arriving. They might not be here yet. If we have no joy by tomorrow we'll go to Old Bill.'

'All right,' she said. 'But on your head be it.'

When wasn't it? I thought, but said nothing in reply.

We ate dinner at the hotel. Not the happiest meal I've ever had, but then I hadn't expected balloons and crackers. I laid off the vino, and after coffee we went back out to the Range Rover and I aimed it in the direction of the festival site once more.

We spent the early evening driving from pub to pub again. More punters were arriving all the time, but we still had no joy. As the summer sun dropped in the sky and twilight moved in over the countryside, I started to share my ex-wife's pessimism about the search.

It was almost full dark when I drove into the car park of the Poacher's Friend, about three miles from Banbury as the crow flies, but about twenty on the tiny lanes I'd been reduced to driving.

The three of us piled out of the motor and we went through the single, half-glassed door marked BAR.

There were half a dozen or so people inside the pub. All men and all local by the looks of it. Country people. Old-fashioned, like we'd suddenly stepped back forty years into one of those Ealing films you get on TV on a Saturday afternoon as BBC2's answer to the sport on the other channels. There were no festival-goers present and the conversation stopped when we entered and every head turned to look at us.

'Fancy a quick one?' I asked my companions.

Even though it wasn't the friendliest of boozers, they agreed. Dawn went for a gin and tonic, Laura asked for a vodka and orange. I sat them down at a table and went to the bar, ordered their drinks and half of lager for myself.

'Evening,' I said to the bloke standing next to me. A fifty-year-old geezer in a tweedy jacket, heavy cords and boots.

'Evenin',' he replied.

'Nice weather.'

He nodded and turned back to the bloke standing next to him.

When the barman served the drinks and I'd asked for the ice he'd omitted to put into the gin and the vodka, I paid for them and said, 'Lots of strangers about.'

He looked me up and down then over to the two women. 'Yes,' he said.

'For the festival.'

'Damn thing. It gets bigger every year.'

'But they stay pretty close to the site. Don't get out this far.'

'They'd better not.'

'You don't like them.' An understatement, but one I had to make to keep the sparse conversation going.

'No.'

'You don't get anyone camping out close by then?'

'Why'd you want to know?' This question came from the geezer with the tweed jacket, who'd obviously been listening and took this opportunity to stick his beak in.

'Just interested,' I said.

'We get 'em,' he said. 'But not for long.'

'You move them on?'

'That's right.'

'All private land round here then?'

'All except Hangman's Field,' said the barman, and Tweed Jacket sent him a warning glare.

'Hangman's Field,' I said. 'Where's that?'

The barman didn't reply and avoided my eye.

'Why'd you want to know?' Tweed Jacket repeated his earlier question.

'I'm looking for some people,' I said. 'It's not important.' And I picked up the drinks and went over to the table. When I sat down I saw Tweed Jacket and the barman talking, and they both glanced over in our direction.

'Something's up,' I said.

'What?' asked Laura.

'I don't know yet. Drink up and we'll move on.'

'Where to?'

'Hangman's Field,' I said and drank half my half in one gulp.

As we were standing up to go, Tweed Jacket walked over from the bar. 'Who you looking for exactly?' he asked.

'My daughter. And her friend.'

'What makes you think they be here?'

'I don't. I've been looking all round the area.'

'There's no one here,' he said emphatically.

I shrugged. 'Then we'll keep on looking,' I said.

'You do that.' And he turned on his heel and went back to the bar.

Dawn, Laura and I walked out of the pub and back to the car. I started it and turned it out of the car park. As I did so, a bloke on a push bike pedalled round the corner. I ran down the electric window and called out: 'Excuse me.'

'Yes?'

'Hangman's Field. Which way?'

He pointed back the way he'd come. 'Straight on, through the village and out the other side, then it's about a mile down on the right.'

'Thanks,' I said, and turned the Vogue in the direction he'd indicated and accelerated it through the automatic box.

10

Hangman's Field wasn't hard to find. I followed the geezer on the bike's directions, but before we arrived I saw the reflection of flames on the underside of the trees in the twilight. The field was quite small, entry was by an open gate, and parked inside, around the huge campfire, like a wagon train awaiting the arrival of hostile Apaches, were three cars and an old coach with a dodgy-looking rainbow painted on the side.

'Bingo,' I said. 'The happy campers.'

I pulled the Range Rover up to the gap in the fence and blocked the entrance with it, putting the gear stick into 'Park', setting the handbrake and locking the doors after we got out, but leaving the headlights on full beam and switching on both spotlights.

There was no one in sight and the three of us walked up to the coach, the windows of which had been covered by some dark material on the inside, and hammered on the door.

No answer.

I hammered again, and it slid open and a long, skinny punter, aged about thirty, with thick ginger dreadlocks tied back with a ribbon, a ring in his nose and half a dozen in each ear, wearing a ratty sweater and oily jeans, shoved himself through the gap.

'What?' he said.

'Eno?' I asked politely.

I saw from his eyes in the light from the fire that it was and that he was stoned, but he said, 'Don't know him, mate.'

I grabbed a handful of locks, pulled him from the step of the bus and dragged him over to the fire where I forced him down until his barnet was trailing in the embers.

'One more lie,' I said, 'and you'll get the Michael Jackson memorial medal for the quickest crew cut in history.'

'Fuck, man,' he said. 'Take it easy. What's going on? This is public land . . .'

'Wrong,' I said. 'I'm not here to move you on. I'm looking for my daughter.'

'What?'

I pushed his head nearer to the flames so that the heat

pinpricked the skin of my hands. 'Wake up, Eno,' I said. 'And say hello to the real world.'

'Leave him,' said a voice from behind me. I turned and looked back at the bus, where a young woman with long, black tangled hair, dark lipstick, as much face furniture as Eno, a velvet top that showed off her high, firm breasts and a long skirt that looked like it was made out of granny's tasselled tablecloth was standing in the coach door.

'Why?' I said.

'Because your daughter's in here. And her friend. They're OK.'

'You know who I am?'

'I know her,' she said, nodding her head at Laura. 'The grand lady.'

I dropped Eno on to the ground where he sat knocking the sparks out of his do and walked back to the coach. 'Let's see them then,' I said.

The woman stood aside and I went in, closely followed by Dawn and Laura. It wasn't a centre spread from *Homes and Gardens* inside, but it wasn't too bad. It was just an old coach with all the seats except the driver's ripped out and a sort of kitchen/living room built at the front, consisting of an old sofa, two mismatched armchairs, a sink without a soil pipe and a stove attached to a Calorgas tank. The floor was carpeted and lamps were attached to the walls. There was a ghetto blaster and about a hundred tapes in one corner and a pile of old newspapers, books and magazines in another. The back half of the bus was divided off with a curtain that looked like it had come from Marrakesh some time in the late sixties and hadn't been washed since. The place stank of marijuana and there was an ashtray full of roaches on the floor next to a tray covered in Rizla packets, busted cigarettes and what looked to be about half an ounce of grass.

Curled up asleep in one of the armchairs was a toddler of

about three, a baby gurgled in a cot beside the other armchair and a young girl dressed in leggings, a sweatshirt and trainers sat on the sofa. She had long, honey-coloured hair and a very pretty face spoiled only by what looked like a perpetual sneer.

'Paula McGann I presume,' I said to her. She didn't reply, so I looked at Laura who nodded.

'How did you find us?' Paula demanded.

I ignored her.

'And you must be Spider,' I said to the woman who'd admitted us.

She nodded too.

'So where's my daughter?' I asked.

'In the back,' said Spider.

I walked across the floor, pulled aside the curtain and found Judith.

She was plugged into a Walkman and was rocking gently back and forth on one of the four beds that were jammed together in the back of the bus. She didn't look up when I went in, or when I pulled the headphones out of her ears, just kept on rocking and singing in a breathy voice, 'Es are good. Es are good.' I could hear the same words coming out of the tiny loudspeakers in the phones and I switched off the power to the tape machine, but still she kept on singing the same words over and over again.

I pulled her face round into the light and looked into her eyes. Her pupils were tiny, and when I sat down and hugged her I might just as well have not been there.

I stood up and walked back to the front of the bus. 'What's she on exactly?' I said to both Paula and Spider.

'She's OK,' said Paula. 'She took an E.' She had a broad yet soft Scottish accent.

'Oh good,' I said. 'That makes it all right then.'

'What's an E?' said Laura.

I couldn't believe she was that innocent. 'Ecstasy,' I

explained. 'MDMA. A synthetic that makes you love everyone. At least that's the idea. It doesn't seem to be working too well for Judith. It comes in pill or capsule form. But these suckers don't come with a government health stamp. They're home-made and they're always cut. Sometimes with harmless stuff, but often with speed or acid, or in the case of whatever Judith's taken, smack. Or at least some kind of downer. Look at her eyes.'

Laura sobbed and pushed through the curtain where I heard her croon to Judith who just kept on singing along to the music in her head.

'They're OK,' said Paula. 'Good kit. She'll be all right in the morning.'

'She'd better be,' I said. 'Or someone round here is dead.' I looked pointedly at Spider as I said it, and Eno came through the door, his dreadlocks looking a little tattier than they had before and his face bright red from the fire.

'There was no need for all that violence,' he said. His speech was a little slurred and I guessed it was him that had been at the puff.

'I ain't started yet, son,' I replied. ''Specially if Judith doesn't come back from whatever planet you've sent her to.'

'It's 'armless, that gear. You should try one. It might put you in a better mood.'

'No thanks. I don't take things like that.'

'Don't you?' said Paula. 'According to Jude, you're always at the dope.'

She was right of course. I couldn't argue with that. But it's different when it's *your* daughter. A lot different, believe me. Just have one of your own and see.

'Not when I was her age,' I said.

Paula's sneer became more pronounced.

I turned back to Eno and Spider. 'What the hell were you thinking of, bringing these two with you? Judith's only fourteen and Paula's the same. You realize that the police are looking for them?'

Eno's face turned from red to a sickly green and he looked first at Spider, then at Paula. 'They told us they were sixteen.'

'I hope that doesn't mean what I think it means, son,' I said. 'If anyone's messed with my daughter—'

'No,' protested Eno, taking a step back. 'They said it was all right. That no one would miss them.'

'And if you believed them, you must be more stupid than you look,' I said, and clenched my fists.

'Relax,' said Paula. 'No one's touched her. I made sure of that.' She seemed to be extremely self-possessed for one so young. Much more than I'd been at that age. But maybe they make them tougher north of the border. 'It was just a laugh,' she went on. 'An adventure. Things were boring at home. We fancied getting away for a few days.'

'A bit of a holiday,' I said sarcastically.

She ignored the sarcasm. 'That's right. A weekend break. You know the sort of thing.'

'But your weekend break involved calling in the police of two countries and frightened your mum and Judith's half to death. Not to mention me.'

'You'll get over it,' said Paula.

'Thanks,' I said. 'That makes me feel much better.'

'So what now?' said Eno.

'Now I take these two back where they came from, and if Judith comes down all right, it'll be the last you hear of me. The police haven't been told about you. But if she *doesn't*, or if I find out that anything bad happened to her whilst she was with you, I come back and find you. I don't care how far you run, believe me I'll do it. Then I'll finish what I started outside by the fire. By the time I've done with you, your mates will think you're related to Colonel Sanders. Get me?'

He nodded. He knew that I meant it and I knew he knew.

'Where are the rest of your pals, by the way?' I asked.

'Gone into Banbury in the microbus to get something to eat and scope the pubs. We stayed behind to mind the kids.'

'Right. Paula, get any stuff of yours and Judith's you want to take and let's go.'

'I'm not coming,' said Paula.

'Yes you are.'

'You going to make me?'

'No,' said Dawn. 'I am. I used to be a little bitch like you, now I'm a big bitch. Big enough to take you on any time.'

'Get fucked,' said Paula.

Dawn's right hand snaked out and caught her round the side of the face with a sound like a gunshot. Paula's head flew back and I could clearly see the imprint of Dawn's fingers on her cheek.

'Rule one,' said Dawn. 'Respect your elders.'

Paula put her hand up to her face and tears leaked from her eyes. 'You cow,' she said.

Dawn's other hand caught her on the other side of her face. 'Rule two,' she said. 'Obey rule one or you'll regret it.'

'Get your stuff,' I said. Then raised my voice. 'Laura. Bring Judith. We're leaving.'

Reluctantly Paula went back behind the curtain and I heard a mumble of female voices, and she returned a few moments later with a small carry-all and a rucksack. Laura followed her supporting Judith who was still singing to herself as she came.

At that moment, seeing the two of them there, my heart almost broke.

'Come on,' I said. 'Let's get outta here.'

Everyone but the two babies left the bus and we walked into the glare of the Range Rover's brights, but before we got to the vehicle a voice said, 'Stay where you are,' and half a dozen figures walked from behind the Vogue. I recognized them as the inhabitants of the bar of the Poacher's Friend,

Tweed Jacket at the front. All were armed with shotguns or wicked-looking farm implements that I imagined during the day they used to eviscerate innocent dumb animals.

There were four guns in all. Tweed Jacket toted a serious-looking pump, the bloke he'd been talking to at the bar had a regular double-barrelled shotgun with a lot of fancy scrolling on the metal that might have been a Purdey. There was a young kid, not much older than Paula, toting an old single-barrelled job that looked like it had come out of the ark, and another geezer, a chinless wonder in a green Barbour, had an over-and-under. He didn't look too happy about the whole thing and I fancied he was the weak link in the chain.

'I might've guessed you were with this scum,' said Tweed Jacket.

'I'm with the two women I was with at the pub,' I said. 'And these two girls.' I indicated Paula and Judith. 'One is my daughter and she isn't feeling too well. I'd like to leave now without any unpleasantness.'

I'd've liked to take his pump action shotgun, stick it up his backside and keep firing till it was empty, but I didn't think it was politic to say so.

'You're going nowhere,' said Tweed Jacket.

'And who's going to stop us?'

'We are. These aren't toy guns.'

'And we're not some poor animals you can just blow away at your heart's content,' I said. 'And we're not a bunch of hippies you can frighten off by showing them a couple of shotguns. I've had people point guns at me before, son. They're easy to point but hard to use. Ain't that right, squire?' I aimed the question at the ice cream in the Barbour.

He licked his lips and said, 'Maybe we'd better leave it, Tom.'

'Maybe you'd better,' I said. 'You've walked into a situation that you know nothing about and doesn't concern you. And

I suggest you turn around, go back to the boozer, buy each other a load of drinks and tell yourselves how brave you've been.'

Tom in the tweed jacket didn't take kindly to my advice. He stepped closer and stuck the barrel of his gun in my chest.

I hate that.

'OK,' I said placatingly. 'What do you want us to do?'

Tom smiled. It wasn't a pretty sight. 'You all move round out of the way. We're going to drive these vehicles up to the motorway, then disable them so that you can't come back. If you do as you're told, no one will be hurt.'

'What about our Range Rover?' I asked.

'That too.'

Like fuck, I thought. 'My daughter is sick,' I said. 'We need transport.'

'Too bad,' said the geezer with the Purdey.

'Let them go, Tom,' said the guy in the Barbour. 'The girl doesn't look too well.'

'Probably on drugs,' said Tom.

He was right, but it was none of his business.

'This is public land,' I said. 'You've got no right—'

The geezer with the Purdey swung it at my head, which was his big mistake. Instead of jumping back, I moved in, wrenched it out of his grasp, nutted him on the forehead, which probably hurt me as much as it did him, but surprised him more, turned the gun round and stuck it into Tom's face. 'Drop the gun,' I said.

He made no move to obey and I thumbed back both hammers on my shooter and said, '*I* will fucking use this. I'll blow your head off then piss in your neck.' That told him. Hey, I almost frightened myself.

He did as he was told that time.

'The rest of you, the same. All weapons on the ground now, or I'll use this fucker.'

There was a clatter as the guns and other utensils hit the deck. Dawn went for the pump and came up and covered the men, and shit, the look on her face frightened me more than all of them put together had, so Christ knows how they felt.

'Now get lost,' I said. 'Go back where you came from and leave these people alone.'

They made no move to leave and Dawn shoved the barrel of the pump hard into Tom's stomach, so hard that he bent almost double from the force of the blow. 'Go,' she said. 'There are children here.' The men shuffled where they stood, before silently vanishing into the darkness behind the lights of the Vogue.

The seven of us stood for a moment before Eno broke the silence. 'Thanks, man,' he said. 'You saved us a lot of hassle there.'

'I saved you fuck all,' I said harshly. 'Those cunts were holding guns on *my* family. And they were going to take *our* motor. I need it to get Judith back to our hotel. I couldn't give a fuck for you, you stupid little shit.' And I hit him across the face with the barrel of the gun I was holding. I'd had enough. *More* than enough of arseholes taking the piss and I wanted some payback.

'That was for giving my daughter bad dope,' I said.

The blow probably broke his nose, from the amount of blood and snot that poured out of his nostrils and the way he cried as he fell to his knees in front of us.

I threw the gun down and Dawn tossed the pump beside it. 'Come on, you lot,' I said. 'Let's get the fuck outta here.'

We went to the Range Rover and I used the key to spring the central locking. Paula didn't look too happy, but Dawn grabbed her arm and dragged her along.

I climbed in behind the wheel and stabbed the key into the ignition and fired up the motor, but as it caught I heard the sound of another engine and a VW Microbus pulled in behind us blocking our exit back to the road.

'Shit,' I said as the doors of the bus opened and half a dozen or more hippies piled out.

I whacked the Range Rover into four-wheel drive, slapped the gear stick into second and took off across the field away from the newcomers. As we went I saw Spider kneel, then stand again with a shotgun, long and ugly in her grasp.

Shit, I thought, the guns, I'd forgotten about them. 'Get down,' I shouted. 'On the floor,' and I slammed my foot down hard on the accelerator and as the Vogue fishtailed past her, she fired. The first blast blew in the side window at the back filling the car with chunks of safety glass and shotgun pellets, the second slammed against the back of the truck.

Not a tyre I thought. Please God, not a tyre.

The Range Rover reached the edge of the field, ploughed through the waist-length grass there, then the brush between two trees, and I saw for a brief second in the headlights a fence which disintegrated as the front bumper slammed into it, then the ground dropped and the front of the car went into a ditch, the note of the engine changed and I thought we were stuck. I dropped the gear lever down another notch and the front of the motor lifted and the back wheels went down into the gulley. The car slid sideways, then the wheels caught and we were up the other side, through another fence, the wood bouncing across the bonnet, and speeding through a field full of wheat or corn that rattled against the side of the car as we beat a trail through it. Then the car destroyed a final fence and I wrestled the Range Rover round on to a rutted lane. I spun the wheel to the right and the motor took off like a scalded cat in the direction that led us away from the camp and towards the lights of Banbury that I could see reflected redly on the dark sky in front of us.

'Is everyone all right?' I asked, as I fought the wheel of the Range Rover.

'Paula's got a cut on her face,' said Dawn. 'That's about it.'

'How's Judith?' I asked.

'She seems all right,' said Laura. 'But we should get her to a hospital.'

'No hospitals,' I said. 'That'll bring in the law and I don't fancy talking to them tonight. When we get back to the hotel we'll get a doctor in.'

I thought my ex-wife was going to argue, but for once she kept quiet, and I kept on driving.

After about a quarter of a mile the lane ended at a minor road, which in its turn led us to a roundabout with a signpost for the town centre. I took the second turning off the round-about and within ten minutes drove the Vogue into the car park at the back of our hotel.

11

We all piled out of the car, and I picked up Judith in my arms and walked through the back entrance of the hotel and into the foyer. As I went, she suddenly opened her eyes, looked up at me and said, 'Daddy, I love you.'

I'd never been happier to hear any four words in all my life, and I looked down into her face and said, 'I love you too, baby.'

Inside the reception area a young blonde in a grey suit was on duty. She looked in astonishment at our little band, and I said, 'Is there a doctor in the house?'

Judith giggled, which told me that her rather poor sense of humour, inherited from me, was still intact. 'Sorry?' said the blonde in reply.

'Do you have a local doctor on call?' I said.

'Yes. What's the matter?'

'It's my daughter. She's taken something she shouldn't, and I want her looked at.'

'There's a hospital in town with a casualty department.'

'Not a hospital,' I said, echoing my earlier words to Laura. 'Not unless the doctor thinks it's absolutely necessary. She seems to be all right, but I want her checked over.'

'We do have an emergency number we can call.'

'Then call it. I don't mind paying. We'll be upstairs in ... What's your room number, Laura?' I said to my ex-wife.

'Two-twenty-eight.'

'Two-twenty-eight,' I said to the blonde. 'Tell him to be as quick as he can,' and still carrying Judith, I went to the stairs and up to the second floor, closely followed by the rest.

Laura opened the door of her room and turned back the bed. I laid Judith on the bottom sheet and said, 'Get her undressed and tucked up. Dawn, take Paula to our room.'

Dawn did as I said and left, taking Paula with her, and as Laura stripped Judith down to her T-shirt and pants I said, 'We'll see what the doctor has to say. If he says hospital, then hospital it is. Otherwise she can stay here. I'll sit up with her. You can go in with Dawn and Paula, unless you'd rather I got you another room.'

'That's all right,' she said. 'I'll be fine. But I still think hospital would be best.'

'I think she's OK,' I said. 'She's awake, just about, and doesn't seem any the worse for wear.'

'We could have been killed out there,' said Laura. 'All of us.'

'But we weren't. Except for a couple of scratches we're fine.'

'Are you going to tell the police we've found her?'

'Sure. As soon as the doctor's gone,' and as if on cue the phone rang. It was reception telling us that the doc was on his way up.

He knocked at the door a few moments later, and Laura opened it to admit a sixtyish man in an olive mac carrying a Gladstone bag.

'Doctor Saunders,' he introduced himself. 'I believe there's a young lady here who's not feeling too well.'

'Our daughter, Judith,' I said. 'She's been fed some drugs. An E spiked with heroin.'

'A brown beefburger,' he said. 'We get lots of them round here.'

'Will she be all right?' asked Laura.

'I'll have to see. No history of epilepsy, asthma or heart disease?' asked the doctor.

'No,' my ex-wife and I said in tandem.

'She should be OK then,' said Doctor Saunders. 'Let's have a look-see.'

He pulled back the covers from Judith's bed and did an examination, talking to her as he went, and eliciting at least some response, which seemed hopeful. After ten minutes he tucked her back under the duvet and said, 'She'll be all right. She's a very healthy young female. But she might not be if she keeps taking the tablets.'

'We'll try and make sure she doesn't,' I said.

'Good. Times have changed. Once it was a drop of alcohol or a joint. Now little children are taking drugs that can kill a bull.'

'Thanks, Doctor,' I said. 'What do we do?'

'With Judith. Nothing. She'll sleep it off by morning. Just try and make sure someone stays awake with her all night. If there's any change in her condition, get her down to the hospital.'

'We'll do that,' I said.

'Any other patients?' he asked me. 'Apart from you of course. You look like you've bumped your head.'

I felt the knot in the middle of my forehead where I'd given

71

the geezer with the double-barrelled shotgun a Glasgow kiss. 'I'll survive,' I said.

'I'm sure you will. But let me look anyway,' he said back, and took me under the light and made a humming sound in the back of his throat as he checked me over. 'Not too bad,' he said. 'There's a small break in the skin. Do you want me to dress it?'

'Don't bother,' I said. 'But there's another girl in a room down the corridor. She got hit with some flying glass.'

'Quite an evening you've had,' he said.

'Not one of our best.'

'Let's have a look at her then,' he said, and I took him out of the room and down to the double room that Dawn and I were sharing, where she and Paula were drinking coffee and digging into a huge pile of sandwiches that they'd ordered from room service.

'All right for some,' said Doctor Saunders, but refused the offer of a snack. I wasn't so shy, and helped myself to some food and drink, and Dawn took a cup of coffee and a plate of beef and ham on brown up to Laura, whilst the doctor took a look at Paula's neck where there was a dry trickle of blood that disappeared into the top of her sweatshirt.

'She'll be fine too,' he said after a minute, when he'd cleaned the slight wound, dabbed on some antiseptic and put on a plaster. 'But might I suggest that you and your friends and family try and lead a quieter life in future?'

'That's not a bad idea, Doc,' I said in reply. 'I'll see what we can do.'

'Well, I'll be off now,' he said. 'Unless someone else in your party is lying with flesh wounds in another part of the hotel.'

'No,' I replied. 'That's your lot for tonight. How much do I owe you?'

He shrugged. 'My usual fee for a call at this time is twenty-five pounds.'

I took out my depleted wad of notes and peeled off five twenties. 'There's a ton,' I said. 'Not a word to anyone.'

He smiled. 'My confidentiality is assured.'

'Good.' And I wished him a very pleasant night as he left the room.

'I'm going to stay with Judith tonight,' I said to Dawn. 'You stop here with Paula and I'll get Laura another room. OK?'

Dawn nodded and Paula sneered again, but not with the same vehemence as earlier, and I left, going downstairs to reception again to use the public phone.

I dialled the number of Gipsy Hill police station from memory and asked for Inspector Robber. He was in. I'd've been surprised if he wasn't. 'Robber,' he barked as he picked up the phone.

'Sharman,' I said.

'There's still no news—'

'I've found them,' I interrupted.

'*What?*'

'I've found them,' I repeated.

'How the hell did you do that?'

'I got a call,' I lied.

'Where were they?'

'They'd run off to join the circus.'

'Are you taking the piss?'

'It's a long story. I'll explain later. I just wanted you to know so's you could call off the hunt.'

'Where are you?'

'Banbury.'

'What the hell are you doing there?'

'I told you, I'll explain when I get back to London.'

'And when's that?'

'Tomorrow probably.'

'Are they all right?'

'Just about. Can you get word to Paula's mother? She's not

73

on the phone. There's a copper named Todd, an inspector who's been dealing with the case in Aberdeen. I don't want Mrs McGann worried another night.'

'I'll see to it,' said Jack Robber.

'Thanks.'

'And you'd better come in and see me when you get back.'

'I will, Jack,' I said, and put down the phone on any more questions.

I went back to Laura's room, where Judith seemed to be sleeping peacefully.

'I've called the cops,' I said. 'Someone I know in London. He's going to get Todd to let Mrs McGann know we've found them.'

'What did he say?'

'Not a lot. I didn't let him. Have you spoken to Louis?'

She nodded. 'I called him from here.'

'What did *he* have to say?'

'Not a lot. Just like your friend. But unlike you I gave him every chance.'

I looked at her. 'It's not working out, is it?'

She shook her head. 'Just my luck,' she said. 'I go from one husband who never grew up to another who was born with a pension book in his hand.'

I shrugged. What was there to say? We stood together looking at our daughter's sleeping form and eventually I said, 'Shall I see if there's another room free for tonight?'

'I want to stay with Judith.'

'You need some sleep,' I said. 'I'll stay here. If there's any change I'll let you know.'

'Where's Paula?'

'With Dawn in our room.'

'I'd rather stay here with you two.'

'Please yourself,' I said.

She sat in the single armchair provided, and I found a spare blanket in a cupboard and put it around her, and as I stood at the window looking out at the lights of the town as they winked out one after another, her breathing became more regular as she dozed off, then I went and made myself as comfortable as possible on the edge of the bed, where Judith's steady breathing gradually lulled me to sleep too.

12

When I woke up it was light and I was lying stretched out on top of Judith's bed with one arm round her. As I opened my eyes, so did she, and I saw the look of amazement in them as she saw me.

'Daddy,' she said. 'What are you ...?' She looked round the room. 'Where am I?' Then she saw Laura, still asleep in the chair at the bottom of the bed. 'Mummy ... Oh God.'

'Ssh,' I whispered. 'Relax. It's all right.'

'But where am I?'

'In a hotel room in Banbury.'

'Banbury,' she repeated, and I saw it all flood back. 'Oh, Daddy, I took something.'

'You did. You had us all very worried. How are you feeling?'

She thought about it for a second. 'Fine,' she said.

'Thank God. We had the doctor in.'

'Did you? I'm sorry, I don't remember.'

'Listen, Jude,' I said. 'I'm not the greatest example to you as a father, I know, but you've got to be careful with that sort of thing.'

'It was the first time,' she protested.

I had to smile. 'I'm sure it was.'

'They said it would be all right. Eno and Spider.'

'They probably thought it would.'

'But what happened? Where did you and Mummy come from?'

'And Dawn too,' I said.

'Dawn. Great. I like her. Where is she? And where's Paula? Is she all right?'

I put on my Max Bygraves voice, which always made Judith laugh, and said, 'I'm going to tell you a story.' And I did. Everything from Laura's first frightened phone call until the present. The sun rose over the town as I told it, and Laura still slept the sleep of utter exhaustion in her uncomfortable chair.

Not that I was that comfortable myself, so I made it short, and when I'd finished Judith said, 'I'm sorry, Daddy, I didn't realize we'd cause such a fuss.'

'Why did you do it?' I asked.

'It's been awful at home this last year. Mummy and Louis aren't getting on and Mummy takes it out on me. She won't let me wear what I want, or see who I want. Everything I do is wrong.'

Blimey, I thought, I could remember saying exactly the same things when I was her age about my mum and dad.

'Are you cross?' Judith asked shyly.

I shook my head. 'No. I'm just glad to see you.'

She gave me a kiss on the cheek. 'Good. Will Mummy be cross?'

'No.'

'Will Louis be cross?'

'God knows. If he is, just let him be. There's nothing much any of us can do about that.'

'He's horrible.'

'I'm glad to see we still agree on certain basics even though you're getting older.'

'I've got to pee.'

'Bathroom's in there,' I said and flipped my thumb over my shoulder at the bathroom door.

Judith pushed back the covers, jumped out of bed and ran for it. I got up, stretched the kinks out of my neck and back, and went and woke Laura.

She came awake with a start, and her eyes went straight to the empty bed. 'Where is she?' she asked, fear in her voice.

'In the loo.'

'Is she all right?'

'As bright as a button.'

'Thank God.'

'We were lucky.'

'I know.'

'But keep an eye on her. Those pills can do strange things to the brain.'

'You should know.'

'*Laura*.'

'Sorry.'

Right then the door to the bathroom burst open and Judith flew in wearing a huge white bath towel wrapped around her. 'I took a quick shower,' she said. 'I felt yukky.' She stopped dead when she saw that her mother was awake. 'Hello, Mum,' she said.

'Hello, darling,' said Laura, who got to her feet, and, after a split second, went to Judith and put her arms round her.

'I'm all wet.'

'I don't care,' said Laura, and held her tighter.

Judith started to cry. 'I'm sorry, Mummy,' she sobbed.

Laura started to cry too, and I wasn't far off it myself, but was saved by the phone ringing. I went and picked it up. It was Dawn.

'Hi. Are you awake?'

'Yes.'

'How's Judith?'

'Weeping in her mother's arms.'

'I mean *how* is she?'

'I know what you mean. She seems fine.'

'We're going down to breakfast. You coming?'

'Sure,' I said. 'See you in a minute,' and put down the phone.

'Who was that?' asked Laura.

'Dawn. She and Paula are going for something to eat. I'll join them. You coming?'

Laura peered into the mirror and pulled a face. 'I look a sight,' she said. 'I'll have to do something to myself.'

In fact she looked better than I'd seen her in years. Gone was the grand lady, as Spider had called her, and in her place was a human being.

'You look all right to me.'

'That's a nice thing to say,' she said, and reached over and took my hand.

'I'm a nice person. Or trying to be.'

'I think you're succeeding.'

'Thank you.'

'No. Thank *you*. I haven't said thank you properly for all you've done for us.'

I was embarrassed. 'There's no need,' I said. 'Look, I'm going to the loo. I'm dying for a pee too.'

I went in, took a piss, used the toothbrush that was in a glass on top of the washbasin and looked at myself in the mirror. 'Not too bad,' I said to my reflection. 'You've done good, son.'

When I came out, I left Laura and Judith together to mend what fences they could, and went down to the restaurant. Dawn and Paula were sitting at a table by the window. I buttonholed the waitress and ordered coffee and Dawn asked if I wanted juice.

'I'll get it for you,' volunteered Paula, and went off to a table on the far side of the room where a cold buffet was set up.

'She seems in a better mood this morning,' I said, as I studied the menu.

'We had a long talk last night,' said Dawn. 'She's all right. She just needs a little attention.'

'Don't we all?'

'Some more than others. She's the eldest of a large family without a father. She thinks she's put upon. She saw the way that Judith lived and got jealous.'

'Is that why she took Judith with her? Jealousy? Trying to get her into trouble?'

'I don't think so. They're friends. Good friends. Opposites attracting. You know the sort of thing. Paula looks after Judith. She really cares. Aberdeen can be a tough town apparently. I know this is corny, but what Paula did was a cry for help.'

'Like attempted suicide?'

'No. Paula's too tough to take that way out. She wanted to give everyone a shock.'

'She certainly did that,' I said.

'So it worked.'

'And now?'

'Who knows? You talk to her.'

Paula and the waitress arrived at the table simultaneously. I poured coffee and ordered a full English breakfast. When the waitress left I sipped at my icy juice and looked at Paula. 'How's it going?' I asked.

'Not too bad,' she said in her soft accent. 'I didn't mean any harm to come to Jude.'

'I know.'

'Is she all right this morning?'

'Seems to be.'

I saw Paula relax. 'Good. I mean it, Mr Sharman—'

'Nick,' I interrupted. 'Call me Nick.'

She smiled. She had a lovely face when she wasn't trying to be toughest kid on the block. She'd be a real beauty in a couple of years. 'Nick,' she said. 'Judith thinks you're so cool.'

'And you?'

'You sorted that lot last night, though I wish you hadn't hit Eno. He wasn't so bad.'

'I was angry. I'm sorry.' And I was.

'He'll survive,' she went on. 'Is Jude coming down?'

'She's getting dressed.'

'And her mum?'

'She'll be down too. She's going to be harder to convince that you meant Judith no harm.'

'I know.'

'But she's not too bad when you get to know her.'

'Is that why you're divorced?' The iron wasn't too far beneath the velvet.

'No,' I said. 'It was my fault. Judith probably told you something about it.'

'She said that you were a copper.'

'I was.'

'That you got into trouble.'

'I did.'

Thankfully, we were interrupted when Laura and Judith came through the door of the restaurant and made for our table.

'Hello, Jude,' said Paula. 'How'ya feeling?'

'OK,' said Judith.

'Hello, Mrs Rudnick.' Paula again.

'Hello, Paula.' Laura was cool, but not as icily cold as I'd feared.

'I'm sorry we caused so much trouble.' Today young Paula was the soul of contrition.

'It could have been worse,' said Laura, and took a seat opposite me.

'So what happens now?' asked Dawn.

'I get these two back up to Scotland,' said Laura, as she

poured herself a cup of coffee. 'There's a small matter of school to be considered. Nick, can you drop us at Heathrow?'

'Sure,' I replied.

'Is Paula coming with us?' asked Judith.

'Of course,' said Laura. 'We're hardly going to leave her down here.'

'In a plane?' said Paula. Suddenly fourteen again. 'I've never been in a plane before.'

'Then it'll be a treat,' said Dawn. 'By the way, has anyone thought to inform the police that we've found these two?'

'I called Robber last night,' I said. 'He's a copper,' I explained. 'He's letting your mother know you're safe, Paula.'

'Good,' she said, but her mood had changed. 'I suppose I'll be in for a row when I get home.'

'I don't think so,' I said. 'Not much of one, anyway. When I saw your mum she just wanted you back.'

'You've been round there?' said Paula.

'Yeah. When I was up in Aberdeen.'

'I didn't know you'd *seen* my mum. How was she?'

'Like I told you last night. Upset. But like you told me, she'll get over it.'

'I didn't mean all that.'

'I know,' I said. 'Forget it.'

Paula smiled at me.

'I'm surprised the police haven't been round here,' said Dawn.

'I didn't actually tell them where we were. Just the town. I didn't fancy being interviewed this morning. Robber wants me to pop in when we get back to London.' I looked at Paula and winked. 'I think it'll be me that's in for the biggest row. I was warned to keep out of it.'

'If it hadn't been for you, we might never have found them,' said Laura, springing to my defence for the first time in years.

'How *did* you find us?' asked Paula.

I winked again and laid my finger against my nose. 'Ask no questions . . .' I said, 'and you'll be told no lies.'

She smiled again. 'It doesn't matter anyway,' she said. 'I'm glad you did.'

13

We left the hotel straight after breakfast. Whilst Dawn packed my stuff and settled up our bill, I went to check the Range Rover. It was a mess. There was a big hole where the rear window had been, the offside back light and indicator cluster was history, the paintwork on the tailgate and flanks of the car was pitted with buckshot scars and the crash cage at the front of the car was buckled from where we'd taken out the fences escaping from Hangman's Field. Plus there were all sorts of assorted scratches on the body that I'm sure hadn't been there when we'd borrowed the motor. Charlie was going to have a cow. Luckily I had enough money in the bank to buy a couple of Vogues, but it was still annoying. On the plus side, all four tyres were hard, so at least we could get home. When our little party gathered in the car park I saw Laura blanch at how close we'd been to disaster.

'How's that cut on your neck?' I asked Paula, to forestall any hysterical reaction from my ex.

Paula touched the plaster that the good doctor had put on the slight wound and said, 'Fine.'

'Good,' I said. 'All aboard then. Next stop Heathrow.'

We slung the baggage in the back, everyone piled in and I headed out of Banbury in the direction of the motorway south. I put my foot down on the thinly populated road, took the M25 turnoff and we were at the airport by eleven. Laura,

Judith and Paula hopped out at the terminal, and under the eagle eye of a turbaned traffic warden we made our farewells.

'Call me when you get home,' I said to Laura. 'And keep Louis off Judith's back.'

'I'll try,' she said. 'Thanks again, Nick. You've been marvellous. And you've got a good woman there,' glancing at Dawn who was busy hugging the two girls. 'Treat her better than you treated me and you might have someone to take care of you in your old age.'

'No worries,' I said.

Whilst Laura said goodbye to Dawn, I gave Judith a hug. 'Take care,' I said. 'And watch those mother's little helpers. They bite.'

'I will, Daddy,' she said. 'Thanks for coming to our rescue. No one's going to believe it.'

'Then keep shtoom.'

I turned to Paula. 'No more weekend breaks on your own,' I said. 'Next time Judith comes down to visit, you come too, all right?'

'Do you mean it?'

I nodded, and she surprised me by jumping up, putting her arms round me and kissing me full on the mouth. There was some tongue in there too and I felt myself blush. At my age. What a tough guy.

I untangled myself from her embrace and said, 'Go on. There's a plane in a few minutes. If you hurry you'll catch it.'

Paula smiled, and I clocked Dawn looking at us and I swear I blushed again.

After we'd waved the trio off, got back in the Vogue and headed for the tunnel back to the motorway, Dawn said, 'You've got a fan there.'

'Who?'

'Come on, Nick, don't act the innocent. Paula of course.'

'Get out of it.'

'God. You men.'

'I believe that could be construed as a sexist remark. If I said, "You women" I'd get a clout from every politically correct arsehole in the room.'

'This isn't a room, it's a car. And we're all alone.'

'I stand corrected.'

I looked over and she was smiling. 'Don't change the subject,' she said. 'You've got a fan and you love it.'

I smiled back. 'Still got it, babe. That old magic something that knocks the women dead.'

'Well keep it locked up, or I might get jealous and cut it off.'

'Christ, Dawn. She's only fourteen.'

'A dangerous age, Holmes.' Then she took my hand. 'But I must say I'm quite proud of you. You did very well, finding them.'

'We,' I corrected her. 'You're not too bad yourself, the way you clouted that geezer in the belly at the camp.'

'I enjoyed it.'

I drove straight back to Charlie's car lot. He was standing, leaning on the bonnet of a 7 Series BMW as I drove up. He took one look at the Range Rover and his face fell.

'Morning, Charles,' I said as I dismounted from the driver's side.

'Don't "morning" me,' he said, looking at the front of the motor. 'What the fuck have you been *doing*?'

'You haven't seen the back,' I said.

When he walked round his face went bright red and when he spoke his voice was apoplectic. 'What happened?'

'Slight altercation with the landed ... Well, I won't say gentry. But they *were* packing shooters.'

'Do you know how much this is going to cost?'

'Put it down to me.'

'Put it down to *you*.'

'Yes. I'd blame the wife's driving, if she wasn't here.'

'Christ, Nick.'

'Just a joke, Charles,' I said. 'Where's your sense of humour gone?'

'Same place as the profit on this motor,' he moaned.

'We got the girls back,' said Dawn, who'd got out of the passenger side. 'I knew you'd be delighted to hear that, Charlie.' I think I might have mentioned that Dawn can get a little sarky from time to time.

He looked up at her and then at me. 'Did you?'

'Yeah. Would you rather Judith had collected the rounds?' That was Dawn again.

'No,' he replied.

'Listen, mate. I'm sorry about the motor,' I said quickly. I didn't want World War Three on my hands over a car. 'But it saved our necks. Get it fixed and I'll stand for it, plus any reasonable amount for loss of business.'

He nodded. 'Are they all right?' he asked. 'The girls?'

'As rain,' I said.

'Good. Sorry, Nick, sorry, Dawn. It's only scrap iron after all.'

'No, mate,' I said. 'It's your living. I shouldn't mess about with it.'

'What the hell? It'll be right as rain in a couple of days. And talking of scrap iron, I suppose you want *your* motor back?'

I nodded.

'Dave,' he called.

A voice replied from out back. 'Yeah?'

'Bring round the Batmobile, will you? Bruce Wayne is back.'

'Sure thing,' the voice said, and within a minute the Chevy arrived dribbling grey smoke from its exhaust.

'Hello, Mr Sharman, Mrs Sharman,' said Dave. 'Have a nice

time in the country?' Then he saw the state of the Vogue and he grinned. 'I see that you did.'

'Shut up, Dave,' said Charlie. 'Haven't you got a car to clean?'

Dawn and I drove back to the flat, and from there I rang Chas.

'Not a word has been mentioned about you,' he said when I'd told him what happened in Banbury, after I'd got his promise it would go no further. We go back far enough to know that our promises to each other are good.

'Let's keep it that way,' I said.

'If you want,' he said back. 'She's not going to make a habit of it, I hope. Or her friend.'

'Me too. But I think she might have learned her lesson. The other one I'm not so sure about.'

'Well, if you need a missing persons story any time, just let me know.'

'I hope I don't,' I said and hung up.

So that just left Robber. I'd made him the last call because I knew that I was in for a bollocking and I wasn't wrong. When I got him on the line, he said, 'Where are you?'

'At home.'

'Get in here now.' And he left me holding the dead dog.

Dawn drove the car, and parked up in a block of flats opposite the police station where a notice on the wall threatened the clamp for any car left unattended without a permit. I fancied I was in for the rack myself, kissed her on the mouth, and went over to the red-brick building where Old Bill did their business.

The desk sergeant called Robber up on the phone, then buzzed me through the security door, and the inspector met me at the foot of the stairs that led up to the canteen and the CID offices.

'You prat,' he said as he led the way up. 'You silly, stupid prat.'

'What did I do that was so bad?' I asked when we were sitting down on opposite sides of his paper-strewn desk.

'You did what you always do,' he said. And the way that he said it, tiredly, made me suddenly feel sorry for the man in late middle age, dressed in a bad suit, sitting in front of me. 'You got involved in something that was none of your business.'

'It was my daughter,' I protested.

'OK, Sharman,' he said. 'It was your daughter, and from what I hear you could've got her killed up there in Banbury, yesterday.'

'What did you hear?' I asked.

'I hear that the gunfight at the OK Corral was replayed in a field just outside of town last night.'

'How do you know that?'

'It's my job.'

I shrugged. 'You win,' I said. 'I almost blew it, but I got them out.'

'More by luck than judgement, from what I could ascertain from the local CID.'

'But I did it.'

'Yes, you did. And you know that I should charge you.'

'For what?'

'Let me name the many and various ways: obstructing the police in the course of their duties, assault, assault with a deadly weapon, ABH, dangerous driving, destruction of private property. Do you want me to go on?'

I held up my arms, fists clenched, wrists together, as if waiting to be handcuffed. 'Book 'm, Danno,' I said.

He almost smiled, but not quite. 'But I had a word with an old pal of mine who's a chief super up there.'

'And?'

'And they're prepared to forget the charges. Apparently you prevented quite a nasty incident taking place. The hijacking of a band of travellers by some armed vigilantes.'

'Who told them that?'

'A couple of the travellers and one very frightened vigilante who couldn't wait to make a clean breast of it at the nearest police station.'

'I bet he was wearing a Barbour,' I said.

'What?'

'Nothing. So am I forgiven?' I asked.

He almost smiled for a second time. Once again, not quite, but almost. 'Get out of here,' he said.

So I went.

So that was that. As far as I was concerned it was the end of the case of the detective's missing daughter. But, as so often in my life, I was wrong. Probably more wrong than I'd ever been before.

part two

pills

By the pricking of my thumbs, Something wicked this way comes.

Macbeth

14

So that was that.

The next six weeks or so were quiet. I spoke to Judith a lot, and Laura too. Judith seemed to be getting on better with her mother, which was good. She seemed to be getting on not so well with Louis. Deep in my heart of hearts, where dark things stir, I thought that was good too. I had never liked the man who'd taken my wife and daughter away from me and I never would. Not that I shared that information with anyone. Not even Dawn. Especially Dawn. I just kept it locked away where it could do no one any harm. Except maybe me.

Judith was still seeing Paula. But not as much as previously. Laura had said that it was all right for them to be friends, and as was inevitable, as soon as it was OK with mum, Judith didn't want to do it so much any more. Kids! I ask you.

But they were still mates. Still met on Saturday afternoons in the shopping mall. But as Judith told me several times, she was busy studying and she just didn't have enough time for a social life.

Then, on another quiet Sunday night at the end of September I got a phone call from my daughter and things would never be the same again.

Never.

Not in this world, or the next if there is one.

Dawn and I had spent another of a series of lazy days together as the late summer turned to autumn and the leaves started to fall in the street outside our flat. It was eight-thirty. I think about it often now and there was a silly cop show on TV.

91

I picked up the phone and I heard Judith's voice. But she sounded different. Older. And all the times I've spoken to her since, she's never been the child I once knew. She was learning, you see. The bitter truth that living is losing. She was learning early. But there's never a good time.

'Daddy,' she said, and started to cry.

'What, darling?' I said. 'What's the matter?' Dawn looked over at me and I pulled my face into a mystified expression.

'It's Paula.'

'What about her?'

'She's in hospital. She's very ill.'

'How ill?'

'Very ill. She took something.'

'What?'

'An E.'

'Did you take one?'

'No. I told you I won't take them again. She was with her friend Clare.'

'Clare. The girl I met when I was up in Aberdeen?'

'That's right.'

'Is Clare in hospital too?' I remembered her face when we'd talked and how young and pretty she'd been.

'No, Daddy.' Judith started to sob again.

'What?'

'She's dead.'

'*What?*'

'She's dead.'

'Dead.'

Dawn got up and came over to stand beside me.

'Yes.'

'I'm so sorry, love. Is Paula bad?'

'Not so bad. But she's in a coma.'

'Christ. Is your mother there?'

'Yes.'

'With you?'

'In the kitchen.'

'Get her, will you?'

The phone went down with a clonk and I told Dawn what Judith had told me.

'Clare,' she said. 'Wasn't that the girl who told you about the travellers, and where Judith and Paula were going to be?'

'Yes.'

Then Laura came on the line.

'Nick. Judith had to speak to you.'

'Of course. Is she all right?'

'Not really. It's been a shock.'

'She hasn't been taking anything?'

'No. I'm sure of it.'

'Me too. When did all this happen?'

'Last night. There was a party on the estate. A rave they called it, in an empty flat. Judith was here all evening.'

'Good. Listen, let me know what happens, will you?'

'Of course.'

'Can I speak to Judith again?'

'Sure.'

'And Laura.'

'What?'

'Take care of her.'

'Of course I will. Here she is.'

My daughter came back on the line. 'Do you want me there?' I asked.

'No. There's nothing you can do.'

She was right of course. 'Well you know I'm just a phone call away.'

'I know.'

'Any time. Night or day.'

'I know, Daddy.'

'Good.'

'And Daddy?'

'What?'

'Thanks.'

'For what?'

'Nothing. Just thanks.' And we made our farewells and hung up.

I poured myself and Dawn a vodka each, sat down and lit a cigarette. 'That could have been Judith you know.'

Dawn nodded.

'Dead, or in a coma like Paula.'

She nodded again.

'This stuff that's coming in. These new drugs. They're shit.'

A third nod.

'I think someone needs teaching a lesson.'

A fourth.

'Wanna help?'

A fifth. And so the die was cast.

15

Clare's death made eight lines in the 'In Brief' column in the *Telegraph* the next morning, under the headline DRUG GIRL DIES. The report simply read:

> Clare Stewart (14) died in hospital yesterday afternoon after taking what were assumed to be tablets of Ecstasy at a party near her home in Aberdeen on Saturday night.
>
> A police spokesman said that there was one other casualty who was recovering in hospital.

Not much of an obituary for a kid with all her life in front of her.

After breakfast I phoned Inspector Todd in Aberdeen.

'Nick Sharman,' I said when he came on the line. 'Remember me?'

'How could I forget?'

'No hard feelings?' I said.

'You found the kids. But you could have let me know.'

'Sorry. I didn't want to get all tied up in bureaucratic red tape.'

'I take it you're calling about Clare Stewart and Paula McGann.'

'Yeah. Judith called me last night and told me what had happened. How is Paula?'

'She woke this morning.'

'Is she OK?'

'Seems to be.'

'What the hell did she take?'

'The same as Clare, but not as many.'

'How many?'

'From what we can gather, Paula took three tabs, Clare took five.'

'Jesus. What was in them?'

'You really want to know?'

'Sure.'

'MDMA, LSD, heroin, rat poison, and are you ready for this? Ground glass, probably from old light bulbs.'

'You are joking?'

'I don't joke about little girls dying.'

'Course you don't. Sorry. But ground glass.'

'Nice little cocktail.'

'Did she overdose on the smack?'

'That and a haemorrhage in her stomach.'

'Can't anything be done about this stuff?' I realized I was being naïve as soon as I said it.

'Don't make me laugh, Sharman. Didn't you work on the drug squad yourself down in the Met? As long as there's a demand for anything, someone will make sure there's a supply. And at anything up to twenty-five quid for a tab, it's a very lucrative supply, believe me.'

'Where did those kids get that sort of money?'

'There's ways.'

Of course there were. After I hung up the phone I decided to go and see Robber again.

16

I drove myself to the police station and took the copy of Monday's paper with me. It was about eleven when I arrived and Robber was in his lair.

'What do you want now?' he asked when I'd been led through security and found an empty space on the edge of the chair in his office to perch myself.

'Did you see this?' I asked and tossed the paper on to his desk where it dislodged a pile of reports he obviously hadn't read.

He scanned the item that I'd marked with a felt-tip pen. 'Friends of yours?' he asked.

'Yeah.' And I explained.

'So?'

'You know that Judith took some of that crap in Banbury. It could've been her lying dead.'

He nodded. 'These kids,' he said.

'We all like to experiment.'

'Nowadays it can kill you. But what's it got to do with me? Aberdeen's a long way away.'

'And a lot of drugs come through this part of the world.'

'Every part of the world.'

'I'd like to put a spanner into someone's works.'

'Whose?'

'I don't care, frankly.'

'Let's get this straight,' he said. 'Because your daughter took some ecstasy in Banbury a few weeks ago, and now some kid you met for half an hour in Aberdeen is dead, and your daughter's mate who, from what you told me, is on the slippery slope anyway, ends up in hospital, you want to run a one-man war against the drug trade?'

'Something like that,' I said.

'And you want my help?'

I nodded.

'You just want me to pluck a name out of the air, give it to you and set you loose?'

I nodded again.

'Sharman. I'm a copper. Have been for thirty years. It doesn't work like that.'

'And you're retiring soon,' I said. 'Time marches on. There must be some villain that you've never been able to put away. Some slag you'd like to see come a serious cropper one way or another. Don't tell me there isn't, because there always is.'

'And you don't care who it is?'

'I'd like it to be someone you suspect of bringing in E. Someone who's right dirty. Come on, Inspector, there must be one.'

'And what do you intend to do?'

'Hurt him. Find out what he's up to and screw him.'

'Physically?'

'No. Well maybe a bit. But it's his business I really want to fuck with.'

Robber smiled, showing dirty teeth. 'I couldn't do it,' he

said. Then he punched the keyboard of the computer that stood on the side of his desk. The machine bleeped at him and he said, 'Soddin' technology. Whatever happened to pencil and paper?' and tried again. He squinted at the screen then looked at his watch. 'Elevenses,' he said. 'Fancy a cuppa?'

I nodded, and he got up from his seat. 'I'll be five minutes. Bacon sarnie?'

'No thanks,' I replied, and he walked out of the room closing the door firmly behind him, and I went round to his side of the desk and looked at the computer myself.

The information that scrolled across the screen concerned a certain James Andrew Marshall with an address in Addington, close to Croydon. The posh part of Addington where the TV celebrities and comedians buy smart houses, then get them repossessed when fickle fame deserts them. Marshall's date of birth was in 1960, which made him thirty-six next birthday. He'd been arrested more times than Elton John had been in detox, for everything from shoplifting to possession of Class A drugs, with a little bit of GBH and attempted murder in between, but had never been convicted and had only done time on remand. A fine, upstanding citizen by all accounts, and just the sort of geezer I was looking for. I found a scrap of clean paper on Robber's desk and copied down the relevant details, then went back to my seat.

Robber came in a couple of minutes later and handed me a thick mug of strong, copper's tea, then sat down behind his desk and turned off the computer without a word.

'You want to be very careful,' he said with his mouth full of bacon sandwich.

'How careful?'

'As careful as you've ever been.'

'Why?'

He leant forward, elbows on his desk. 'If you happen to be thinking about paying a certain party a visit, just remember that he's a serious player. He likes body building, martial arts and guns. And he loves his doggie. A very vicious beast by all accounts. The kind that snacks it up on postmen when the Pal meat runs out. *And*, the thing he hates most is anyone trying to stop his God-given right to break the law.'

'Him or the dog?'

'Both.'

'Is that right?'

'It is.'

'Is there anyone else at home I have to keep an eye out for? A homicidal mum f'rinstance?'

'There's a tart there to keep the home fires burning. Make his macrobiotic salads and keep his bed warm. Quite a girl herself from what we know. Karen. From Loughton in Essex.'

'Nice little family.'

'Nuclear. Literally.'

'I'll remember that.'

'Not that you got it from me.'

'Course not.'

'I mean that, Sharman. It's pension on line time.'

'Trust me.'

'Do you think you'd be here now if I didn't.'

I shook my head, drank my tea, fed Robber's nicotine habit with my Silk Cut and nattered about nothing. Then I left. As I went he said, 'I don't want to see you here again.'

'All right, Mr Robber,' I said.

'Good luck, Sharman.'

'And you.'

As I was between Tulse Hill and Croydon I decided to cruise round and scope out Marshall's gaff. I drove the Chevy down to Addington, found the road I was looking for on the southernmost page of the *A–Z*, dumped the motor three streets away and took a stroll. The house was large, secluded and looked like it had cost close to a million. There was a high wall round the garden and a big iron gate in front of the drive. The place was belled up solid. Lots of alarm boxes and blue lights planted across the front of the house, but apart from a solitary squirrel sitting on the branch of a horse chestnut tree, there was no sign of life and the only indication that a guard dog existed was a solitary turd on the closely mown grass of the front lawn. I hung around for a few minutes, but the area was well patrolled by private security as well as Old Bill, so I didn't stay long. I needed an expert to give the place a close going over and I knew just the face to do it.

But first I had to talk to Dawn.

17

So I went home and laid it all out for her. I had to tell her what I had planned. I was in a modern marriage after all. The bonding of equals. And besides, I needed her help.

She jumped at it. I was surprised she was so enthusiastic.

'It's going to be dangerous,' I said. 'These people won't appreciate us putting our oar in.'

'So?' she said. 'It'll be fun.'

Fun wasn't exactly the word I'd've used, but I said nothing.

'But why these people in particular?' she asked.

'Because they're there,' I replied. 'And they're dirty.'

'But they had nothing to do with what happened in Scotland, surely.'

I shrugged. 'I doubt it. But that's not the point. Anyone will do. Anyone who's handy. Does it matter?'

She shook her head.

'So it's a runner?' I said after a moment.

She nodded.

'Great. How's the cash situation?'

I knew that Dawn with her squirrel instincts had stashed some spare dough away. Her fighting fund she called it.

'How much do you need?'

'Five hundred for now.'

She went into our tiny bathroom and came out a few seconds later with a wodge of notes in her hand. Where she manages to hide it without me knowing I can never work out.

'Got an envelope?' I asked.

She dug one out of a drawer. I put the cash inside, wrote Marshall's address on the back, stashed it in my pocket, found the car keys and said, 'I'm going to look for someone. I'll be back later.'

'Do you want me to come?'

'Not this time. The geezer doesn't know you. You'll meet him in due course. Unless he's banged up at Her Majesty's pleasure of course.'

'Like that, is it?'

'Yeah,' I replied, kissed her on the cheek and split.

I was looking for 'Monkey' Mann, a jobbing villain, who'd always been pleased previously to earn a little extra dough to get me into places I shouldn't be. His nickname came from the fact that he could climb anything. *Anything.* And make it look easy.

I took the car down to Beckenham and checked out Monkey's local haunts. That day he was sitting at the bar of the Goat and Cheese, a dark cave of a boozer that had seen better days, located at the back of a huge shopping development where half the shops were empty and the other half were having closing down sales. He was deep in dialogue with a young lady of what I could only gather was easy virtue as I overheard the end of their conversation.

'It's fifty nicker, Monkey,' she was saying tiredly as I came up beside them. 'Cash. I don't take kites or plastic.'

'Listen, doll,' pleaded Monkey. 'I'm a bit short at the present. Cash flow problems. You know how it is. Couldn't you see your way to letting me 'ave one on the slate? I'll see you all right in the week. A geezer owes me a spot of wedge.'

'On the *slate*,' she said. 'On the fuckin' slate. What d'you fink I am? If I let you 'ave it for nuffin', every bleedin' punter in the place will want the same.'

'Not for nothing, love,' explained Monkey patiently. 'Just give me time to pay. Like Montague Burton used to for a whistle.'

'I ain't Montague Burton, whoever he was, Monkey,' said the young lady, who was most fetchingly attired in gold stilettos, black fishnets, a lime green skirt and a strawberry pink angora sweater that, if it had been cut any lower over her chest, would hardly have kept her belly button warm. 'So show us your cash, you cheeky old fucker, or I'm out of here.'

'Not interrupting anything, I hope,' I said as I walked up to the pair of them.

Monkey looked up at the sound of my voice. 'Hello, Mr S,' he said. 'Long time.' He too was dressed for amour, I could tell, in a wide-lapelled safari jacket that went out of fashion just as punk came in, a dark blue sateen shirt with seven-inch points on the collars, pale blue flares and white casuals with gold bars across the fronts.

'Hello, Monkey,' I said back, looked him up and down in amazement and asked, 'Who dressed you this morning? Agnetha from Abba?'

'All the go this gear,' said Monkey in a hurt tone. 'The seventies are back.'

'So they tell me. Want a drink? And one for your charming friend?' I smiled at the girl. 'I'm afraid I haven't had the pleasure.' Although it was a racing certainty that most of the other geezers in the place *had*.

'Sorry, Mr S. I'm forgetting me manners,' said Monkey. 'This is Sonia. Sonia, this is Mr Nick Sharman, an old friend of mine.'

Sonia offered one hand whose black-painted nails were bitten to the quick. 'Delighted,' she said. 'I'll have a large G & T, ice and a slice. I'm a model.'

'I thought so,' I replied. 'Didn't I see you on the cover of *Vogue* last month? Or was it *Vanity Fair*?'

'I do like your friend,' said Sonia, blushing prettily. 'Why haven't I met him before?'

'Not his usual manor, love,' said Monkey, as I ordered Sonia's drink, a large Irish whiskey for him and a pint for myself. 'He comes from Tulse Hill.'

'And I keep losing my passport,' I said. 'You know how hard it is to get across the border at Crystal Palace.'

Sonia looked perplexed. 'I never have any trouble on Network South East,' she said.

'It must be your pretty face,' I said back.

'D'you think so?' she asked as the drinks arrived and I exchanged a fiver plus change for them. 'I do massage too. Would you like my card?'

'I think my wife might confiscate it and put me in the corner for the evening.'

'Are you into domination then?' asked Sonia. 'I do a very good line in punishment for naughty boys.'

'No, not really. If anything, I like to be the one in control.'

'I just bet you do,' she said and licked her little pink tongue across the hot red lipstick she wore. 'And I bet you're good at it too.'

'Sonia, I'm afraid that's something you'll probably never find out, sad to say. I've turned into a very boring and faithful husband.'

'They're the worst kind when they get out on the loose,' she replied, obviously out of bitter experience. 'But never mind. If you change your mind, Monkey knows where to find me.'

'I'll remember that. Now I'm sorry to be rude and I don't want to break up the party, but I need fifteen minutes alone with the man. Could I ask you to excuse us?'

'No problem,' she replied, taking out her cigarettes, lighting one and slipping a length of chewing gum into her mouth at the same time. 'Monkey's skint, and I can see an old boyfriend of mine's just come in. I think I'll go join him.'

'Good,' I said. 'And Monkey might just be coming into some money, so I wouldn't elope with the other fella if I were you.'

Sonia raised her eyebrows, slid off the stool where she'd been sitting and sashayed across the carpet towards a florid-looking individual in a suit that looked like he'd been cleaning streets in it, who'd just rolled in to join the fun.

'Still got impeccable taste in women I see, Monkey,' I said as I took over the stool that was still warm from Sonia's bottom.

He looked over his shoulder at her retreating back appreciatively. 'I dunno, Mr S,' he said. 'I must be gettin' old. Can't even get a bunk up on tick any more.' Then he turned back to me and said, 'So what can I do for you today? You mentioned money.'

'I need to get into a house.'

'No problem.'

'This is no ordinary house,' I said. 'There's lots of security. Burglar alarms. Probably infra reds. And a very big, very fierce dog.'

Monkey shrugged. 'Do the alarms go through to the police?'

'I doubt that very much,' I said. 'This place belongs to a bad man. A very bad man. The Bill would love to be able to get inside for a squint.'

'Security firm?'

'Maybe.'

'Give us the address. I'll take a look round myself.'

'Be careful, Monkey,' I said. 'I mean it. If this geezer finds out you're sniffing around, he'll hurt you. Hurt you seriously.'

'I have done this sort of thing before, Mr S,' Monkey said sniffily as if I was questioning his professional abilities.

'I know.'

'When do you want to go in?'

'Soon as possible.'

'Then what?'

'Then you piss off, Monkey. You get us inside and then you vanish. That's it.'

'Us?'

'Me and Dawn.'

'You're going in with a bird?'

'She's my wife. The only one I trust. And Monkey. We're going in armed.'

He shrugged. 'How much?'

'A grand. Five hundred now, five hundred on the night.' I showed him the envelope I'd brought with me.

'A monkey for Monkey, eh?'

I nodded. 'The address is on the envelope. Memorize it and burn it.'

'You sound like *Mission Impossible*.' Well up on trash TV was the Monk.

'I don't want anyone knowing who went into that house,' I said. 'Ever.'

'You ain't gonna kill nobody.'

'I hope it doesn't come to that.'

'Who's inside?'

'A bloke called Marshall. And his girlfriend. And the pooch. That's it.'

'Why?'

'Why what?'

'Why you going in?'

'It's a long story. Marshall's got some information I want. At least, I think he has.'

Monkey looked over his shoulder again at Sonia, who was comfortably seated next to her other friend with her arm linked through his.

'Gimme the dough,' he said.

'If you take it now, Monks, you go through with the job. No backing out.'

'I don't back out, Mr S. You should know that by now.'

'I know,' I said, and slid the envelope towards him across the pub table. It vanished into an inside pocket of his jacket.

'Righto, Mr S,' he said. 'I'll be in touch.'

'Soon.'

'Soonest.'

'See you then, Monkey. Have fun.' And with that I walked out of the pub, giving Sonia a wave as I went.

18

I went back home again and told Dawn what had gone on down at the pub.

'How much cash have we got left?' I asked her, when I'd finished.

'Here?'

'Yeah.'

'How much do you need?'

'Enough to buy some guns.'

'How much is that?'

'A lot. I need a handgun for each of us, and I thought I'd

invest in a fully automatic machine pistol if I can get hold of one.'

She didn't turn a hair. 'Why not wait for a couple of months? Father Christmas might bring you one down the chimney.'

'No time, love. Have we got three grand?'

'Just about.'

'What, here?'

She nodded.

'You're amazing,' I said.

She ignored the compliment. She knew what she was. 'And there's plenty more in the bank,' she said.

'That's good. Get me what we've got and I'll worry about the rest later.'

Dawn went into the bathroom again and came back with a large Jiffy bag which she upended on the table and a whole bunch of fifties and twenties slid out. We counted the dough and it came to two thousand eight hundred pounds, which we bundled up into four lots of five hundred each and eight single hundreds. That evening I went down a boozer off the Falcon Road in Clapham where I'd been before on a similar errand, taking the cash with me. The same bearded, beer-gutted geezer I'd seen there the last time was hanging out by the bar. He looked at me as I walked in, and followed me with his eyes as I went to the bar. I ordered a pint of lager and looked over at him. 'Drink?' I said.

'Do I know you?'

'We've met before.'

He nodded. 'Lager top,' he said.

I ordered it when my drink arrived. When the barmaid put the second, tall, frosty glass in front of me, Beergut walked over and joined me. 'Something you need?' he asked.

'A new hat. Hats. Two.'

'Going in mob handed, are we?'

I smiled. 'Something like that.'

He fished out a cigarette and said, 'Gotta light?' I pulled out one of the bundles containing a ton and passed it over to him with my lighter. He lit his cigarette and the money vanished. 'Cheers,' he said. 'Gonna be around for a bit?'

'As long as it takes.'

'Keep an eye on my drink.' And he walked out of the boozer.

I stayed put for half an hour before he came back, tasted his beer pulled a face and added some ice from the bucket on the bar. 'The cab outside,' he said. 'Same as last time.'

I finished my pint. 'Cheers,' I said and left.

Outside in the warm, autumn air sat a black London taxi with its 'FOR HIRE' sign turned off. As I approached it, the rear door cracked open slightly. I pulled it all the way and climbed in. Before I could close it properly again, the cab pulled away. I fell into the back seat next to a large figure wrapped up unseasonably in a heavy coat, scarf and hat. The driver was equally bundled up and he had his mirror turned so that I couldn't see his face.

'Hello again, dear,' said the figure sitting next to me. 'Back in business?'

'That's right.'

'Whatever happened to that nice little piece I sold you the last time?'

'It got mislaid.'

'So much of my merchandise does. What do you need?'

'A couple of pistols. An auto and a revolver. Small calibre revolver. Nine-mill auto. Plus some clips for the auto and ammo for both.'

'I hope you've emptied your piggy bank.'

I said nothing, and the large figure awkwardly pulled a cardboard box from beside him. There wasn't much room for the pair of us on the seat, but he managed. He opened the top of the box and pulled out a Browning niner semi-automatic.

'Been used a few times,' he said. 'But I've changed the barrel. It's been test fired and is *very* accurate.'

He passed it over and I hefted it in my hand.

'Fifteen-shot clip,' said the figure. 'A very fine weapon.'

'How much?'

'Six hundred.'

'Ammunition?'

'A hundred rounds, a hundred pounds.'

I put the gun in my lap. 'Got spare clips?'

He nodded.

'Revolver?'

'A thirty-two?'

'Sounds fine.'

He put his hand back in the box and drew out a Colt Detective Special with a two-inch barrel. Not much of a stopper, but handy for Dawn's handbag. He passed it over. It was an old gun with the blueing on the barrel worn away in places. I told him so.

'It's a good gun,' he said. 'And a bargain at one-fifty.'

'Ammo?'

'Fifty rounds, Smith and Wesson long. Fifty notes.'

'All together?'

'Nine hundred sovs.'

'No discount for bulk? And an old customer?'

I heard him chuckle. 'Eight-fifty.'

I pulled out one of the five-hundred-quid bundles and four more of the tons, split one of them in half and held the money out to him. As he reached for it, I pulled it back. 'There's something else I want,' I said.

The fat man looked at me and the money. 'Like what, dear?' he asked. 'Always happy to oblige if I can.'

'A machine pistol,' I said. 'Fully auto, with a suppressor, and more ammo to go with.'

His eyes narrowed. 'We are getting ambitious, aren't we, dear? That's a very heavy request.'

'I'm dealing with very heavy people.'

'It's not really my type of merchandise. Those type of weapons are more for the younger, wilder element of society. Crackheads, etc.' He pondered for a moment. 'But I can give you a name. However, let me warn you. The gentleman is not fond of people of our ethnic persuasion, although we have done business on one or two occasions. And his abode is in one of the less salubrious areas of this fair city of ours.'

'I'll take my chances,' I said.

'And chances they will be, I can assure you. The individual you want is called Darkman.'

I gave the fat man a quizzical look.

'Yes. Just Darkman,' he said. 'And he conducts his affairs from an apartment on the Lion Estate.'

Shit, I thought. 'The Lion,' I repeated.

'That's correct.'

I'd had dealings on the Lion before. It's down Deptford way, and is without doubt the worst estate in London. A stinking drain for every lowlife in south London.

'I know it,' I said.

'Who doesn't, dear?' The fat man gave me a flat number in one of the highrises that dominate the place, and I gave him the cash, which he counted off with his chubby fingers. When he was satisfied, he tapped on the glass partition between us and the driver and we headed back towards Clapham. The same as last time he told me he'd buy the guns back at 25 per cent of the price he'd sold them to me for. And just like the last time we'd done business too, he dropped me off about five minutes' walk from the pub. A careful man.

I watched the cab speed off towards the river as I walked back to my motor, and his final words echoed in my ears. 'Good luck, dear,' he said. 'You'll need it.'

19

I took the guns back to the flat, cleaned and dry fired both of them, loaded the clips for the automatic and tried to give Dawn some idea of the basics of using the .32. Now, it's difficult to teach someone to shoot without actually using the gun. Sure, any fool can hold a pistol and pull the trigger. Everyone's seen it a million times on TV and at the cinema, but it's a lot different when the gun is loaded with real bullets. First of all they make a hell of a noise, and they kick, and finally you've got to remember that bullets do serious damage. They hurt. Dawn had seen *what* sort of damage and hurt before, but had never actually fired a gun, even if she'd looked pretty cool toting that shotgun in the field outside Banbury.

'We'll try and get some practice in soon,' I said. 'But the constabulary in this country doesn't take kindly to people blasting away with illegal guns all over the scenery. So we'll wait until we get the machine gun, if I can get hold of one, and we'll test it out somewhere quiet early one morning.'

At least Dawn didn't seem scared of the piece. She held it confidently, dry fired it happily, clicked out the cylinder and spun it like an expert, but I still wanted her to get the feel of *real* shooting before we got serious. Right then there was nothing I could do about it. In this life, I've found, you work with what you've got, and vamp the middle eight.

I told her what the fat man had told me about the geezer who could supply us with a machine pistol, and we decided to go visit him the next day.

* * *

I got Dawn to drive me to the estate around noon and left her in the car on the outskirts with the doors locked, the loaded thirty-two tucked into the waistband of her jeans and the Browning under the driver's seat, cocked and unlocked. She also had a wicked-looking kitchen knife with a nine-inch blade under her bra strap at the back. On the way we stopped at our bank and withdrew another couple of grand, which Dawn put in her handbag. I didn't know what the deal was going to be, if in fact a deal there was. I knew it was dangerous for us to carry that sort of money in that sort of area, but I needed some cash handy just in case.

'Give me an hour,' I said. 'If I'm any longer, I'm in trouble. Then you should call the cops.'

She shook her head. 'If you're more than an hour I'll come and get you.'

There was no point in arguing. 'Don't cut yourself getting out of the car,' I said, leant over from the passenger side and kissed her.

I was wearing my old Schott leather, blue jeans, a denim shirt and soft slip-on Timberlands. I'd left my watch at home. Around this estate they'd mug you for an old Swatch, let alone a solid gold Rolex, and my wrist felt naked without it. I carried no weapons, cigarettes, matches or money. Nothing, except my driving licence for ID, for what it was worth. I was going in cold and I was scared stiff.

I walked away from the car with as much swagger as I could muster but I could already feel the sweat running down from my armpits.

I strolled on to the estate proper and picked my way through the broken glass, dog shit, and fast-food wrappers that littered the streets. It was quiet between the highrise blocks. Too quiet, as the Lone Ranger would have remarked to Tonto. I wasn't crazy about it, I'll own up to that.

I found the right block and walked up the four flights to

the floor I was looking for. It was quiet inside the block too. No music or screaming and shouting. I was willing to bet it wasn't this quiet come Saturday night when the pubs chucked out.

The flat I wanted was protected by a metal fire door and the one window that looked out on to the corridor was screened with mesh.

I hammered on the metal of the door and the noise boomed down the stairwell.

After a few seconds a slot in the fire door opened and a pair of brown, bloodshot eyes gave me a blimp.

'Whaddya want?' said the voice belonging to the eyes.

'I want to see Darkman.'

'We all darkmen in here, man. Aincha heard?' And he laughed.

'Darkman,' I said again.

'You filth?'

I shook my head. 'My name's Sharman. Nick Sharman.'

'Who sencha?'

'A geezer in a taxi. Sells hats.'

The slot closed with a bang and I stayed where I was. I didn't have much choice.

After a couple of minutes I heard the rattle of chains and the sound of bolts being pulled back, and with a screech from the hinges, the fire door opened outwards, and the biggest black geezer I'd ever seen stood in the doorway. 'Got any ID?' he said.

I showed him my driver's licence. I felt like I was trying to cash a cheque. But if this fucker bounced, I probably would too, on the concrete pavement four floors down.

He looked at it, then at me, and sneered, 'This don't mean nothin'.'

I shrugged. 'What do you want?' I asked.

It was like we were having a friendly chat over a pint in our

113

local, instead of standing outside a crack house where I was trying to buy an automatic weapon.

'Tell me about the hat man,' he said.

'He's fat, sounds like an old queen and drives around in the back of a black cab.'

'Why'd he send you here?'

'He said the Darkman could get me what I want.'

He made a sizzling sound with his teeth against his lips. 'He got that right,' he said. 'You better come inside.'

He stood back to allow me entry, and when I was inside tugged the fire door closed with another screech of metal.

The front hall of the flat was dark, with a dingy carpet on the floor and the walls decorated with graffiti.

A big black woman came out through a door and stood looking at me. She wore a short, scarlet dress cut low at the front to show off most of her big, hard-looking boobs. Her hair was in dreads and caught up in a pineapple look, and she carried an open flick-knife in one hand.

The black geezer pushed me up against the wall.

'Jacket,' he said.

I took off my Schott and he examined it inside and out, checking all the seams. When he was satisfied he dropped it on the floor.

'Shirt.'

I unsnapped the front of my western-style shirt, took it off and passed it over. He checked the pockets and the double yoke, then dropped it on top of my jacket.

'Shoes and socks.'

I slid out of my loafers and, as he examined them, took off my socks and stood barefoot on the crummy carpet.

'Strides.'

I looked at the woman and she looked back at me and cleaned her long, scarlet fingernails with the point of the flick-knife blade.

I unbuttoned my 501s and took them off, hopping awkwardly from one foot to the other as I did it.

The black geezer checked them thoroughly too, pulling out the pockets then consigning them also to the growing pile of clothes on the floor.

'Shorts.'

'Hey man,' I said, and looked at the woman again.

'You shy?' he asked.

'Sure.'

'You might be wired. If you want to see Darkman, I check everywhere.'

I dropped my shorts and he looked at my groin. 'See, Marsha,' he said. 'White meat is smaller.'

'I seen white meat before,' she retorted.

I could actually feel my balls shrink as they discussed the size of my genitals. It wasn't one of the highspots of my week.

'Don't tell Darkman,' said the black geezer with a frown. 'He don't dig inter-racial sex.'

'Unless he fuckin' some blonde bimbo,' she said, and with a sneer at my privates, went back through the door she'd come in by.

The black geezer turned me to face the wall, then back, and tossed me my shorts. At least he hadn't given me an internal.

'You travel light,' he said.

'Best way,' I replied.

He nodded. 'Get dressed, man,' he said. 'You clean.'

I didn't need to be told twice, and struggled back into my clothes almost quicker than it takes to tell. Then the black guy opened another door off the hall and waved me through politely.

I walked into a hot room that smelled equally of marijuana, stale sweat and Chanel perfume. The curtains were tightly closed over the windows, which I would have been willing to bet were masked with steel themselves, and only one dim light burned in the ceiling fixture. A tired-sounding electric fan moved the air around the room lethargically. There was a quantity of expensive-looking leather furniture, but it was scarred with cigarette burns and knife cuts. A huge, glass-topped coffee table sat in the centre of the room covered with cigarette papers, grass, disposable lighters, two small hand mirrors, shredded cigarettes, crack-smoking paraphernalia, dirty cups and dishes, fag packets, a pile of new fifty-pound notes, a couple of portable phones, some oblong paper wraps for coke or smack, razor blades and all sorts of other shit. Behind the coffee table on a raised dais was a beaten-up-looking, high-backed, gold-painted chair, with red velvet cushions and armrests, that looked like some kind of throne. Seated on it, with one leg over one of the arms, was a skinny, thirty-something black man in a single-breasted silvery-grey sharkskin suit, a white shirt with a tab collar, and a narrow black tie with a gold clip. His feet were immaculately shod in grey, Italian loafers, the one hanging over the arm of the chair tapping to the beat of music that only he could hear.

'He's cool, chief,' said the huge geezer from behind me.

The man in the chair nodded and said, 'Come in. Welcome to my world. If you're Babylon you're dead.'

'No,' I said. 'I've got more sense.'

He nodded sagely, and I walked further into the room and the huge geezer followed me, closed the door behind him and took up position leaning against the wall next to it with his arms folded. I looked over my shoulder at him and he nodded, like he was saying, 'Now you're in, you stay here till we say you can go.'

I turned my head back to the guy in the chair. 'Darkman?' I asked.

'In the flesh. What brings you to my kingdom?'

So he did think it was a throne.

'I was sent here.'

'By the mad hatter.'

'Right.'

'We've done business.'

'So he said.'

'I hope that was all he said.' His tone was menacing.

'It was,' I reassured him.

'Good. So what can I do for you?'

The door behind me opened again and the woman in the scarlet dress came in, walked over to the table, knelt down, opened one of the wraps, dumped the contents on one of the mirrors and started cutting out lines with a razor blade.

I looked at her, then at Darkman.

'Don't be shy,' he said. 'Spit it out.'

'I want to buy a machine pistol. An Uzi or an Ingram, and some ammunition. Plus a silencer. That's very important.'

'And why should I sell to you?'

The woman finished cutting out half a dozen fat lines and rolled up one of the fifties into a tight tube. She took the mirror and the banknote over to Darkman and offered it to him. He scarfed up two lines, threw his head back and swallowed hard, then looked at me again.

'Why?' he repeated.

'Why not?'

He thought about it as the woman stood silently beside him. After a moment he flapped his hand and she snorted two lines herself, then walked over and offered the mirror and note to me.

I touched the tip of the pinky on my right hand to the end of one line and licked off the residue. I got a freeze right away, plucked the note from between the woman's fingers and snorted a line up each nostril. I felt the coke kick in immediately and the taste of aluminium at the back of my throat as my mouth filled with saliva and I swallowed.

'Good stuff,' I said.

'Only the best for Darkman. And you're careful. I like that.'

I said nothing in reply.

'You know a cat called Emerald?' Darkman asked after a moment.

'Sure,' I said. 'We're old friends.'

Darkman nodded. 'Do up a blunt, bitch,' he said to Marsha.

The woman knelt down in front of the table again and started to put a five-skin, all-grass joint together.

'Can I have a cigarette?' I asked.

Darkman flapped his hand again and Martha took a Marlboro Lite from a crumpled packet, lit it with one of the disposable lighters and passed it to me. The tip was red with her lipstick and I could taste the tang of the cosmetic as I took a drag. She went back to rolling the joint.

'You helped him out a while back,' said Darkman.

'That's what friends are for.'

'How much cash you got?'

'On me. None. How much will it cost?'

He shrugged. 'A lot,' he said. 'Dangerous things, machine guns. Who you gonna shoot?'

'Some drug dealers,' I said. Honesty being the best policy.

Darkman frowned, and Marsha stopped rolling and looked up at me.

'I a drug dealer,' said Darkman.

'I'm not interested in you, except for the gun you can get me.' Maybe next time, I thought.

'So who ya gonna use the gun on? Black men or white men?'

'White men,' I said. 'At least I think they are.'

He grinned, showing a mouthful of pearly teeth. 'Pity,' he said. 'You could get some of the black trash off the street for me.'

I smiled. Marsha finished rolling the joint and lit it with another of the disposable lighters. She took down a huge

118

mouthful of smoke, held it until she almost choked then let it out in a long grey plume that drifted up to the ceiling before being dispersed by the fan.

'Draw,' said Darkman, and Marsha passed him the joint and he took a long hit of his own. I finished my Marlboro and stubbed it out in an ashtray.

'Want some?' asked Darkman, holding up the joint.

I shook my head. 'No thanks.'

'Leave your number, man. I call you soon. Make sure you've got your cash handy.'

'I'll do that,' I said, and with a wave he dismissed me.

The huge geezer showed me the front door, where I gave him my phone number and I walked back to the Chevy and Dawn.

20

Darkman called up the next morning. He didn't introduce himself, just said, 'Got what you want, man.'

'Good. How much?'

'A long 'un and a half.'

'Good kit?'

'The best.'

'It'd better be. Where and when?'

'Brockwell Park. In front of the big white house. Be alone. One o'clock.' And he put down the phone.

I collected fifteen hundred nicker from Dawn and put it in a brown envelope which I tucked into the left-hand pocket of my leather. In the other I put the Browning, cocked and unlocked, with one in the chamber.

At twenty to one I got Dawn to drive me to the Norwood Road and Brockwell Park Gardens entrance to the park. She turned the car round so that it was facing the main road and put the .32 under the sun visor, butt outwards for a quick draw. I gave her a kiss, exited the motor and took a stroll amongst the flowers. I walked up the hill towards the white house that sat on top. On a wooden bench in front of the place, I saw Darkman sitting, dressed in a Burberry mac. On the seat beside him was a briefcase and two Tesco's carrier bags. I couldn't see anyone else close. I walked up and sat next to him and let the sun warm my face for a moment.

'How's every little thing?' he asked. I looked at his eyes. He'd been at the charlie again, or maybe a rock of crack.

'Just dandy,' I said.

'Got the dough?'

'Naturally.'

He pushed the briefcase towards me. I picked it up. It wasn't light, wasn't heavy.

'Let's take a walk,' he said.

We wandered away from the house on a path that led to a copse of trees.

'No one waiting for us is there?' I asked.

'No, man. When I make a deal, I make a deal. I don't want to be waiting round for people to rip me a new arsehole. Anyway, you a friend of Emerald's. I'd never be able to go home again if he thought I done you up.'

There was another bench by the trees. Darkman sat down, so did I. I slipped the catches on the case and opened it. Inside it was lined with foam cut out in the shape of an Uzi machine pistol which gleamed with oil. Above it, also sunk into the foam, was the phallic length of a suppressor. Four empty clips were next to the gun. I shut the case. Darkman passed me the Tesco bags. I looked inside them. In each were five cardboard ammunition boxes. I took one out. A white sticky label was pasted on the end of the box. Printed on it was '9mm × 50'. I opened the box and saw the brass cases nestling there.

'Good enough,' I said, and took out the envelope and passed it to Darkman. He took out the money and counted it in a nanosecond, then smiled.

'Good enough,' he echoed, stood up and walked in the direction of Brixton. 'Drop by for a taste any time,' he said over his shoulder as he went. 'And stay chilly. The Darkman likes his friends to be cool.'

I picked up the briefcase and the bags and cut across the grass in the direction of the car. The only people I saw on the way back were two old biddies taking their springer spaniel for a walk.

21

Dawn drove me home and we went up to the flat. I took out the Uzi, broke it down, cleaned, dry fired it and screwed on the suppressor to make sure it fitted. It all seemed kosher, but there was only one way for sure to find out. I took out the mags and showed Dawn how to load them. A tedious job, which didn't suit her long fingernails, but she soon got the knack. We loaded the four sticks with one hundred and twenty rounds of nine-mill ammo and I put them, the silencer and the pistol back into their foam-filled coffin.

As I was doing it, I saw that one corner of the foam was loose. I pried it open. Underneath was a wrap with about a half gram of coke inside and three ready-rolled grass joints. So that's what Darkman had meant. I smiled as I lit up one of the joints.

'Nice people to do business with,' I said. 'What's the time?'

'Nearly four.'

'Let's go eat.'

We went to the local Chinese. Before we left the house I stashed the case and the two handguns in a hidyhole I'd long ago discovered under the eaves of the roof. I didn't think we'd need to be armed at the restaurant. That was unless someone got ugly over the Peking duck.

No one did.

After the meal we went home, broke open a couple of beers, smoked another joint and went to bed. We had to be up early.

I set the alarm for five, but was awake and up long before. I made strong black coffee and split out two lines of coke for us. Just the thing to get the sleep out of your eyes. Once fortified, I rescued the case and the .32, which I wrapped in a yellow duster, went down to the Chevy with Dawn, stashed the guns away in a compartment at the back of the wagon and headed for Epping Forest.

We were there just before six. I found a secluded parking area off the A11 and dumped the car, took the guns out of the back and we hiked into the forest. It was very quiet in there at that time. Quiet enough for what we wanted. After about ten minutes' walking we came into a clearing that suited our purposes perfectly. In one corner were two young trees, one maybe twelve inches in circumference, the other slightly bigger. I opened the case, took out the Uzi, screwed on the suppressor, loaded a clip, set the gun to full auto, winked at Dawn, aimed and pulled the trigger. The gun kicked back at me and tried to pull up and to the left, but the silencer worked perfectly and I doubted that the noise from the shots reached more than a few yards into the trees surrounding us. I emptied the clip in a couple of seconds and the smaller of the two saplings crashed to the floor of the forest as a stream of hot, brass cartridge cases spewed out of the ejector at the side of the gun.

'Tim-ber,' I said.

'I must remember to cancel your subscription to the Friends of the Earth magazine.'

'Funny,' I replied, took the Colt out of my pocket and handed it to her. 'Your turn. Don't forget, fire the gun, don't let the gun fire you. Aim at the other tree.'

She took the pistol, held it two handed, bent her knees slightly and opened fire. The sound of the shots was loud in the clearing after the pop of the Uzi and birds rose in clouds from the treetops around us. All six bullets hit dead centre, clustering in a group that I could cover with one hand.

'Christ,' I said, walking over and examining the evidence. 'You're a natural. Or a lucky beginner. Do it again.'

And she did. Reloading quickly from the bullets I gave her and transferring the empty cartridge cases to the pocket of her coat, emptying the cylinder for the second time and narrowing the spread of the hits even more.

I felt like a right prat for lecturing her about shooting. She was a damned sight better shot than me. 'Uncanny,' I said. 'You sure you've not done this before?'

She nodded.

'Amazing.'

'Jealous?'

'No. Relieved. Want a go with the Uzi?'

'No,' she replied. 'This is more my speed,' and she spun the Colt around her forefinger like a western gunslinger.

'Please yourself.' I unscrewed the suppressor from the machine pistol, popped the clip and put it, the silencer and the still warm gun back into the briefcase whilst Dawn busily collected the nine-millimetre cartridge cases from the ground. 'Come on,' I said. 'Let's go, before anyone gets curious.'

We went back to the car, which still stood alone in the

parking area, and I put the guns away again and drove off in search of breakfast.

Just down the road we found a Little Chef that was opening, and we both went straight to the toilets to wash the powder stains off our hands.

When we were sitting at a corner table, with our food ordered and coffees in front of us, I said, 'That's it then, babe. What do you reckon?'

'Brilliant. Better than sex.'

'Thanks.'

'You know what I mean.'

'Sure I do. But don't get hooked on it. It can get to be a habit. And remember, it's different firing at people than at trees. People have a nasty way of firing back.'

She covered my hand with hers and squeezed it. 'Don't worry,' she said. 'I won't.'

'I know.'

'So what do we do now?'

'Eat breakfast, then go home and wait for Monkey to get in touch.'

Which is exactly what we did.

22

He called that same evening.

'Mr S?'

'Monkey?'

'Yeah.'

'What's up?'

'I 'ad a little shufti round that gaff.'

'Did you?'

'Yeah. The BT man had to call. Fault on the line. The bird was there. Didn't even know there was anythin' wrong wiv it.'

'And was there?'

'Course. You know me, Mr S. I didn't want the bleedin' fing to ring while I was explainin' myself.'

'And?'

'And she was right tasty. Might've bin able t'do a bit o' good for meself if I'd've 'ad more time.'

'I think you've got a Casanova complex, Monkey.'

''Ave I? Is that good?'

I ignored the question. 'What about the house, Monkey?'

'Oh yeah. You was right about the alarms. Go through to some security firm's got a couple of geezers runnin' round in radio-controlled vans. I know the mob. Not bad, but a bit pricey, I reckon...'

'*Monkey.*'

'Sorry. No problem to fix. We'll go in through the patio doors at the back. The side door through to the garden ain't wired up.'

'What about Rover?'

'The doggie. Soldier, 'is name is. A lovely Dobermann. 'E's all right. More of a pet than a danger I reckon, whatever they say. 'E likes treats. And I've got just the thing for 'im. There's a big flap on the kitchen door so's 'e can get in and out at night and patrol the back garden. But like I said, 'e's a big softy. We got on like a house on fire. 'E'll remember me, I 'spect. That'll confuse 'im. And because 'e's around there ain't no infra reds, so once we're in we're in. Piece o' cake.'

'That's good, Monkey. You did well. Thanks.'

'No problem, Mr S. So when d'ya wanna go inside?'

'Soon as possible. But they've got to be there.'

'Friday night, tomorrow, Mr S. Football's on satellite from Italy. Big match. Cup winner's cup or sumfin'. Milan versus Arsenal. 'E's a big Gunners fan. She's pissed off. She wanted to go up west to a club. But she reckons 'e'll be legless by midnight whoever wins, so's they'll 'ave an early night.'

'You're a genius, Monkey.'

'Reckon I am. I fink she wanted me to ask 'er out, but I never.'

'Just as well.'

'So tomorrow?'

'Sounds good to me.'

'What time?'

'Two. Three.'

'That's best. Give 'em a chance to get well into the land of nod before we go in. There's a boozer round the corner. The Love Lies Bleedin'. Know it?'

'I've seen it.'

'Meet you outside at two sharp.'

'We'll be there. I'll have the rest of your money. You get us in, Monkey, then scarper. All right?'

'Suits me.'

'Tomorrow night then.'

'I'll be there.'

And on that we finished the call.

I told Dawn what was happening and broke down the weapons we'd be taking and gave them a clean.

23

We were at the boozer right on time, Friday night. I wore my leather jacket, black Levi's, Doc Marten's and a woollen balaclava rolled up like a watch cap on my head. On my hands I was wearing a pair of black leather gloves. I carried the Browning in one of my jacket pockets, and the Uzi was in one of the Tesco's shopping bags that Darkman had brought the bullets in, with the silencer in my other jacket pocket. Dawn was all padded up like the Michelin Man, which was exactly what I wanted Marshall to think she was – a geezer. She was wearing a couple of T-shirts, one of my Levi shirts, a denim jacket and a big down-filled jacket on top. On her legs she wore two pairs of jeans, a tight pair underneath and a baggy pair on top, and a pair of Doctor Marten's of her own. She had rolled her hair up tightly and wore a balaclava too. Her .32 was stuck in her belt with the hammer resting on an empty chamber. I didn't want her blowing a hole in her own belly, and, not surprisingly, neither did she. She also wore gloves and kept moaning that she was melting in all the clothes. With a bit of luck, and if she kept her mouth shut, we might confuse Marshall enough to think that we were a pair of blokes. If not, tough. I parked the Chevy opposite the car park entrance to the pub, and a minute later Monkey materialized beside the driver's door.

I wound down the window and he hunkered down next to me, nodded at Dawn and said, 'Ready?'

'Sure,' I replied.

'Let's go then.'

Dawn and I left the car together. I'd already taken the precaution of taking out the bulbs in the interior lights so that no one would see inside the car, and as we went I discarded the Tesco bag and screwed the suppressor on to the barrel of the Uzi. Monkey looked round at it and shook his head.

When we got to Marshall's front gate, we slid inside and stood in the shelter of the tree in the front garden. I reached into my pocket and took out the second part of Monkey's money and handed it over. He was dressed in dark clothing too, with a bag hooked over one shoulder. He put the envelope into one of his pockets without looking at the contents.

Trust. I like that.

We padded along the grass beside the drive and crept round

to the side of the house. Monkey found a pair of surgeon's rubber gloves in his bag and pulled them on. He slipped the lock on the side door and pushed it open, gesturing for us to stand back as he did so. Then he reached into the bag again and pulled out a raw hamburger pattie. 'Hey, Soldier,' he whispered. 'Come on, boy.'

Even as he said it, the huge Dobermann appeared at the end of the alley formed by the garden wall and the side of the house.

'Hey, boy,' said Monkey, 'catch,' and lobbed the meat at the dog, who caught it in his mouth and swallowed it in one motion.

Monkey held up his hand, and the three of us stood looking at the dog, for the longest ten seconds of my life until he keeled over silently and lay still.

'I told you he likes his treats,' said Monkey. 'Come on round the back.'

He led us round to the rear of the house, where the garden stretched away until it was lost in the darkness. We stood on the paved patio in front of a set of sliding double doors side by side in their aluminium frames and locked in the middle with a small round Chubb. Monkey took a tiny torch from his pocket, switched it on and checked the framework. Once satisfied, he stuck it in his mouth to leave his hands free, then hunted around in his bag once more and came out with a pair of tiny rubber suckers connected by a very long length of thin wire, which was attached by more wire to a tiny plastic junction box. He examined the frames of the patio doors and carefully attached one sucker on to a metal strip on the left-hand frame and the other to a similar strip sunk into the glass of the right-hand door, and allowed the connecting wire to drag on the ground. When he was satisfied, he touched a button on the box and a red light glinted into life. He tapped the left-hand door gently, took the torch out of his mouth and whispered, 'That knocks out the alarm on this door. Easy. I told you. But don't break the contact or the alarm'll go off. You can leave it connected when you go. It's not traceable.'

I touched his arm in response.

Next, from his bag he produced two more rubber suckers, this time roughly the size of lavatory plungers with metal handles on the tops and butterfly nuts sticking out of the ends of the handles. He stuck first one then the other to the glass of the left-hand door, tightening the butterfly nut each time, and with a hiss of air a vacuum was formed inside the suckers fixing them firmly to the window. Finally he produced a leather case from the bag, extracted a metal pick from it and dealt with the Chubb. Then he stood legs apart, gripped the handles of the suckers in each hand and lifted the patio door clean out of its frame, making sure it didn't touch the wire, turned it and with a slight grunt placed it silently on the patio and leant it against the wall.

'All yours,' he said, with another look at the Uzi. He unfastened the big suction pads from the window and put them back in his bag. 'I'm out of here. The master bedroom's on the first floor. Door on the right. That's where they'll be.'

Monkey obviously *had* done his homework. I touched him on the shoulder. 'Thanks, Monk,' I said. 'See you.'

'You *don't* see me, Mr S,' he said, picked up his bag and vanished silently into the gloom of the side passage.

24

I tapped Dawn on the shoulder, pulled my balaclava down over my face and she did the same. I checked the magazine was firmly home in the Uzi's butt, she drew her Colt, we both stepped over the thin wire that was preventing the alarm system from advertising our presence and into the living room of Marshall's house. I pulled a small torch of my own from one of the pockets in my jacket and switched it on. Before leaving home I'd taken the precaution of masking off most of the crystal with black tape so that only a thin beam of light emerged, and using it I led the way across the expanse of expensive tan carpeting to the door that led to the rest of the house.

I eased open the door, moved silently into the hall and shone the light up the stairs. At the top a dim glow came from a small wattage bulb set in the ceiling and I switched off the torch and returned it to my pocket. Slowly and quietly Dawn and I started to climb the flight to the first floor.

When we reached the top there was a wide corridor facing us. The first door on the right was ajar and I padded across the floor and pushed it gently open with my gloved hand. The room was illuminated by the splash from a street light from outside through undrawn curtains and I saw that the emperor-size bed was inhabited by two still forms. I could hear the sound of snoring from one of them. Marshall, I assumed, sleeping off the beers he'd drunk whilst he watched Arsenal slaughter Milan four–nil. I hoped that was going to be the last good thing to happen to him for a long time.

I pointed to the window, and Dawn crossed the room and drew the curtains with hardly a rustle from the material. When she was done I flipped on the light switch by the door and shouted, 'Wakey, wakey,' walked over to the bed, the Uzi in front of me, and booted the side of the mattress. Hard.

There was a man and a woman in bed, and at my shout and the jolt to where they were sleeping, the man sat bolt upright and made as if to get out from under the covers.

'Not so fast, fucker,' I said, and cocked the Uzi. The sound of the bolt being thrown froze Marshall where he was.

'James Andrew Marshall,' I said. 'Your worst nightmare just came true. A pair of lunatics with automatic weapons have invaded your house. So wake up, son, we've got things to talk about.'

'What . . . ? What . . . ?' he mumbled through lips still numb with sleep.

'You 'eard, shitcunt,' I said, making my voice deeper and camping up the cockney accent. 'Wipe the sleep out of your eyes, matey. We ain't got all night.'

'Jimmy. What is it?' said the woman, sitting up and allowing the sheet to slide off a quite spectacular pair of breasts.

'Cover yourself up, Kazza,' I said. 'You'll frighten the animals.'

'Do it,' said Marshall, and she did, looking from Dawn to me with terror in her eyes.

Marshall did the same, but he wasn't frightened. Not yet. That was to come. 'Where's Soldier?' he demanded at the mention of animals.

'In the land of nod. It was something he ate.'

Marshall looked as if he was ready to jump out of bed and have a go, guns or no guns, so I said, 'Don't worry, Jimmy. He's OK. He's dreaming of a nice juicy piece of beef. So come on. Out of your lazy beds, time's a-wasting.'

They both did as they were told, slid out from under the covers and stood together under the twin barrels of our weapons.

It was quite a sight. They were both stark naked. Marshall looked like he'd been gobbling anabolic steroids big time. He was the colour of a tandoori chicken straight out of the oven, from repeated visits to Spain or somewhere, topped up with a sunbed, and every muscle on his frame was pumped up till it looked like snakes were wriggling under his skin. His neck was wider than his head and the whole effect was only spoiled by the fact that his mouth resembled a pig's arsehole and his dick was the length of one of those little chipolatas that come on a stick at weddings.

His girlfriend, on the other hand, was pale and smooth, with her pubic hair shaved into the shape of a heart. She wasn't bad as it happens. I could see why Monkey'd been attracted.

'Put something on, the pair of you,' I said. 'You look like you're auditioning for a sex education video.'

I picked up a white towelling robe from the bed and tossed it to Marshall. He put it on, his eyes never leaving mine all the while.

Not scared yet, James, I thought. Stick around.

'What do you want?' he asked. 'There's nothing here for you.'

'You'd be surprised. Come on, Karen, get your knickers on.'

She picked up a robe of her own from off the dressing table stool and shrugged into it.

'How do you know so much about us?' asked Marshall.

'You're my hobby. Some people spot trains, I spot you. Now come on, downstairs. This place stinks like a brothel.'

All four of us filed out of the bedroom and down to the ground floor. I went first, walking backwards, gun pointing upwards, then Marshall, then Karen and finally Dawn at the rear, well out of my line of fire. She was learning fast.

We went into the living room once more. I switched on the chandelier that hung from the ceiling. The curtains were already drawn, and I motioned for Marshall and Karen to sit on the sofa. The room opened into the kitchen, which was all ice-white surfaces and chrome accessories. There were two bowls on the floor, one containing chopped up dog food, the other water.

'Where's the dog?' said Marshall.

'Outside. He's all right. I told you.'

'He'd better be.'

'You're in no position to threaten me, Jim,' I pointed out.

132

'What kind of position am I in?'

'The worst kind. But tell me what I want to know and you'll be just fine.'

'So. What *do* you want to know about?' said Marshall.

'Drugs,' I said.

'Bollocks.'

'Don't bollocks me, Jimmy,' I said. 'You're a player. Everybody knows you. You've just got away with it so far.'

'Who are you then? Pinky and Perky?'

I didn't like it that he could still make jokes. 'You're not taking this as seriously as you might, Jimmy,' I said. 'Now that's silly. I know you're all webbed up with a bunch of big operators, but they're not here, are they? There's no one to protect you and your girlfriend.'

'What are you goin' to do then?'

'Nothing, I hope. All I want is some information from you, then we'll leave, and you can get on with your little lives.'

'What kind of information?'

'Where you get the stuff from and the movements of the next consignment.'

He shook his head. 'Can I have a fag?'

There was a packet of Benson's on the coffee table, a lighter and a half-full ashtray.

'No. But I will.' I took the packet, fished a cigarette out, stuck it in the hole in my balaclava, lit it and inhaled. 'Very nice. You can have one yourself if you're prepared to co-operate. It'll settle your nerves.'

'Piss off.'

So there we were. Stalemate. I didn't want to actually shoot the geezer, or his girlfriend, but I needed something to galvanize his attention. As if on cue, the dog flap in the kitchen door was pushed open and Soldier stumbled through the gap and weaved his way across the kitchen towards us. He didn't seem any too happy at being fed a Mickey in his midnight snack, and had the kind of look in his eyes which said that Dawn and I might be next on the menu, if he could summon up the strength in his legs to attack.

Instinctively I turned the barrel of the Uzi in the dog's direction and fired it on full auto. I must have spent half the magazine before I eased my finger off the trigger of the bucking machine pistol in my hand. The silencer absorbed most of the sound of the shots and the Dobermann exploded into meaty chunks that resembled its dinner, which were hurled all over the kitchen, where they lay and stank the place out as the contents of Soldier's bowels and bladder spread across the shiny plastic that covered the floor, and the bullets that had passed through him chopped neat circles in the MFI kitchen cabinets.

I saw Dawn's eyes glitter through the slits in her mask as she glanced over at me.

'So I'm a cat lover,' I said.

25

'Will you speak to me now, Jimmy?' I asked mildly through the pall of smoke and the stink of used gunpowder and animal offal which filled the room. 'Or do I have to do the same to Karen to get you to talk? Because I will.'

'You filthy bastard,' he shouted, coming halfway out of his seat until I turned the machine pistol back on him and let the knuckle of my forefinger whiten on the trigger.

'Sticks and stones,' I said as he fell back on to the sofa, tears in his eyes, whilst Karen stared at the carnage that had overtaken their pet. She put her hand over her mouth and gasped as her skin paled to grey, and her whole body began to shake as if in the grip of a *grand mal* epileptic seizure.

'You fucking cunt,' Jimmy said through clenched teeth. 'If it's the last thing I ever do—'

'Sounds like the script for a bad film,' I interrupted. 'Shut your fuckin' gob, you slag. You and your mates are killing *people* every single day of the fuckin' week with what you deal. Kids. Kids who don't know no better. And you think I'm going to worry about fuckin' Fido. Sod him, and her and you. You want to live, talk. You don't, don't. Simple.'

I think he got the message. When he looked up again there was fear lurking in the corners of his eyes. Excellent.

'Whaddya want to know?' he asked.

'You deal E.' It wasn't a question.

'Amongst other stuff.'

'It's the E I'm interested in right now. Where does it come from? You got a factory here or is it imported?'

'Imported. It's easier.'

'Quality control?'

'If you like.'

'You should get on to the manufacturers. People are dying of this stuff.'

'There's nothing wrong with it. They just take too many tabs. Don't drink. Dehydrate.'

'Not the stuff I'm talking about. Would you know anything about rat poison? And ground glass?'

'That's not ours. We're not the only ones bringing gear in.'

'Proud of the product, are you? Too bad. You got the short straw. You're taking the can back for all the rest.'

'I don't get it.'

'You don't have to. Let's just say that the wheel of fortune stopped at your number.'

'If it's money you want . . .'

'Fuck off.'

'You reckon you can get more by stealing the stuff?'

As he had the reasoning power of a mouse on helium I explained. 'I'm not going to nick the stuff, or turn it over to the authorities. I'm going to destroy it personally. Just let me know when the next lot's coming in.'

'Why?'

'None of your fuckin' business. Just let's say it's personal. Now tell me.'

He licked his lips. 'I can't do that.'

'No such word as can't, Jimmy.'

'I can't.'

I moved the barrel of the Uzi over to point at Karen's chest. 'She'd look lousy in a shroud,' was all I said.

She looked at Marshall. 'Jimmy,' she pleaded.

'All right, all right,' he said.

I waited for a moment and he licked his lips again.

'So?' I said.

'It comes in from Amsterdam.'

'That's better. How?'

'By truck. Artic. Hidden in a regular load.'

'What kind of regular load?'

'Self-construct furniture. Tables and chairs with chromed tubular frames. You know the sort of thing. Packed flat. The chrome tubes that make up the legs of the things are hollow. The dope is packed in them. The driver stops at a place in Wembley. A bunch of our lads meet him and offload the stuff, refasten the packs and the driver drops them off at the furniture warehouse like nothing had happened.'

'When?'

He hesitated again.

'Come on, Jimmy,' I said. 'In for a penny.'

He closed his eyes, shook his head, then coughed the lot. I could almost hear his bottle go as he spoke. 'Once a month. The last Saturday. The driver catches the late-afternoon ferry that gets in at midnight so's to be in London by Sunday morning first thing. That gives us all day to get the gear off the truck and the driver delivers the straight stuff the next day. There's no hassle about the extra time that way. As long as the furniture arrives by seven a.m. Monday, he can travel any time over the weekend. As far as his guv'nors are concerned he's got a mystery he visits for a fuck. It's simple.'

'The last Saturday of the month, you say. So the next load's due tomorrow?'

Marshall nodded.

'Lovely. Which port?'

'Harwich from the Hook of Holland.'

'And it's the midnight landing.'

Marshall nodded again.

'What about customs? If this is so regular, don't they ever get sus?'

'They're sorted.'

Typical.

'Old Bill?'

'Them too.'

Lovely. I could just picture Robber's face if I ever told him.

'So it's a milk run.'

He just looked at me.

I grinned under my mask. 'So let's keep it that way, Jimmy, and no one will get hurt. What's the name of the trucking firm by the way?'

He sighed. 'Barnhoff.'

'How much gear?'

'Two million tabs.'

'*How* many?'

'You heard.'

'How much does that cost you?'

'Fiver a tab, maybe a bit less.'

'And you sell for?'

'Tenner to a wholesaler.'

'And they sell on at how much?'

'Whatever they can get. Fifteen quid bottom, twenty-five tops.'

'Lucrative business.'

He nodded.

'So there's about ten million quid tied up in this shipment initially.'

'Something like that.'

'I hope you haven't got a big investment in it, Jimmy.'

'Enough.'

'Not enough to do anything silly I hope.'

'Like what?'

'Lots of things. See, you could be lying to me now. No shipment. No Barnhoff. No nothin'. Or you could call it all off. Tell your bosses or partners or whatever they are what happened here tonight. And they could simply hold up the truck or send it through with just what's on the shipping note. Or worse, they could load up the back with a bunch of hard cases who wait for us to do what we're going to do and jump out with guns blazing. But remember how easy I got in here tonight, Jimmy, and remember also that if anything like that does occur, whatever happens to us, there's a bunch of mates of ours who can get in just as easy another night, and they won't do any talking. They'll hurt you, Jimmy, and Karen and as many more doggies as you get in here to protect you. There's no alarm system can keep them out and believe me they've got long memories. You'd never be able to rest easy again in your bed upstairs. Never. Get me?'

He nodded.

'Good,' I said. 'And besides. If you *did* admit to telling us what's going on, even if you phoned up the minute we're gone and told your pals that you only spilled the beans to get shot of us, they'd *know*, wouldn't they? They'd know that you and her were vulnerable, and it might be easier just to shut you up permanent so that you couldn't do it again. Think about it, Jimmy. Think about it and go back to bed and fuck little Miss Essex here, and forget we ever called. All right?'

He said nothing in reply and I leant over and poked him in the throat with the barrel of the Uzi. 'All right?' I repeated.

He nodded again, and I thought that was enough for one night.

'Good,' I said. 'Now turn off the alarm system, we're going out the front door.'

Marshall got up from the sofa and I took him into the hall where he disabled the alarm system, then I took him back, got him seated again and left him in Dawn's care whilst I went to the patio doors and ripped the wires and connections that Monkey had fixed to the alarm terminals and stuffed them into my pocket.

Then we split. I didn't bother making threats as to what would happen if either of them followed us. I didn't think that they would. And they didn't. I broke the silencer down from the Uzi before we got to the street and tucked it and the gun inside my jacket, but I needn't have bothered for all the activity that was going on outside. We didn't even see as much as a stray cat on the short walk back to the car, and within five minutes we were clear of the area and heading home.

26

'Did you have to shoot the dog?' said Dawn after a bit.

'Got Marshall's attention,' I replied.

'It was horrible.'

'He would've tried to see us off.'

'I know, but it seems such a shame. He was a beautiful dog.'

'And he would've eaten you for his dinner, given half a chance.'

'But you didn't have to do that to him.'

'Seemed like a good idea at the time. And it worked.'

'Yeah, OK. So what do we do now?'

'Now we go home for a few hours' kip, then tomorrow we go to Harwich and meet the boat.'

'And you think Marshall will let it go at that?'

'Yeah, I do. I think he's shitting himself right now. And if we move fast we can catch the next shipment before he has time to get brave again. We're lucky it's tomorrow and not three weeks' time.'

'I think he gave in too easily.'

'Get out of it. He'd just seen one of his pride and joys splattered all over the kitchen walls and I was threatening to do the same with another. He gave in because he couldn't take the chance that I'd've killed Karen.'

'And would you?'

'What do you think?'

'I don't know, I really don't.'

'And nor did he. That's why he talked.'

'I don't know.'

'I do, Dawn. I'm off to Essex tomorrow to do what has to be done. Now you can come along or not as you want. No hard feelings like, but I'm going with you or without.'

'You're a hard bastard, Nick.'

'No I'm not. For all I know Marshall's on the blower to his mates right now telling them what happened. But I don't think so. I think he'll swallow what we gave him and bury Fido in the back garden and try and imagine it was all a bad dream.'

'And if he doesn't?'

'We're armed and extremely dangerous, Dawn,' I said as

we pulled up in front of the house. 'And whatever happens we'll let these people know they can't get away with what they're doing indefinitely without some interference. So, are you coming or what?'

'I'm coming. You'll need someone along with a bit of sense.'

'Good,' I said. 'And by the way, I wouldn't've – shot her I mean.'

She kissed me then, and we went inside and up to bed.

Saturday morning I was awake early. Earlier than I should have been after so little sleep, but as old Sherlock would've said, the game was afoot, and I was raring to go. I washed and shaved and woke Dawn with a cuppa.

'So what's the plan?' she asked.

'We drive to Harwich, meet the truck and blow the fucker to kingdom come.'

'Just like that?'

'Exactly like that.'

'And no one will try and stop us.'

'They might try, but they won't succeed. We've got enough firepower to start a small war and we'll use it if necessary.'

'Some plan. I must say you've got every contingency covered.'

'We'll play it by ear.'

'And what happens if Marshall was lying, or if he spills the beans?'

'You keep asking that. I'm telling you like I told him, if he tells his pals what he told us, he's a dead man. These fuckers don't mess around, there's too much at stake. If Marshall owns up to letting the cat out of the bag, they'll whack him. Big-time drug suppliers aren't noted for their forgiving natures.'

'That's what I'm afraid of.'

'You don't know the meaning of the word.'

'If you say so.'

'I do.'

'OK. Are we going in our car?'

'No chance.'

'What then?'

'I'll nick one.'

'What, you? We'll still be here at Christmas if we leave it to you. You couldn't even get into our car when you were locked out.'

'I'm good at pinching cars,' I protested. 'I was in the Met remember. I was taught by experts.'

'I'll believe it when I see it.'

'Stick around. I'll show you later.'

And I did.

As it goes I'm *not* very good at hoisting motors. Hopeless as a matter of fact. But I'd borrowed a key off Charlie. It's guaranteed to open any car without a dead lock. The key's of dubious legality, but can be obtained through the motor trade. So round about one we loaded the Chevy up with weapons and ammunition and went looking for a fast car, full of petrol to take us up to Harwich.

I left Dawn in our motor parked up in a side street in Clapham. There's still a bit of money round that way and I figured I could find the kind of car I wanted without much trouble. How long it would be before it was reported stolen was another matter. I saw the transport I wanted almost immediately. It was an Audi Quattro automatic on a J-plate. Young enough still to be poky, but old enough to let me and my magic key in. I checked for an alarm but couldn't spot one, so with a quick glance up and down I worked the key into the lock with my gloved fingers and popped it sharpish. I was in and away within ten seconds, the Audi starting on the button, sounding sweet as a nut. It had a three-quarter-full tank. Someone had looked after their jam jar. It almost seemed like a shame to nick it.

I drove the Audi back round to where the Chevy was parked and flashed the lights as I went by, leaving Dawn to retrieve the ordnance and meet me on the next corner away from our motor. She threw the bags into the back and sat next to me.

'Jesus, Nick,' she said, 'but we're asking for trouble driving around in a stolen car with enough guns to keep Rambo happy.'

'But having fun,' I said, and aimed the Audi in the direction of Essex.

27

I nicked a set of number plates in the car park of a shopping centre near Romford from a J-registered Nissan Micra without too much pissing about. I hid the Audi's plates under the front carpet beneath Dawn's feet and we hit Harwich in the late afternoon. Plenty of time for a fish supper, a few drinks in a charming pub down by the sea front and a scout round to find out exactly where the ferry would discharge its cargo.

After all that we drove to a petrol station on the outskirts where I gassed up the Audi and bought a metal petrol can which I filled with two gallons of premium four star and stashed behind the front seats of our car.

At eleven-fifty-five precisely, with a few mournful hoots from its whistle, the ferry from the Hook arrived, and shortly afterwards a long blue and white trailer with 'BARNHOFF' printed in capital letters along both sides in red, hauled by a six-wheeled Volvo caterpillar tractor, pulled out from one of the customs sheds and took the slip to the main road where Dawn and I were waiting. She drove and I checked the weapons.

We followed at a polite distance. There seemed to be only the driver in the cab which was good news.

I imagined he would take the A120, bypassing Colchester, then pick up the A12 to the M25 junction just past Brentwood, then anti-clockwise round to Wembley. It's a bastard journey with no motorway, but that suited me fine. There were a lot of quiet turnoffs on the way, and I didn't intend he'd make it as far as Chelmsford. The only problem being how to get him to turn off the main drag so's we could get acquainted.

But then fate stepped in at an all-night services near a place called Horsley Cross just a few miles down the highway. The artic indicated and pulled into the parking lot, and we drifted after him and Dawn stopped the car half a dozen spaces down from the Volvo, and we watched as the driver shut down the truck and went into the restaurant. We followed and were one place behind him in the queue at the counter as he purchased a full English breakfast.

'Hungry?' I asked Dawn.

'Not very.'

'Have some coffee.'

'OK.'

I bought two pots of coffee, and a Danish for myself which seemed fitting under the circumstances, and we moved over to a table behind the driver and I nibbled at my pastry as Dawn lit a cigarette.

'Everything looks all right,' I said. 'We'll have him over soon.'

'I love your optimism. He might just drive through us.'

'I'll think of something,' I said.

I'd finished my pastry and then lit a cigarette of my own whilst the driver was wrestling with the last of his pork sausage and fried slice, when Dawn decided she needed to visit the ladies. She was back quickly and said, 'There's a copper looking at our car.'

'Shit,' I said, got up and followed her out to the front of the place where a brand new Ford Mondeo decked out in full Essex County Constabulary livery was standing right outside, about fifty yards from the shop where you paid for the fuel, where one uniformed officer was drinking a cup of tea and nattering with the geezer behind the counter. A second uniform was walking slowly up the line of cars, vans and trucks that were parked up outside the restaurant giving them a good screw.

He vanished behind the Barnhoff truck then reappeared clocking a Suzuki jeep, an old Vauxhall Cavalier and our Audi.

I pulled Dawn back through the door as the truck driver walked past us and off to his lorry. If the sight of the Old Bill interested him, he didn't show it, as he unlocked the door of the Volvo, opened it, climbed in, started his engine and switched on his lights. And if the sight of the truck interested the coppers they didn't show it either.

The truck and trailer reversed out of the parking space, swung round, then straightened out and headed across the tarmac away from us, disappearing behind the bulk of a shut down garage workshop before joining the main road again.

'We'll lose him,' moaned Dawn.

'We know where he's going,' I said. 'There's no rush. We can catch him easy. It's that copper and his radio I'm worried about. If he calls in for a PNC on the Audi we're fucked. The registration doesn't match the car and all our guns are inside. If he gets smart we'll be hitchhiking home empty handed with a full terrorist hue and cry after us.'

'We probably will anyway,' said Dawn drily, but I ignored her.

Luck was with us. The copper was just being curious and after a few minutes he wandered off to join his mate at the petrol station and cadge a cuppa off the geezer behind the cash desk for himself.

'Come on, let's split,' I said and we walked arm in arm across the blacktop towards our car. On the way I glanced inside the police car and saw the keys gleaming in the ignition and the lock button on the driver's side in the unlocked position. 'Shit,' I whispered. 'That cop car's up for grabs.'

'No, Nick,' said Dawn, grabbing my arm and hurrying me along.

'Yes, Nick,' I said. 'That's how we'll stop that fucker in the truck.'

'No,' said Dawn again.

'No problem,' I said. 'We won't need it for long. We can dump it straight after and hoist another motor. Get the Audi round by the slip road back to the main drag and dump it. Get the guns and the petrol out and I'll meet you in a minute.'

'Nick . . .' she wailed.

'Quick or they'll be out,' I urged her. 'Come on, hurry.'

Dawn shook her head but got behind the wheel of the Audi, started the motor, reversed out herself and went in the same direction as the Volvo whilst I ducked down behind the parked cars and headed back towards the restaurant.

I passed round the front of the Mondeo, clocked that the two Old Bill were still deep in conversation with the proprietor of the garage, opened the door of the police motor and slid into the driver's seat.

The still warm engine started with a whisper and I was off with just a slight squeal from the back tyres, and I was almost out of sight behind the garage building before the cops tumbled out on to the petrol station forecourt almost tripping over each other in their haste. The police radio was buzzing away and I turned down the volume.

I flipped on the headlights as I turned the corner and spotted Dawn standing beside the Audi, the bags of guns in her arms and the petrol can between her feet. I skidded into a broadside beside her, knocked up the button on the rear door and she

146

hoisted the can on to the back seat and threw herself and the weapons in after it, and I banged in the clutch and screeched away before she'd even had time to shut the door behind her. I hit the main road doing fifty and accelerating in third gear, and the Mondeo fishtailed wildly as I crossed both lanes heading west towards London, and set off after the truck and trailer.

28

'You're fucking mad, Nick,' gasped Dawn as she clambered into the front passenger seat beside me.

'But such charming company,' I replied as I pushed the Mondeo down the deserted A120. 'Let's just hope there's no other squad cars close. Now get those guns out, we'll catch the truck up in a minute.'

Dawn did as she was told, tossed me the Browning, tucked the Colt into the belt of her jeans and was screwing the silencer on to the Uzi when the Christmas tree lights that went right round the back of the Volvo's trailer came into sight, as we pulled up behind the rig which was doing a steady fifty-five in the left-hand lane in front of us.

'Done,' she shouted.

'Great,' I said as I spotted an exit sign that told me we were a mile and a half from the turnoff to the B1029 and Ardleigh and Thorrington beyond.

'There should be a switch here,' I said, fumbling on the dash, until I found it and with a screech the siren erupted. Next to the screamer switch was another that put on the flashers mounted on the top of the motor, which illuminated the road around us with their eerie blue light.

I accelerated again, pulled alongside the length of the artic, then in front of it, and slowed down so that it was forced to stop behind us.

'Come on,' I said, grabbing the Uzi and stuffing the Browning into the pocket of my jacket. 'Let's introduce ourselves.'

I turned off the tones but left the flashers and the engine on, and we both got out of the police car and jogged back towards the cab of the lorry.

As we arrived on the driver's side, the window rolled down and his head appeared. 'Officers,' he said in English with just a trace of an accent. 'What is the matter?' He didn't seem very perturbed and for a moment I was afraid it was all a wind-up, and all that he had on board was a load of build-it-yourself furniture.

'Put your hands where I can see them,' I ordered. 'Flat on the windscreen in front of you.'

'There is no need, everything has been organized. Officers, please.'

Then I knew it wasn't a wind-up at all.

'We're not fucking officers,' I snarled, and fired the Uzi at the trailer where the bullets stitched a neat line across the paintwork. 'Now put your fucking hands where I can see them or you'll get the next lot.'

He did as he was told then, and I opened the cab door as Dawn trained her gun on the driver.

Then I went round to the passenger side and got in beside him whilst Dawn kept him covered. Once inside I told her to lead the way off the main road and find somewhere quiet where we could both park up, and turn off the flashers.

She slammed the driver's door shut, ran to the Mondeo, got in, killed the lights on the roof, pulled away and on to the turnoff.

'Follow her,' I said to the driver.

'Who are you and what do you want?' he asked.

'Who we are doesn't matter, and we want the drugs in the back.'

'What drugs?'

I dug the Uzi into his side. 'Don't fuck about,' I said, 'you know as well as I do. Now get going.' He looked at me in the light from the dashboard of the truck, worked the clutch, put the stick into low gear and we lurched away after Dawn, off the main highway and into the darkness of the B-road, until we came to a lay-by which took both the Ford and the artic comfortably.

'Turn the engine off, but leave your lights on and get out,' I told the driver, who hadn't said a word in the short drive, when Dawn was back in front of the cab, gun in gloved hand. 'And don't get any bright ideas. We're both prepared to kill you.'

He did as he was told, and within a few seconds all three of us were standing on the road in front of the Volvo in the harsh glare of its main beams. The driver was wearing a set of dark overalls, and I shouldered the Uzi and, keeping well out of Dawn's line of fire, patted him down. He was unarmed.

'Watch him,' I said to Dawn and took a look around. There was no sign of life in the pitch black that surrounded us. If there were any houses they were dark and it seemed like the perfect place for what I had planned.

'Turn your motor round,' I said to Dawn, 'while I watch him. I want to look in the back, so get the lights on the doors.'

She did as she was told again, ran back to the Mondeo, screeched it in a tight U-turn, back past us, then into another tight turn so that the police car's headlights were trained on the back doors of the trailer.

I shoved the driver along the length of the articulated truck until we got to the back doors which were secured by a padlock the size of my hand, where Dawn was waiting for us. 'Right, you,' I said to him, 'open it up.'

'I don't have the keys.'

I hit him round the head with the silencer on the Uzi then, and he went down on one knee in the mud at the side of the road. 'Don't fuck me about again,' I said. 'I'm serious, son. I'll kill you stone dead in a second. Bet on it. Then I'll find the fucking keys wherever they are and open it up myself.'

'OK, OK,' he said, and pulled himself to his feet using the handle on the trailer doors, wiping blood from his cheek. 'Just don't hit me again.'

'Not unless you ask for it.'

Slowly and carefully he put his left hand into one of the pockets of his overalls, brought out two keys on a ring and handed them to me.

'That's better,' I said, then to Dawn, 'Take him out of my way and keep him quiet. If he tries any shit, shoot him in the belly.'

The pair of them moved to the side of the Mondeo and I found the key for the door locks, then the padlock, wrestled it off, dropped it at my feet, worked the door handle, stepped back and pulled open the massive doors. Inside, packed front to back, were large, flat cardboard boxes bearing the brand name of a Scandinavian furniture manufacturer. I pulled down the first box and tore it open. Inside were the makings of a small dining-room table neatly wrapped in bubble sheeting. I tore that apart too and found two pairs of U-shaped chrome-pipe legs. At the bottoms of each leg were black rubber grommets, one of which I wrestled out of the tube it sealed, put my fingers inside and pulled out a plum. A neatly packed, long clear plastic sausage crimped at both ends with metal clamps, and containing what looked like ten thousand or so red and black capsules.

'Bingo,' I said. 'We have contact.'

'Is it what you thought?' asked Dawn.

'Oh yeah. No problem.'

I stood up and went over to the driver and hung the packet of drugs in front of him. 'So what's this, pal? Scotch mist?'

'I know nothing about this stuff. I am just paid to drive.'

'Just obeying orders, huh?' I said. 'Fair enough.'

'So what do you do now?' he asked.

'Now we blow this stuff to shit.'

'That is not a good idea.'

'As good as I've come up with lately.' Which wasn't saying much.

'And what about me?' he said.

'You? You fuck off. Get lost. Vanish. Disappear.'

'Where?'

I pointed the Uzi at the dark field beyond the fence on the edge of the road. 'Thataway will do.'

'There's nothing there.'

'Just keep going. Eventually you'll get somewhere.'

'No.'

'Sweetheart,' I said to Dawn. 'If he doesn't move, shoot the fucker.'

I saw Dawn pale, but the driver didn't notice, or if he did he took it as a sign of her eagerness to blow lumps out of him.

'All right, I go,' he said. 'But you'll be sorry.'

'Don't be petulant,' I said. 'And don't threaten me. You're in no position. Just shut up and go, and don't come back.'

He walked away from us, towards the fence, looked into the darkness beyond and hesitated.

'Give him some encouragement,' I said to Dawn.

'How?'

'Shoot at the cunt.'

She raised her Colt revolver and fired twice over the driver's head. He ducked and ran towards the fence, vaulted it in one movement and crashed through the undergrowth away from us.

'Very ladylike,' I said. 'Right, let's get busy.'

29

I hung the Uzi by its strap over Dawn's shoulder and told her to keep an eye out in case the driver came back to try and do something smart. Then I took the petrol can out of the back of the Mondeo and ran to the front of the truck, undid the top of the can, made a trail of petrol about ten yards long on the road and up to the front of the Volvo, got into the cab where I splashed petrol over the seats and dashboard, out again, more petrol on to the front tyre, the running board, the twin back tyres of the tractor, the hydraulics, along the side of the trailer, the wheels and up into the back and over the contents. Finally I picked up the carton I'd ripped open and threw that into the back, complete with all its contents, put the top back on the can and threw it up into the trailer too, and pushed the doors shut.

'Come on, darlin',' I said. 'Let's go.'

We both piled into the Mondeo, and Dawn drove it up to where I'd started the petrol trail. I bailed out and lit the fuel with my Zippo. The petrol caught and the flames shimmied along the blacktop until they ran up the front of the tractor, jumped to the tyre, then suddenly engulfed the interior of the cab in flames. At that I hopped back into the Mondeo and Dawn drove it to a safe distance where we could watch the progress of the fire without being in any danger. We both got out of the motor to watch. By that time the cab was burning merrily and the flames had danced along the side of the trailer and into the cargo compartment. I turned and grinned at Dawn in the light from the fire and made an O with the thumb and forefinger of my right hand, just as the windscreen of the

Volvo blew out. The pyrotechnics continued as the diesel tanks blew and the tractor and trailer parted company. Then the petrol can in the back exploded and tore a hole in the side of the trailer which allowed fresh air inside, and within a few minutes the complete length of it was blazing.

'Time to split, honey,' I shouted above the sound of the flames. 'We'll be getting company soon.'

As if to confirm what I'd said, I saw a tiny light blink on about a quarter of a mile away across a darkened field, as a householder in a previously invisible dwelling woke up, and decided to see what all the excitement was about.

We got back into the Mondeo and took off down the secondary road in what I guessed to be a southerly direction for a few miles until we came to a village called Frating Green, where the A133 bisected the B1029, and we swapped cars again. I found a Volkswagen Golf GTI neatly parked on a grass verge, whose doors opened to my hoister's key. We transferred the guns to the back of the VW, left the police car down the next lane with the keys in the ignition but no thank you note, took the A133 to where it joined the A12 at Colchester and we were back in London before it was light. I drove sedately across town, dropped Dawn and the guns off at the Chevy, then parked the VW in exactly the same spot, give or take a couple of yards, where I'd nicked the Audi the previous afternoon. That would give Old Bill something to think about when they found it and traced its movements back.

I strolled round to where my wife was waiting behind the wheel of the Caprice, she drove us home, and we were in bed as the birds were waking up.

30

Sunday we laid low. There was a mention of the truck fire on the local news, but they didn't go into much detail.

On Monday I bought the *Telegraph* and found this item on page five:

Mysterious Fire in Essex

An unexplained fire destroyed an articulated lorry and its load of flat-packed furniture valued at over £150,000 en route from Amsterdam via the Hook of Holland to a showroom in Wimbledon, south London, early on Sunday morning.

The fire started at approximately one-thirty a.m. in a lay-by on the B1029, just off the A120 close to the village of Frating Green, and the truck and contents were completely gutted by the time emergency services arrived at the scene.

The driver of the vehicle has not been traced although a police spokesman reports no sign of any casualties. The same spokesman refused to comment on suggested links between the fire and the theft of a police patrol car shortly before the incident, from a service station on the A120, but it is known that investigations are taking place in Frating Green itself where a Volkswagen Golf GTI was stolen the same night.

> Forensic experts are studying the wreck-
> age as to the cause of the fire which is sus-
> pected to be arson.

I passed the paper to Dawn. 'We've had a result,' I said. 'That truck's history.'

She read the piece.

'They suspect arson,' she said.

'You amaze me.'

'No mention of the drugs.'

'There wouldn't be, but I wouldn't put it past forensics to find some remains.'

'You think they might?'

'Depends on how much of the cargo is left and how hard they look. I dunno, love. If we're lucky they'll put it down to an insurance fraud and blame the driver. Depends if they catch up with him.'

'And if they do find the driver and he tells them what happened?'

'He's going to have a hard time explaining why a heavily armed man and woman hijacked his load of cheap furniture and destroyed it. What's he going to tell Old Bill? That we were from the good taste in home furnishings police? No. He's long gone if you ask me. And even if they do catch up with him, so what? There's no way of tying any of it in with us.'

'Except for a trail of stolen cars from Clapham to Harwich and back.'

'There's a lot of villains in Clapham.'

'So that's it finished?'

'Looks like it. The case of the private detective's daughter webbed up in the rave scene has come to a satisfactory conclusion.'

'You don't seem very happy.'

I shrugged. 'That's not all that's finished,' I said.

'What else?'

'Judith as a child. She's nearly a woman now. And I don't think I did the best job in the world as a father.'

'So what father does?'

'Some do. And time's going past so quickly. There's not much left to make it up to her.'

'Poor Nick. What did you do in the beat boom, Daddy, when the Beatles and the Rolling Stones were fighting it out for domination in the top twenty hit parade?'

'What are you talking about?' I said. 'I'm only . . .' Then I looked up and saw that she was laughing at me. 'All right. I get you, I'm acting like an old fart.'

'An extremely boring old fart at that. And you could have another chance.'

'What are you talking about?' I asked.

'Me and you and the patter of tiny feet.'

'Do what?' Then it dawned on me what she was saying. 'You don't mean you're . . .'

'Well I'm not thinking about taking up breeding chihuahuas.'

'You're *pregnant*.'

She nodded.

'And you came out with me and beat up that truck.'

'I'm only a little bit pregnant.'

'How little?'

'A couple of months. I don't even show yet.'

I got up and held her. 'You're mad,' I said. 'Why didn't you tell me?'

'I'm telling you now. Aren't you glad?'

'Course I am. It just takes a bit of getting used to.'

'We'll need to get a bigger place.'

'Whatever you want.'

'It's not what I want, Nick, it's what we need.'

'Then we'll do it.'
'Are you really pleased?'
'Of course I am.'
'Then hold me tight. I'm scared.'
'You don't have to be scared when I'm around.'
Which of course was patently untrue.

part three

dark is the night

It will have blood, they say; blood will have blood.

Macbeth

31

They murdered Dawn one night in March. Dawn and her best friend Tracey. Dawn was eight months' pregnant at the time.

The three of them – I say three, because as far as I was concerned the child was a human being too, though still in Dawn's womb – were driving back from Tracey's mother's place in Milton Keynes, down the M1. Dawn was too big with child to drive by then. She couldn't fit behind the steering wheel. So they went up for the brief visit in Tracey's little Renault. They drove back late. Very late. It was three o'clock in the morning when they left for London. Three o'clock on a clear, bright night with an almost full moon and lights down the motorway. Tracey's mother told me that Tracey hadn't had a drink or anything else all day. I believed her. Tracey was going to be godmother and she loved Dawn and she loved the child inside her. They couldn't do a blood alcohol test, because her body was too badly burned. But if they'd been able to, I'm sure it would have come up totally negative.

The crash happened just before junction eleven, the Dunstable turnoff, where a road bridge crosses the motorway, at about three-thirty a.m. There were no witnesses of the actual incident, but another car arrived as the Renault was burning fiercely. But I believed that there were witnesses. I believed that another vehicle was involved, that forced Tracey's car off the motorway and into the buttress of the road bridge where it burst into flames. But of course there was no proof.

Not then.

I didn't get the news until around nine that morning. I

wasn't expecting Dawn back until later that day. Tracey's mother called me. The fire brigade had dowsed down the car, and although it was completely burnt out, the rear number plate was readable. The Renault was registered at Tracey's flat in Wandsworth. It took that long for the police to do a PNC, get round there, find the place empty, get hold of a neighbour with a spare key, get in, find Tracey's mother's address and get hold of her.

She was crying when she telephoned to tell me what happened. I was crying by the time I put down the receiver.

It was then, at nine o'clock on that March morning, with more than just a hint of spring in the air, that I might just as well have died myself. I did. I was dead, but I didn't lie down. That's the way it goes.

I drove Dawn's Chevrolet Caprice station wagon up to Milton Keynes right away. I don't know how I made it without racking that car up too. I couldn't stop the tears welling up in my eyes and running down my face. I couldn't swallow for the lump that was stuck in my throat and I wanted to scream.

I was there by eleven. I took Tracey's mother to the mortuary in Dunstable. On the way we passed the spot where they'd died, but we didn't stop. What would've been the point? At the mortuary they didn't want to let us view the bodies. I insisted. I argued that they needed positive identification by a member of family. The pathologist told me that the bodies would be impossible *to* identify. I insisted some more. I threatened violence at one point, I think. Eventually the pathologist agreed. At one o'clock he took us into a room to see the charred remains of our loved ones.

Now I've seen some bad shit in my life, but this was the worst. They were still in the sitting positions they'd been in when they died in the car, but the fire had shrunken the bodies to pygmy size and the only way I could tell one from the other was that beside Dawn was the tiny, blackened skeleton of our baby that they'd removed from her body. God alone knows why. The pathologist told me she would have been a little girl. That made it even worse. Knowing that. We didn't want to know previously. But we'd agreed that if our child was a girl, we'd call her Daisy. I looked at those little bones and promised all three of them that I'd find out what really happened, and if anyone else was involved, avenge them.

What with seeing the bodies, and the smell of charred flesh and bone that hung like a miasma over the room, I had to leave or I'd've thrown up. I went outside with Tracey's mother and we both lit cigarettes. Mine tasted of burned flesh. I think hers must have too, because we both only took one drag before putting them out. We were both crying again by then, and I felt so cold and lost that I held on to her for comfort. She asked me why they hadn't tried to escape from the car but I couldn't answer.

Police forensic scientists checked over the remains of the Renault. It wasn't an easy job, being so badly damaged by fire. The front nearside was a mess from hitting the bridge, but as far as they could ascertain the steering had been OK. The tyres had all melted, so there was a possibility of a blow out, but they'd never be certain. Otherwise the car seemed mechanically perfect. I guessed that it had been.

The coroner at the post mortem two days later gave a verdict of accidental death.

I didn't.

Tracey, Dawn and Daisy, who was replaced inside the body of her mother, were buried in Greenwich, side by side, next to the graves of Dawn's first husband and her first daughter, ironically also killed in a car crash on a motorway.

It would have been too dark a gesture to have had them cremated.

I talked with Tracey's mother, hard and long, about whether she wanted *her* daughter buried closer to where she lived. But she said that as Tracey and my wife had been together in life, and together in death too, they should lie together for ever.

She was a brave woman. Braver than me, I think.

The funeral took place on a bright, sunny day, with the Thames running sluggish and brown along one side of the cemetery.

There were about fifty people at the service. The organist played 'Amazing Grace', and I cried. Afterwards a lot of us went for a drink at the pub by the side of the river. I wanted to get drunk but couldn't. Someone drove me home. I can't remember who.

32

Laura and Judith came down to visit whilst I was sorting out the arrangements for the funerals and stayed on for the service. They were great. As supportive as anyone could be. But they both had lives to live in Scotland, and after a week or so they went home. That was when things got really bad, because after they'd left I had nothing else to do but wonder who the 'they' were that had murdered my wife and child and my wife's best friend.

I decided to try and find out, but came up with zip.

Inspector Robber had retired to his sister's on the coast, so I had no friends left on the police force, and when I went to scope out Marshall's house I found that a young family were living there and nothing was known about the former owner or his girlfriend's whereabouts.

I wondered what they'd done with the remains of the dog.

Monkey Mann had vanished from his usual haunts too. I spoke to several of his drinking cronies, including the lovely

Sonia, but the only information I managed to extract was that he was last seen heading towards Euston and a train bound for the north of England, as relationships between himself and the local police were, to say the least, strained. And to say the most, he was wanted for questioning about a string of second-storey break-ins that had plagued the area for some months.

I even drove to Harwich on a number of Saturdays looking for another Barnhoff truck and trailer, but none appeared on any of the ferries I met.

And that was where the trails petered out.

After that I didn't do much. I sold the Chevy and my old E-Type Jag to Charlie. I wasn't planning on driving anywhere. For once he didn't make any jokes about the motors and told me that if I needed transport he was always there. I suppose I could've moved, but I couldn't bear the hassle. In a strange way I needed to stay in a place that reminded me of Dawn, and Tracey too for that matter. You've got to realize I was going crazy then. Quietly out of my head. Maybe if I hadn't been, all that happened later wouldn't have. But I'm getting ahead of myself.

Then spring came, and not far behind it the summer. I wasn't in the mood for company and I let the place go. I didn't wash much, and when I came in from my sporadic trips out, you could tell a man lived in the flat. I dined mostly on take-outs brought to the door. It's amazing what varieties of cuisine are available for delivery in Tulse Hill. But in the end it was mostly pizza or Chinese that I settled for, and my garbage was full of disposable dishes and cardboard boxes by the end of each week. Disposable dishes, cardboard boxes and bottles, for a disposable life. I was drinking a lot. Hard liquor too. But I was keeping my standards up. No cheap supermarket own-brands for me. It was Jack Daniel's or nothing. Luckily I had the money. Dawn had been well insured. We'd both taken out policies shortly after we'd found out she was pregnant. Big ones too. And after the coroner's verdict they paid out a double indemnity on hers.

And I didn't stop drinking. For weeks I wandered from bar to bar, and the bars were like churches to me. The sacrament came out of a bottle, and I'd drink until the pain went away, but it never did. So I drank some more.

I knelt in these churches too. Knelt in the toilets or in the gutters outside and puked up my guts.

I don't know how I survived.

My memory of that time isn't so good. Sometimes days went by that I can't remember at all, and that's possibly for the best, because some mornings I woke up with blood on my hands.

By midsummer I was up to a bottle of bourbon a day plus the occasional beer, I hadn't had my hair cut for months and had grown a beard. A proper one, not just stubble. There was a little grey in it, but when you've been through all that I'd been through, a few grey hairs were about to be expected. I was smoking a lot of dope too. I needed a joint to get me out of bed in the morning, several to see me through the day and a big one to help me sleep at night. I dreamt of Dawn a lot that summer. Sometimes in the dreams I didn't know that she was dead and sometimes I did. Those ones disturbed me the most and I'd often wake up with tears drying on my pillow.

And I listened to music. Fucking stupid things that were lying around the flat. Stuff that Dawn had brought with her when she moved in and I'd never properly noticed before. Some were her favourites and some weren't. One song in particular I would play over and over again. 'Dark Is the Night' it was called, by Shakatak. It had a line that went: 'Where is the star that lit my skies?' God knows why she had it. It wasn't her style at all. Fucking hairdresser's music from the eighties.

But I kept playing it, and I knew where my star had gone. Gone to feed the worms, that's where.

A pretty sad life, or what? And don't think I didn't know it. I thought about topping myself as it goes. Seriously. I had enough guns to make a first-class job of it, and they were the only things I cleaned as the long hot days shortened and autumn loomed.

But I didn't. I didn't have the bottle. Enough times I stuck the muzzle of one of the handguns into my mouth and tried to pull the trigger. But I couldn't. I knew that Dawn and Tracey would never forgive me. Nor Daisy if she could comprehend. And also, even at the worst of times, I had the feeling that one day sooner or later something or someone would turn up that would lead me to the killers of those I had loved, and still did. Maybe they'd try and kill me too. I was up on offer. But they didn't. Alive I was suffering. Dead, maybe I'd find some peace. And they didn't want that.

So the year continued until Christmas reared its ugly head, and with it came the bombers.

Even in the state I was in, I'd heard all about the big peace plans in Northern Ireland that year. The newspapers and TV were full of it. The IRA had ceased active terrorism a year or so before and all was right with the world.

But a lot of people were unhappy about it. Work it out for yourself. There was a whole bunch of loose money floating about when the terror campaign was on line. Cash from sympathizers in the US and agitators in the Middle East. Cash from protection rackets. Cash from the sales of arms and cash from the robberies that part funded the Republican movement. Cash from sodding MI6 for all I knew. When the clandestine activities ceased, so did the flow of money, and a lot of people suffered.

And money wasn't all of it. Some of the real hardliners thought that the whole deal had gone sour. Soft. Twenty-five years wasted. So a splinter group was formed. Heavy duty bad guys. They called themselves FIRE. The Free Irish Republic Executive. They left the six counties alone and targeted the mainland. London specifically.

The security services had pretty well closed off the City of London behind a ring of steel, so the bombers moved their operation to the West End. They blasted the shit out of it that winter. The worst incident took place on a Saturday morning in November. The terrorists phoned a Sunday paper to say that there was a car bomb outside a store at the western end of Oxford Street. The coppers evacuated the place and got all the shoppers behind police lines. Then, just where the crowds were densest, a large bomb in the back of a hijacked Luton van belonging to a shopfitting firm in Basildon was triggered. It was mayhem captured on video for the world to gawp at. How many times did the TV stations repeat the pictures of the explosion that had been caught on the camcorder of a fourteen-year-old from Tufnell Park who was filming his mum and sister out doing their Christmas shopping? He earned a lot of money from that film. Other people didn't come out of it so well. Seventy died that morning, over three hundred were treated for injury and a lot who saw it still can't sleep.

On the Monday morning following I went down the road for a paper. I was all bundled up in my double-breasted overcoat, and just as I reached the end of the street before turning right to go to the newsagent a car pulled up beside me.

'Mr Sharman,' a voice said.

I froze, then turned. If someone was going to kill me so be it. I didn't have to make the decision myself and I was grateful.

The window of the car was down and the passenger repeated his question: 'Mr Sharman?'

'That's right.'

He smiled and brought his hand up from behind the door.

I winced until I saw that all he was holding was an envelope.

'This is for you,' he said.

'What is it?'

'Read it and find out. Here you are.'

I walked over to the car and accepted the envelope. Maybe another time I wouldn't have, but I knew that this was it. Don't ask me how, I just did.

33

I bought the paper. The headlines were all about the bombing. I went home and made some tea and opened the envelope. I wanted to savour the moment. Inside was a letter and five grand in fifties. Good ones. The letter read:

Dear Mr Sharman

It has come to my attention that we have a common concern. I wonder if we might meet at a convenient time for you. My office number is 0171-622-3200. I am available there, five days a week, from 9.30 am until 5.30 pm. I have enclosed a non-returnable retainer as proof of my good faith.

I look forward to hearing from you soon.

Yours sincerely

It was signed Jason D'Arbley.

Although he'd mentioned an office, there was no letterhead. The paper was best quality, creamy white bond with a seahorse as a watermark.

I counted the money again. Still five grand. Non returnable. That was good. I looked at my watch. Nine on the dot. Half an hour to go. I made another cup of tea.

At nine-thirty-five I gave the number in the letter a go. It was a direct line. 'D'Arbley,' said a man's voice.

'Nick Sharman,' I said.

'Oh. Mr Sharman. Good. You got my note.'

'Yes.'

'I wonder if we might meet.'

'What common concern?' I asked.

'I'd rather tell you in person.'

'I might be wasting my time.'

'I'm sure you'll've been adequately compensated by my retainer.'

'I'm an expensive boy.'

'So I understand. When would be convenient for you?'

'Today.'

'You don't waste any time.'

'I hate mysteries.'

'That's why you're a good detective.'

'Who says?'

'People.'

I knew if I asked 'What people?' he'd give me the run-around. So instead I said, 'Three o'clock?'

'Splendid.' He gave me an address in Bloomsbury and rang off.

I put down the phone and had a bit of a think.

But not too much of one. Instead I went and had a shower and shaved off my beard.

And it hurt.

34

I took a cab to the meeting. I figured with five grand burning a hole I could afford it. I wore the same suit I'd worn for my wedding and Dawn's funeral. I hadn't worn it since. Navy blue wool. With a pale blue button-down shirt, a flashy tie, black boots and my Burberry on top. I wasn't armed. Not so much as a toothpick.

The taxi driver dropped me off outside a renovated Georgian terrace between Russell Square and the Euston Road. The address I was looking for was in the middle of the row. There was no indication of what went on inside on the outside. Just an entryphone with a single button. I pressed it at three o'clock precisely. Someone answered. A man. But as usual on those things, he might have been on Mars for all I could understand. 'Nick Sharman,' I said.

A minute later the door was answered by the geezer who'd handed me the envelope from the car that morning. He was bigger standing up, dressed as sort of half bouncer, half butler, and said, 'Mr Sharman. How nice to see you again so soon. Come in. Mr D'Arbley is expecting you.'

I did as I was told, and he led me through into what looked like part office, part living room. By the window was a large desk with a couple of phones on top. Next to that was another with two computers, both switched on and scrolling some sort of stock information down their screens, two fax machines and a paper shredder. The usual shit. Opposite the window an open fireplace, complete with a log fire that crackled away quite happily. In front of the fire were a pair of matching sofas, a low coffee table between them. It was all very cosy. The room was empty, and the butler/bouncer said, 'Mr D'Arbley will be with you directly,' and backed out of the room closing the door softly behind him.

Half a minute later it opened again and another bloke walked in. He was wearing a grey pinstripe whistle, blue-and-white-striped shirt, discreet striped tie, a diamond in each cufflink and highly polished black casuals. He was about fifty I guessed, with grizzled dark hair and a face that had something of Peter O'Toole in it.

'Mr Sharman,' he said, sticking out his mitten and coming at me fast. 'So glad you could come. Let me take your coat. Do sit down.'

I shook the proffered German, gave up my mac without a fight and sat on one of the sofas.

'Coffee, tea, a drink?'

'Coffee would be good.'

'And a brandy, I dare say.' He had an Eton and Oxford voice, and I nodded.

He pushed a bell on the wall and the butler/bouncer came back. 'Coffee, please,' said D'Arbley. 'And brandy.'

'Sir,' said the butler/bouncer, and withdrew again.

'I wanted our talk to be private so I've let all the office staff go early,' said D'Arbley. 'I just kept Simon on to keep us supplied with refreshments.'

'Nice name,' I said. 'What common concern?'

'Straight to the point,' said D'Arbley. 'I like that.'

The coffee must've been brewing, because Simon came straight back in with a china pot of the stuff, two cups and saucers, silverware, cream and sugar. Plus a bottle of brandy that looked as if it had been around since Napoleon kicked off and two massive balloon glasses.

'No interruptions, Simon,' said D'Arbley as he started to be mother. 'I'll ring if I need you.'

'Sir,' said Simon and went out again, and D'Arbley and I were alone.

He put my coffee and a good slug of brandy on the table between the sofas, sat on the one opposite me and said, 'Let me put my cards on the table, Mr Sharman. Over the past few months I have been making discreet enquiries about you.'

'I thought that was *my* job.'

'Not always discreet from what I can gather, and that's a plus. And may I commiserate with you on your loss.'

I raised an eyebrow. Years of practice made it perfect.

'Your wife and unborn child, and your wife's friend.'

I said nothing.

'They were murdered,' he said.

I'd been right. This was it.

'How do you know?'

'I'll come to that. Let me start at the beginning.'

'Do you mind if I smoke?' I asked.

'Of course not.' He got up and found me an ashtray whilst I fired up a Silk Cut.

'Right,' he said when we were both comfy again. 'I had a wife and daughter once myself.' A look of ineffable sadness came over his face as he went on: 'I met my wife in New Zealand almost twenty-five years ago. After I left university I went round the world. Working manual jobs. Gaining experience. Looking for something to do with my life. I found it near Christchurch. Her name was Jennifer. I married her and we came back to England where I started an import/export business. Things went well and we had a daughter. We called her Susan. Susie.' He smiled at that. 'Things went even better and I built an empire. In the eighties I made frightening amounts of money. Frightening. I had a company in the City of London. My speciality was finding holes in the market and filling them. A wine lake in France would be exchanged for a

173

glut of coffee beans in Brazil. A butter mountain in Finland would go to the old USSR, in exchange for gold in a Swiss depository, which would be used to buy tobacco from America, which would pay for rubber from Indonesia. You know the sort of thing.'

I didn't, but I let it pass.

'We flourished. Then my wife died almost four years ago.' He saw my look. 'Natural causes. She was never strong, which is why we had only one child. I was left in charge of Susie's upkeep, and I failed miserably. I thought that money was a substitute for love and attention. I was wrong. My daughter fell in with the proverbial "bad crowd". Other children, because they were no more than that, with more money than self-discipline, and the parasites who fed off them. Susie was just fifteen when Jennifer died. A heroin addict by the time she was seventeen, dead before her nineteenth birthday.'

'I'm sorry,' I said.

He nodded. 'That was in the spring of this year. She had a boyfriend at the time. A man called Noel Tyson. He introduced her to the stuff. He worked – still works – for a man named Schofield. Derek Schofield. He's a big-time drug importer. He is the man who had your wife murdered.'

'Why?' I asked.

'Because you and your wife destroyed a shipment of ecstasy that he was bringing in from Amsterdam last autumn.'

Bingo! All the right answers. 'How do you know all this?' I said.

'Information is my stock-in-trade. It's how I managed to make so much money.'

'So?' I said.

'So. I want you to kill Schofield and Tyson. You've done it before, haven't you? Killed people, I mean.'

'Yes,' I replied.

'So will you?'

'You want a button man. A contract killer. I'm not sure I'm up for that.'

'Even after all I've told you?'

'Even after all that.'

'Then let me show you something.'

'Go ahead.'

He stood up and went over to his desk. He opened the top left-hand drawer, and just for a moment I had the terrible feeling he was going to pull out a gun and shoot me. I stiffened in my seat, but all that he had in his hand when it reappeared was a brown folder. He came over, gave it to me and sat down again.

'Please,' he said, and gestured towards it.

I opened it.

Inside were a bunch of photocopies of newspaper clippings and a pile of photographs.

I looked at the pictures first. They were of a woman and a girl. The oldest looked to have been taken about ten years previously from the clothes. The woman was about thirty, the girl, who I assumed to be Susan, had to be nine. That fitted.

It was a happy photo, as were the others that appeared in obvious chronological order.

That was until the woman no longer smiled so easily and appeared haggard and old before her years. Then she was no more, and it was the girl on her own. At first just unhappy, then sullen, then sullen and wasted. Then there were no more photos.

The clippings were in chronological order too. Reports of the death of Susan D'Arbley, the inquest, which showed a verdict of accidental death from a heroin OD, and the funeral. There were other, smaller clippings, from what seemed to be financial journals, although these weren't dated, about a mysterious player named Derek Schofield and all the money he had made.

'I'm sorry,' I said again. 'But this doesn't change anything.'

D'Arbley poured himself another brandy and looked at me over the rim of his glass. 'There's someone else I'd like you to meet,' he said.

'Who?'

He got up, went over to the desk, picked up one of the phones and whispered something into it.

A moment after he'd replaced the receiver the door behind me opened and I looked round. I didn't recognize the man who entered for a moment, until he said, 'Hello, Nick. Remember me?'

35

'*Toby?*' I said unbelievingly. 'Toby Gillis.'

'That's right.'

'Jesus. I don't believe it. What are you doing here? I haven't seen you since that night on the Lion Estate in Deptford.'

What I didn't say was, it was the night he'd saved my life, when two particularly vicious bent coppers who'd rampaged their way across London had the drop on me, and Toby blew them away.

'Where've you been? How's Jackie?' I demanded, as I got up, went over to him and shook his hand. Close up he looked the same as I remembered him, just older. The same athletic build, the same mop of blond hair that fell down over one eye. Except now there were lines on his face that hadn't been there the last time I'd seen him.

Jackie had been the daughter of another copper. A straight one this time. She'd been the victim of abuse from her uncle, who was yet another member of the Met. Her father had killed him, then himself. It had all been pretty sensational at the time. Front-page news. Toby was the minder who looked after her for a Sunday tabloid. He was ex-SAS. Quite a tough nut. They'd fallen for each other hard and left the country to start a new life together. I hadn't heard from either of them since. It had to have been two years.

'Jackie's dead,' said Toby bluntly.

'What?'

'She killed herself.'

I couldn't believe it. Not Jackie too. 'Why?' I said. 'What happened?'

'Long story. She got some money when her dad died. We got married and sunk it into a boatel-cum-motel in Florida, down on the Keys. Someone didn't want us there. They put on the pressure. Jackie wasn't up to it, so we left. We lost everything. She blamed herself. One night she shot herself with my gun.'

'Jesus,' I said. I still couldn't take it in.

'She was never right after her father did the same thing. But then you know all about that.'

I did. I'd been there. 'Toby,' I said. 'I'm so sorry. Why didn't you get in touch?'

He shrugged. 'I don't know. I thought you'd been through enough. I knew how close you were to Jackie.'

'I was. Who forced you out?' I hardly had to ask.

'A bloke called Derek Schofield. The place we bought was where he was landing cocaine from South America. The previous owner had taken a cut for turning a blind eye. We wouldn't. It was a screw-up all along the line. Everything fell apart. After the funeral, Mr D'Arbley here got in touch. He's taken me on to deal with Schofield.'

'Terminate with extreme prejudice,' I said.

'If you like. I heard what happened to *your* wife. I'm sorry.'

'Thanks.'

'Now Mr D'Arbley wants you to help me. Two heads being better than one.'

'I know,' I said. I turned to D'Arbley. 'But why Schofield too? If it was Tyson turned your daughter on to smack.'

'Because he's an evil man,' replied D'Arbley. 'I've done a lot of digging into his career. I know what he did either directly or indirectly to a lot of people.'

'So why just us?' I said. 'Why aren't there a bunch of people here?'

'Because you are the only two who have both the motive and the necessary background to carry it off.'

I looked from one of them to the other.

'So are you in?' said Toby.

'It could be your daughter next,' said D'Arbley.

'What do you know about her?' I said. He was walking on extremely thin ice.

He held up his hands in a placating way. 'Don't get excited, Mr Sharman. I know how you feel about her. Very much like I felt about Susie, I imagine. But Schofield won't be happy until you're on your knees. He doesn't have a forgiving nature. Believe me, I know. He'd rather hurt those close to you, than you yourself. Then watch you suffer.'

'What's wrong with going to the police?'

D'Arbley almost smiled. 'It's been tried. He's wanted by the authorities in a dozen countries. Including Great Britain, under a score of names. But he has a large wallet and the civil service are not the most generous of employers.'

'He just buys them off, right?'

'One way or another. Those he cannot buy, he corrupts, then blackmails. Those he cannot buy or corrupt, he has killed.'

'Just like that.'

'Just like that,' he agreed.

'And I'm supposed to agree to try and kill this particularly powerful individual just on your say so.'

'And mine,' said Toby.

'And you saw the clippings,' said D'Arbley.

'I saw that your daughter died, not who was responsible.'

'Trust us,' said Toby. 'Think of your wife.'

Trust. I've always said that is a big word.

'Say I'm in,' I said. 'What's the deal?'

D'Arbley nodded. 'Simple. I pay you half a million pounds between you for the job. One third up front. The rest on completion.'

I nodded back. 'So where is this bloke Schofield? He doesn't sound like he'd be easy to get next to.'

'He isn't. This minute, who knows? He comes and goes like a shadow. But on New Year's Eve he will be at his country house in East Anglia.'

'Country house. Nice work. How do you know?'

'We have our methods.'

'Isn't that rather risky for a man who's so wanted?'

'What better night for it? Most of the police in Great Britain are out looking for drunken drivers. The rest are drunk themselves.'

'And Tyson will be there too?'

'Where Schofield goes, Tyson goes.'

I looked at Toby and he looked back at me. 'OK, Mr D'Arbley,' I said. 'Count me in.'

36

'I think you and I'd better go and have a chat,' Toby said to me. 'There's a pub just round the corner.'

'I think you're right,' I agreed. 'This is a lot to take in, in one afternoon.'

'We'll be in touch, Mr D'Arbley,' said Toby as I collected my coat and my wits, and the man himself showed us to the door.

The pub was small, with lots of plants in hanging baskets outside. They must have been a riot in the summer, but right then, on that November afternoon, they were bare and brown. A bit like the way I felt. Inside it was all neat and clean, with just a couple of customers. There was an open fire in there too. But a fake one this time, giving off more light than heat. Toby bought a couple of pints of lager and I sat at a table close to the fire and lit a cigarette. My head was still spinning from information overload and sorrow at the news of Jackie's death.

When he joined me I said, 'Tell me about Jackie.'

'I already did.'

'Details.' I realized how that sounded. 'Sorry,' I said. 'But we're both in the same boat. I don't want to sound callous, but since Dawn died, I'm not exactly filled with the milk of human kindness.'

'I understand,' he said. He looked inside himself and started. 'You know that when we left England we headed for the Caribbean?'

I nodded.

'We travelled around the Gulf and the eastern seaboard of

the United States and liked what we saw. The climate, the lifestyle, everything. So we decided to settle down there. Big mistake.' His mouth twisted. 'Like I told you we sunk our money, her inheritance and my savings, into a place in Florida. Near Key Largo. A nice place. Interstate highway one side, an estuary the other. A dozen rooms. A little shop for bait, beer and groceries. A couple of pumps for fuel for the boats and cars and a small diner. It had everything, or so we thought. We ran it with the help of a kid who looked after the pumps and the shop and a couple of local women who ran the diner. We looked after the hotel itself. It could've worked out fine. The water formed a natural harbour where people could tie up and recharge their batteries. Literally. That was the trouble. The harbour was perfect for landing contraband. Secluded and quiet. Oh hell, everyone knew about it. It's a cottage industry down there. It's kind of a depressed area. The eco-structure is shot to hell, from over-development and just plain greed. And every little helps. The guy who sold us the place took a kickback. Had done for years. Only he declined to tell us about it. I guess he just assumed we'd carry on. But Jackie and I didn't see it that way. We were both tired of corruption. We'd seen enough of it in this country. We decided to make a stand.'

'And?'

'And our staff quit. The local sheriff started hassling us. We were getting bogged down with visits from the health and safety. Then the bookings dried up. Christ knows how he did it – Schofield. But he did. We'd taken out a loan at the local bank. Suddenly they wanted paying all at once. The manager must've been in Schofield's pocket. We were broke within a year. So we sold the place for a loss and moved to Miami. I got a job running security for a little carburettor factory on the local industrial park. Jackie went into decline. She was never that strong. Not physically or mentally, after what she went through as a kid. I had a day off and went to the market for groceries. Just another day, or so I thought. Whilst I was gone, it was only an hour or so –' he sounded desperate – 'she got the gun I carried at work, stuck it in her mouth and pulled the trigger.'

I looked at my untouched drink on the table in front of me. 'I've got to take a piss,' I said, and went to the gents. I stood by the sink and looked in the mirror. My face without the beard was old and hard. I'd aged ten years since Dawn had been killed, and the blood ran bitter and sour through my veins. Now another friend was dead. How many more? I thought, before this is all over?

I went back to Toby and said, 'What do we do?'

He took a thick envelope out of the inside pocket of his dark overcoat and passed it to me. 'The plans of the house and its grounds, and photos of Tyson and Schofield. Schofield's is lousy. He doesn't like publicity for obvious reasons. It's the only one of him in existence as far as we know, and it took months to get. They're for you to keep. Read, learn and inwardly digest.'

My old granny used to say that. 'You must've been pretty sure of me,' I commented.

'I was.'

I nodded and opened the envelope. The maps and plans I laid aside for later, and concentrated on the photographs. One was clear: an eight-by-ten of a handsome young bloke of about twenty-eight. If I had anything to do with it, he'd never see thirty. The other was smaller. Snapshot size and grainy. Not very clear. Taken on the run. The man photographed could have been any age between forty and sixty. Dark haired, with a face you wouldn't look at twice. *You* wouldn't maybe, but I would. He was the man who'd had Dawn, Daisy and Tracey killed. My heart was cold as I looked at it.

'How do we do it?' I asked.

'Leave that to me. Have you got a bank deposit account?'

'Sure.'

'Do you have the account number handy?'

'I've got a card.'

'Let's have a look.'

I pulled out my credit-card holder, found the card for my high-interest account and passed it over. Toby took down the details and said, 'Check it later in the week. You should find that half of one third of half a million quid has been deposited.'

'What *will* the taxman say?'

'Tell him you had a win on the horses.'

'Sure.'

'Listen, Nick,' he said. 'It's been fun, but I've got a lot to do. I'll be in touch with you later. I've still got your number.'

'I'll wait for your call.'

With a brief goodbye, he left the remains of his pint and split.

I sat and made pictures in the flames of the fake fire. Bad pictures, like bad dreams, so I left too.

37

I used a phone box on the corner to phone Chas in Wapping.

'Long time,' he said.

'Yeah. Can I see you?'

'When?'

'Now?'

'It's been months, Nick, and now all of a sudden —'

'Yeah,' I interrupted. 'I've got a lead on who killed Dawn and Tracey.'

'Where are you?'

'Bloomsbury.'

'Do you know a boozer called the Queen of Spain underneath Holborn Viaduct?'

'I'll find it.'

'Be there in half an hour.'

I was. Chas rolled in ten minutes later.

'You look terrible, Nick,' he said.

'Nice to see you too, Chas.'

He smiled, and I bought him a scotch.

'So tell me,' he said.

'Does the name Derek Schofield mean anything to you?'

'Christ, you love to mess around with the big boys, don't you?'

'Meaning?'

'Big-time entrepreneur. And I mean B-I-G. Billionaire. You know the deal.'

I didn't, but I was learning. 'Know what he looks like?' I asked.

'No. No one does. He makes Howard Hughes look like a party animal. Doesn't like publicity, big time. Has lawyers on the case twenty-five hours a day. It's even said that he has half a dozen ringers all over the world at any one time, living in his houses or booked into hotels under his name to confuse the issue.'

'Why?'

'Fuck knows. The geezer's mental maybe. But what's he got to do with Dawn and Tracey?'

'I heard he had them killed.'

He looked amazed. 'Schofield? Jesus. If that's right, it's the story of the year.'

I could see the headlines in his eyes, and I leant over and gripped his hand. Hard. 'Not a word on this, Chas. Not to anyone. Understand?'

'OK, Nick. Take it easy. That's my typewriting hand you're grinding to pulp.'

I looked down, saw that he was right and relaxed my grip. His skin was white with pressure and he eased his fingers.

'Sorry, mate,' I said. 'Bad day.'

I took out the envelope Toby had given me and extracted the picture of Schofield. 'Know him?' I asked.

Chas looked at it and shook his head.

'That's Schofield,' I said.

'You're kidding.'

'No.'

'Jesus. Can I have this?'

'No, Chas,' I said. 'I just wanted your confirmation.'

'I can't confirm a thing. I've never seen him.'

'Exactly.'

38

Chas wanted to know the whole story. I wouldn't tell him any more, but did promise that if I found out any further information he'd be the first to know. It was only then that he'd let me go.

I went home and drank myself stupid. More stupid than usual. I rolled a couple of joints and watched TV. I woke up at three a.m. in my armchair with the screen full of snow and an irritating whine coming from the closed down station, and decided that it was at last time to go and see where Dawn, Daisy and Tracey had died. Then I fell asleep again. I woke up at seven and felt just fine. Apart from a mouth that tasted like a dead dog's armpit, and a nasty headache.

I made some tea, and at a more reasonable hour called

Charlie on the phone. 'I need a motor. Now,' I said when he answered.

'And a very good morning to you too, Nick,' he said back.

I suddenly felt shitty again. 'Sorry, mate,' I said. 'Nought out of ten for communication skills. How are you?'

'Just fine.'

'I really need a car for a couple of hours. Maybe all day.'

'I said there'd always be one here for you. Anything in particular?'

'No. Just as long as it goes.'

'All my cars go. At least till they get to the bottom of the road.' And he laughed his car dealer's laugh. 'I've got just the thing. Another Range Rover. A special. It's got a big block Chevy V8 lump through a Blazer turbo 400 auto four-speed gearbox. Beefed up suspension and brakes and the biggest tyres you've ever seen. I got it as part of a debt from some nutty bastard who thought that the end of the world was coming before Christmas.'

'And isn't it?'

'His did, when the VAT men went in.' And he laughed again.

Charlie continued to tell me all about the high-performance cylinder heads, but I really wasn't interested, even though I pretended to be, because I always had been in the past. Frankly a rusty Fiesta on a T-plate would've done me that day.

'Sounds great,' I said. 'Is it ready to roll?'

'I'll get it gassed up, check the oil and water and you can have it when you like.'

'About half an hour.'

'You got it.'

And we rang off.

I walked up to his place. It didn't take long and helped clear my headache.

I saw the motor before I saw Charlie. It was parked half on and half off the pavement outside his lot. It stood very tall on wide, chromed wheels with tyres that had enough tread to rip up tarmac as it went. The Rover was sprayed a sort of muddy green, and huge matt black crash bars were mounted front and back to protect the lights and frighten cab drivers. There was a power hump on the bonnet and the windows were tinted dark grey. All in all it looked like something you'd use for a bit of recreational ram-raiding if the shops were shut and you needed an extra pint of milk.

Charlie was leaning against a black 8 Series BMW drinking a cup of tea out of a Styrofoam cup, taking the winter air, with an eye out for likely punters, when he saw me. He was tarted up in a beige cashmere overcoat with a black velvet collar over a purple mohair three piece, pink tab-collar shirt and Guards tie.

'Don't move,' I said. 'I want to remember you just like you are.'

'Nick.'

'Charlie.'

'Your carriage awaits.'

'Subtle.'

'Shit off a shovel, son.'

'Am I insured?'

'Sure. I've put you on the books as a consultant.'

'Consultant on what?'

'Christ knows. Trouble probably.' He took a set of keys out of his coat pocket and lobbed them over. 'Enjoy,' he said.

'Cheers.'

'Cuppa before you go?'

'No thanks. I want to get there.'

He didn't ask where and I was grateful. I just unlocked the driver's door and got in. The interior was pale beige leather.

I settled behind the wheel, adjusted the seat for height and rake and switched on the engine. The big Chevy lump came to life with a rumble like a bear being woken early from hibernation, grey smoke belched from the exhausts and the needle on the fuel gauge swung round to F. I put my foot on the brake and engaged 'Drive'. The Rover tried to leave without me at less than a thousand revs, and I knew I was going to be in for a fun day. I tooted the horn, Charlie raised his hand, I took my foot off the brake pedal and dribbled another few hundred r.p.m. The Rover's huge back tyres squealed and before I knew it I was thirty yards down the road, and a rep in a Cavalier had aged ten years as I cut him off. I drifted the motor down Norwood Road, getting the hang of the power steering. By the time I got to Brixton I was used to the car and let it have its head on the Stockwell Road and up to the river. By the time I hit Park Lane I was showing off and almost forgetting the point of my journey, as I enjoyed the power that the Range Rover put through the huge tyres that sounded like tank tracks on the road.

The Edgware Road was as crowded as usual, but when I hit the motorway, I put my foot down hard and before the rev counter got to five thousand I was doing close to a hundred and thirty m.p.h.

It took no time at all to get to Dunstable, and it was only when I saw a signpost for junction eleven that I remembered why I was there.

I went past it, under the bridge where the crash happened, and it started to rain. All the way up the motorway the sky had got darker and I could see the wind coming up, as the tops of the trees alongside the road began to dance and sway. By the time I reached the next turnoff I needed the wipers on double time. I came off at junction twelve, swung round the slip roads and came back on to the highway, heading south. Within a couple of minutes I was back at the bridge, indicated left and pulled on to the hard shoulder, switched to emergency blinkers and got out of the car.

I pulled up the collar of my leather jacket against the weather and walked up the grassy embankment towards the support of the bridge above me that Tracey's car had hit. There were some scars on the concrete and black stains from the smoke. Behind me, the traffic rushed towards London and I could feel the draught of its slipstream and the boom of the engines that echoed around me. From somewhere across the fields that stretched towards the town I heard the motor of a light plane or helicopter, but couldn't see it for the ceiling that the bridge made above my head. At least under there I wasn't getting soaked, just feeling some peripheral drops that the wind blew under it. I stood on the grass and looked for tyre tracks, but the grass had had all summer and autumn to fill them in and I could see nothing. Not that I could've seen much anyway, because my eyes filled with tears, and I leant my head against the cold concrete and wished I was dead myself.

39

That's where the Old Bill found me. They drove up in a Range Rover of their own a couple of minutes later. It was dripping with emergency gear and had its blue light flashing, but the siren was silent. They parked theirs behind mine and two coppers wearing lime green fluorescent jackets got out. They walked across the grass to join me.

The first one to reach me was the shorter of the two, puffy faced, with a dark moustache and eyes that were too close together. This one's going to be trouble, I thought as he spoke.

'What's going on?' he said.

'Nothing much.'

'Has your car broken down?'

'No.'

'Do you know it's an offence to stop on the hard shoulder unless it's an emergency?'

I did. I could've even quoted the subsection of the Road Traffic Act that he was referring to, given a little time.

I nodded.

'So?'

'So?' I said back.

He sighed and turned to his mate, who was a few years younger, a good many pints and meat pies slimmer, and who I could see had blond hair under his peaked cap. 'What do you reckon, John?' Moustache said.

The blond one shrugged, then looked at me. 'It'll be a lot easier if you just get into your car and go,' he said to me.

'And if I don't?'

'Then we nick you,' said Moustache. There was a trace of a country boy accent in his voice which made it hard for me to take him seriously.

'So nick me,' I said. 'I'll come quietly.' Stupid. I told you that.

Before he had time to make his move, the one he'd called John said, 'What's the attraction?'

'Of what?'

'This place.'

I pointed at the scarred and stained concrete buttress. 'My wife was killed here last March.'

'Jesus,' said John. 'What time of day?'

'Middle of the night.'

He wrinkled his forehead. 'A Renault? Two female casualties? DOA?'

I nodded. 'My wife was pregnant.'

'I remember it,' said John, then turned to his mate. 'You were on sick leave. I was teamed up with Bob Young. It was a sod of a shout.' He looked back at me. 'Sorry.'

I shrugged. 'S'all right.'

'So why are you here now?' said Moustache.

'I thought it was time to take a look-see.'

'You haven't been before?' John again.

'No.'

He nodded thoughtfully. 'You still can't park there.' He gestured back towards the road.

'Fair enough,' I said. 'Sorry to be a nuisance.'

'Yeah. The chopper spotted you. Wondered what was going on.'

He seemed like a reasonable bloke. 'You got a minute?' I asked.

'For what?'

'To tell me what you saw that night.'

'I saw a car burning. That's all.'

'I'd be obliged.'

He looked at his mate and made a decision. 'OK,' he said. 'But I might get a call.'

'Whatever,' I said.

He looked at his mate again, who by the look on *his* face obviously thought that it was a waste of time, and said, 'You take the motor, Pete. I'll go with this gentleman. Follow us. We'll park up by the next junction. If you need me, flash the lights.'

We went back to the two Range Rovers. Pete got behind the wheel of his and started the engine. I got into mine, with John in the passenger seat, and switched on the ignition.

'What engine?' he asked, when the motor rumbled into life.

'Chevy. Big block. Belongs to a friend of mine in the motor trade.'

I switched off the blinkers, indicated right, waited for a gap in the traffic and pulled out, the police car behind me. The police helicopter was swinging from left to right, like the weight on the end of a pendulum, half a mile away across country. I drove at a leisurely pace down to junction eleven, moved on to the slip road and stopped at a lay-by on the roundabout above it. I switched off the Range Rover's engine and heard the cold rain drumming on the roof.

'So?' said John.

'So,' I said back. 'Did you ever think it was anything else than an accident?'

'Is that what you think?'

'Dunno,' I lied.

'They do happen. I see them all the time.'

'I can imagine.'

'It was a bad one. I'm sorry for your loss.'

'Thank you.'

'But you'd have to have a lot of enemies for someone to do something like that. Your wife being pregnant and all.'

'I know.'

'Have you?'

'What?'

'Got a lot of enemies.'

I didn't answer and he didn't press it. Instead he said, 'And it's not a clever idea to start haunting that place. Next time Pete might have another mate. One who wasn't there that night.'

'I won't,' I said. 'It was just something I needed to do.'

'I'd probably do the same under the circumstances.'

In the rear-view mirror I saw the brights on the police car flash. 'You're wanted,' I said. 'Duty calls.'

He looked over his shoulder through the back window and waved. 'I'll be off then,' he said. 'Take it easy.'

'I will. And thanks for being there. That night I mean.'

'It's my job. Sorry I couldn't've done more.' And with that he jumped out, ran back to his vehicle, climbed into the passenger seat, and took off with the siren braying and blue lights flashing.

I stayed where I was for a few minutes, thinking, as the cars rushed by my window in the rain. I looked at them, all full of people with places to go, things to do. Reps off selling office furniture or corn flakes before going back to the wife and kids with tales of their day on the road. I thought of my wife, rotting under a few feet of earth in Greenwich, and my ex-wife and daughter up in Scotland. And all the other women I'd known. Where were they now? All gone. Dead or alive. All gone. Disasters every one. If they weren't, why was I alone now? But then look at the ones I picked, or who picked me. Junkies, thieves, self-mutilators, whores, persistent victims. Fucked up bitches every one, who'd sooner put their finger in your eye than say something nice. Whose fault was it that every relationship I'd ever had went to shit? Theirs or mine? Who the fuck knew? And I wasn't going to find out by sitting on a rain-washed roundabout near Dunstable, so I switched on the engine again and headed south.

40

I drove the Range Rover straight back to Charlie's car lot, thanked him for the loan of it, had a cup of tea and a natter. Then walked home. He didn't ask me where I'd been and I didn't volunteer the information.

I sat around the flat for the rest of the afternoon, but things had changed. I felt restless and unable to settle to my usual nightly chores of eating something brought in or out of a can, and surfing the TV channels until I fell asleep. And I was thinking about where I'd been and what I'd seen and the copper I'd met, and I didn't want to. So around six, I showered, shaved and got dressed in clean clothes, polished my cowboy boots and went out for a drink. I started up west, but it was too crowded and I felt like a ghost drifting between the packs of brightly dressed women and predatory men looking for . . . what? To get drunk, forget about the drudgery of work and maybe score some easy sex. So I headed east and ended up in Clerkenwell, an area I don't know well, but its very strangeness made it seem safe. A hiding place in the big, mean city, where no one knew me either.

I drifted into a pub that was part of an office block, somewhere off the Gray's Inn Road. The bar was softly lit, clean, with a CD jukebox that wasn't too loud, and almost empty. I went up to the bar, snagged a stool and ordered a bottle of Rolling Rock and a Jack Daniel's chaser. So far, so good. Two stools down, a girl in a red dress was sitting with another girl in a black two-piece suit. The one in red had long, thick dark hair that she kept tossing about all over the place as if she knew it was her best asset. She was young. Far too young for me, and her friend wasn't much older. As I paid for my drinks, the one in red looked round at me, tossed her mane of hair one more time and turned back to her pal, said something and they both laughed. I felt even older as they did it. I should have got up there and then, left my drinks and gone home. But I didn't. It was the first time someone had made a move on me for so long, that I felt flattered.

After a minute, the one in the suit got up and went over to the jukebox and Red turned towards me again.

'Is it raining out?' she asked.

It was obvious by the fact that my jacket was dry, that it wasn't.

'No,' I said. Not friendly. No smile. Minimum eye contact.

But I could feel the palms of my hands spring out with sweat as I said the word.

'They got it wrong again.'

That time I did smile. I couldn't help it and I turned towards her. 'They usually do.'

'Do you work upstairs?' she asked.

By that I imagined she meant in the office building. I shook my head.

'I didn't think so. Not many of the men who do wear boots like that.'

I looked down at my best, hand-tooled, imported from Texas, underslung-heeled, needle-toed, black ranch boots. 'Is that so?' I said.

She nodded. 'Come up,' she said, patting the stool next to hers. 'I can't hear you properly.'

I thought about it for a second, shrugged, pushed my bottle and glass along the bar and moved up until I was next to her. She pushed back her hair again and I could smell the shampoo in it and the perfume she wore on her body. Close up she *was* young. No more than twenty. Fresh and alive and I felt near to tears. Her skin was smooth and white, and it suddenly occurred to me that it had been months since I'd touched any skin apart from my own, and how much I missed doing it, and how much I just wanted to touch hers. I'd been starved of basic human contact for too long.

'My name's Diane,' she said, and put out her hand with its long, slim fingers and nails lacquered the same colour as her dress.

I wiped my right palm on my jeans and shook it. I got my wish. I got to touch her skin and it was as soft and smooth as I'd thought it would be. 'Nick,' I said.

She smiled. 'How do you do, Nick. My friend's name is June.'

I nodded. 'Do *you* work upstairs?'

'Worse luck. I hate it. I'm a secretary.' She pronounced it 'Seckertary', and put a nasal intonation into her voice as she did so. She was OK.

'Been working late?' I asked.

'Not really. We're meeting some people.'

So that was that, I thought. I'd read it wrong. Not surprising really with my track record.

'Boyfriends?' I asked.

'No.' She was very certain. 'Blokes from the office. They're down the gym. We usually get together on a Tuesday. It's a bit of a drag really. But it's better than being at home watching telly.'

'I wouldn't have thought you had much problem filling your social diary.'

The hair again and a smile. 'I'm choosy,' she said.

Then her friend came back.

'June, this is Nick. He's a . . .' I hadn't told her. Besides I wasn't sure.

'Company director,' I said.

'In boots like that?' said June, as if she doubted it. 'I've met some of them where I live. Walthamstow. Usually means they've got a portable phone.'

She was sharp, I'll give her that. Any sharper and she'd cut her glass.

I laughed. 'Not me.'

'What kind of company?' asked June.

'A detective agency.' Wasn't I grand?

'A detective,' said Diane, and tossed her hair for the hundredth time. 'That must be exciting.'

'Don't you believe it.'

Then the door to the pub opened to let in a gust of cold air and four geezers in suits carrying gym bags.

'Here's the boys,' said June.

'Oh good,' said Diane, and pulled a face at me.

196

The boys were all under thirty, big built and boisterous. They must've had a good time in the showers together. Probably comparing the size of their dicks.

They bounced over, dropped their bags on the floor and shouted for the barman.

'Kenny, John, Paul, Mike. This is Nick. He's a private detective,' said Diane.

The four looked at me like I was something unpleasant that had crawled out of their muesli, especially Kenny, who said, 'Sure.' I think he had eyes for Diane. Who am I kidding? Of course he did. Who wouldn't?

'It's true,' I said and took a hit on my JD. Now what was *I* trying to prove? That I could be every inch the kind of arsehole he was?

Kenny moved round so that he was between me and Diane and ordered a round of drinks, leaving me out. What did I care? I could buy my own booze.

When the drinks were in he didn't move, and Diane sort of stuck her head round him and said, 'Sorry about this.'

I shrugged. Frankly I could have cared less, but I didn't know how.

So then old Kenny decides to step back and stand on my feet. You know how it happens. Purely accidental. But I was fond of those boots and I didn't want them scuffed. And also I had a bit of a corn on one toe and it hurt like hell when he stomped all over it.

'Careful,' I said. But mildly. I wasn't looking for a fight. Just a quiet drink, and I'd been getting kind of fond of Diane's company.

'Sorry,' he said. But with a big grin, like he was telling me to fuck off, there and then.

'There's plenty of room,' I said.

'So use some of it,' he said straight back.

Not friendly.

'And if I don't?'

'Maybe I'll make you.'

'You'll have me gibbering with fear if you carry on like that.'

'Get back to your wife.'

Now why he said that I'll never know, and I've thought about it some since. Why he picked that particular way to try and get rid of me. Afterwards, when I got home I checked in the mirror to see if I had something tattooed on my forehead so that he reacted as he did.

I stood up. I could feel sweat breaking out on me again. This time not just on the palms of my hands, but all over.

'What?' I said.

'You heard. You're married, aren't you?'

I shook my head.

'You're wearing a ring.'

'So what? That doesn't mean anything.' I was starting to justify myself. Bad move.

'See,' he said, and looked round at his mates and Diane and June.

I mean, what was this geezer? My moral arbiter?

He stuck his forefinger in my face and said, 'No one wants you here. Just get out and stop bothering us.'

I saw that Diane was about to say something, but I beat her to it. I grabbed his finger and bent it back until I heard the ligaments creak, and then I forced it back a bit further. He screamed and went down on one knee. 'Listen, cunt,' I said. 'If I break this you'll go into shock and maybe die. Do you want that?'

He didn't answer quick enough, so I gave the finger a bit more pressure. Enough for tears to come to his eyes and for him to scream again, loud enough to drown out the music on the jukebox and bring the barman running. I shook my head at him and he stopped on the other side of the bar. One of

Kenny's mates, the one nearest me, made a move in my direction and I kicked him on the outside of his left knee. Not hard enough to break it, but hard enough so that he went down on it with a crack.

I looked across at the other two geezers. 'Leave it,' I said. 'Or your pal'll be signing cheques with his left hand for a month.'

They looked at each other and raised their hands in surrender.

'Walkies,' I said, and exerted a little more pressure on Kenny's finger, and pulled him with me as I backed towards the door.

'Bye, Diane,' I said. 'It was nice meeting you. Maybe another time.'

'Walters and Williams, Investment Brokers,' she said. 'They're in the book.'

I let go of Kenny's finger and he fell forward on his face, sobbing, and I ducked out of the door of the pub and cut across the main road, through the traffic and took the first turning I came to, then another, and into the next boozer I saw.

Excellent behaviour, Nick, I thought. Just what the doctor ordered. Maybe you could take it up for a living, going from pub to pub beating up on kids. Perhaps you should phone one of those agencies. Ask them if they've got a vacancy for a Thug-O-Gram.

The bar was small and deserted except for a barmaid and one male customer watching TV. No pretty women with lots of hair.

I ordered a lager. Obviously I was going to go home alone.

41

I hung around till closing time, then took a cab home. The driver dropped me off opposite my place, and I strolled across the road, took out my keys and just as I was inserting the Yale into the lock, a female voice with a Scottish accent said, 'Thank Christ you're home at last. I've been waiting for hours, and it's bloody freezing here.'

I almost dropped the keys in surprise. The voice came from the direction of the concrete half-shed where the dustbins for the flats in the house were kept. I recognized the voice, but when she stepped into the dim light that spilled from the single bulb in the hallway behind the front door, I hardly recognized the girl.

It was Paula McGann. But since I'd last seen her, just over a year ago, she'd gone through a sea change. Where once there was Rave, now there was Goth. Her hair was dreaded up and gathered on top so that her head resembled a pineapple. Her face was dead white, except for heavily sooted eyes and black lips. She was dressed in black too. A black velvet and lace dress, with a short, full skirt, under a black leather jacket and some sort of black cloak. On her legs were black fishnets, ripped at one knee, and she stood in black high-heeled boots with pointed toes. She had black scarves tied all over herself and a huge amount of chunky silver jewellery. In one hand she carried a small black leather doctor's bag.

I still couldn't quite believe it. 'Paula?' I said. 'What the hell are you doing here?' Not the warmest of welcomes, but she'd given me a hell of a start.

'Aren't you going to say hello, Mr Sharman?'

I shook my head, opened the door and we both went inside. Under better light she looked worse. Her face was tired under the make-up, and her clothes were dusty and stained and looked as if she'd been wearing them for days. But maybe that was the idea.

'You'd better come up,' I said. 'You look like you could use a cup of tea.'

She smiled then, and it was the Paula I remembered. 'You're a lovely man,' she said, and she passed out.

I caught her before she hit the ground, picked her and her bag up and climbed the stairs. She weighed about the same as a carrier full of shopping, so it was no hardship. I wrestled my flat door open and put her on the sofa, pulled her skirt down and wondered if I should call a doctor. I lit a cigarette to help the thought process, and she opened her eyes and said, 'Did someone say something about tea?'

'Are you all right?' I asked. 'And don't mess me about. I'm not in the mood.'

'Sorry. It's just been a while since I had anything to eat.'

'How long?'

'Four days. Five.'

I sighed. 'What do you want?'

'Anything. But no meat.'

Which ruled out a bacon sandwich. I put on the kettle, then found a can of minestrone soup and put it in a saucepan to warm through. 'Are you all right with butter?' I asked. I've known some veggies. Weird fuckers, one and all.

She nodded, and I cut a couple of slices of bread and smeared them with butter. By then the soup was warm, and I put it into a bowl and served it to her where she was sitting. The whole lot vanished in a second, and a little colour came back to her cheeks under the coat of white.

'Want anything else?' I asked, as I made two mugs of tea.

'Not right now. Unless you've got a biscuit.'

I did as it happened. A new packet of milk chocolate fingers. They lasted as long as the tea.

When it was all finished, I said, 'So tell me. What's up? What are you doing here?'

'I ran away again.'

'When?'

'Couple of weeks ago.'

'Jesus Christ, Paula.'

'Rhiannon.'

'What?'

'That's what they call me now. Rhiannon. Like in the Fleetwood Mac song. It's my favourite.'

'Who calls you that?'

'Everyone.'

'Not your mum, I'll bet.'

She pulled a wry face. 'Mebbe,' she said.

I suddenly had a moment's panic. 'And what about Judith?'

'What about her?'

'She's not . . .'

'Course not. You'd've heard, wouldn't you? No. Judith's working hard at her books. We don't see much of each other these days.'

'So why are you here?'

'I just blew into town. I remembered your address.'

'And here you are.'

'Here I am. You haven't got anything to smoke, have you?'

As a matter of fact I did. Plenty. But I wasn't about to share it with her, so I shook my head.

'Pity.'

I felt the same way. There was nothing I fancied right then so much as a spliff. But I had some JD, so I went for that. She wanted some too, but I refused and offered her straight coke, which after the usual in-joke, she accepted.

202

'So,' I said, when we had our drinks. 'What are you going to do now?'

She shrugged.

'Do you want to go home?'

She shook her head.

'How old are you?'

'Fifteen. Sixteen in a few months.'

'I think you should try it.'

'What?'

'Going home. Just for a bit.'

'And share a room with my sister?'

'It's better than walking the streets.'

'Don't you believe it.'

'Is your mum on the phone now?'

She shook her head again.

'Is there anyone you want to talk to up there?'

Another shake.

'What about the police?'

'What about them?'

I was getting a bit pissed off with the cryptic way she was answering my questions. 'Do you think they're looking for you?'

'I don't know. I doubt it.'

'I still think you should give it another try.'

'They think I'm weird up there, dressed like this.'

I could see why, and smiled. 'I'll pay your fare,' I said.

'Can we talk about it tomorrow?'

I knew we were approaching an uncomfortable phase. 'What about tonight?'

'What about it?'

See what I mean? 'Have you got anywhere to stay?'

'No.'

It was late and I was half pissed. 'Do you want to stay here?'

She nodded.

I looked round. It was just a small studio flat. One room with bathroom attached. It contained a bed, a sofa. A few bits of furniture. A lot of mess. Dawn and I had never got around to moving. We were going to do it once the baby had arrived.

'I was very sorry to hear about your wife,' said Paula – Rhiannon, whatever – as if picking up on my thoughts. 'She was nice. Nice to me.'

'She was,' I agreed.

'Judith told me about it,' said Paula. 'And your poor little baby.'

I didn't want to talk about it. 'I'll make you up a bed on the sofa,' I said.

'You don't have to.' She looked at the bed.

Fucking hell, I thought. 'Sofa,' I said.

'It'd be all right.'

'You're only fifteen. The last time I remember looking, that was under age.'

'Where have you been, Mr Sharman? I had my first period when I was twelve and I lost my virginity two years ago.'

'Were you sleeping with that guy?'

'Which guy?'

'That guy in Banbury. The traveller?'

'Eno?'

'That's the one.'

She nodded.

'And Judith?'

This time she smiled. 'No. We told you. She was too young. Too innocent. She only ran away to keep me company.'

I believed her and was relieved. I went and found some sheets, blankets and a pillow. She moved to a chair and I made her up a bed on the sofa. 'Bathroom's in there,' I said, indicating the door inside the kitchen. 'Wait.' I went and found Dawn's robe. I hadn't chucked anything of hers away. It smelt of her, and my guts hurt. 'Wear this,' I said.

When Paula went into the bathroom with her little black bag I sat down and lit a cigarette and poured more JD. The smell of Dawn had been almost too much to bear.

When she came back she was wearing the robe and carrying her clothes over her arm. I grabbed a robe of my own and went off to clean my teeth, take a piss and undress. Which I did, down to my boxers and T-shirt, then shucked on the robe and went back next door. Paula was on the sofa, sheets up to her chin, and fast asleep. I turned off the light, slipped out of the robe and jumped into bed.

Christ knows what time it was when she came in with me, but it was late and I was as fast asleep as Mr Jack Daniel could make me. She woke me up by pushing up my T-shirt and attaching her mouth full of sharp little teeth on to my nipple.

Jesus, but I jumped. Where I was in my dreams I don't know, but when I came awake it was to find I had my arms full of a tiny, slippery little female who wanted a fuck.

So I gave her one. Right or wrong, that's what I did. And I enjoyed it, and so did she. It had been a long time, but I soon caught up. She was extremely horny and had a lot of energy. But I kept thinking of Dawn and wishing it was her I was holding, and because it wasn't, I felt like I was being the worst kind of unfaithful.

But it was good, and I remembered what a woman's skin feels like.

The next morning we did it again, then I put her on a train to Aberdeen. It was the best thing for both of us. I carried memories around like luggage, and something was going on top. Having Paula around would have only made us both miserable. So I paid for a one-way ticket and gave her a ton. It wasn't a payoff, at least I didn't see it like that. If it had been my daughter on the loose, I hope someone would do the same for her. I'm not so sure about the fucks though.

She didn't want to go. She said she'd get off the train at the first stop and come back. I told her that she could if she wanted, but maybe a little time in Scotland might be best all round.

She reluctantly agreed, then told me she'd be back one day, and when she did she'd come and visit. I told her she'd be welcome. And I told her the truth.

She leant out of the window of the train as it pulled away, all young and pretty, even in the Gothic gear that made her look like she was in mourning, and I knew I'd miss her.

And I did.

42

The money was in the bank Friday morning. I phoned in and checked.

Over eighty-three thousand pounds. It doesn't sound like much if you say it fast.

Toby Gillis phoned about an hour later. 'Got the cash?' he asked.

'Yes.'

'Good. We should talk.'

I agreed.

'I'm at the Dorchester. Come over for lunch. Have you studied the maps?'

'I've had a look at them.'

'Good. One o'clock suit you?'

'I'll be there.'

He gave me his room number and told me to come straight up.

I cabbed it to the hotel. I'd spent the morning looking again at the map and plans he'd given me. Schofield's country house was roughly equidistant between Great Yarmouth, Lowestoft and Norwich, in the marshes off the A143. It sounded nice and remote. Just right for our purposes. The plans of the place were detailed. It was big. Massive. Built in the fifteenth century, and added to regularly ever since. I was surprised it hadn't slipped into the marshes long ago.

When I got to the Dorchester, I body swerved through the foyer and caught a lift to the fifth floor. I knocked three times, just like in the movies, and Toby answered the door. He let me into a suite that had to be a monkey a night without breakfast, and we shook hands. He was dressed in a white shirt without a tie, grey suit pants and socks without shoes. He pushed his hair out of his eyes and said, 'I've ordered food up here. Is that all right? It's more private than the dining room.'

'Suits me,' I replied.

'Take your coat off. Sit down. Drink?'

I did as he said and ordered a bloody Mary which he made at his own little personal bar. It seems that if you worked for D'Arbley you went first class.

The food came almost straight away. There was a good mixture. Cold meats and fish, salad, hot new potatoes, apple pie and coffee in the poshest thermos I'd ever seen. Plus a couple of bottles of white wine, that normally I'd need a mortgage to drink. But this was a special occasion, and I was mum with the booze, whilst Toby tipped the waiter and told him we'd serve ourselves.

We didn't talk business until after we'd eaten. Instead we caught up a bit more on what had happened since we'd last met.

It was a depressing conversation and it soon petered out.

Only when the dishes were stacked on the trolley, the wine bottles were empty and the coffee and brandy was on the table did we get down to brass tacks.

'You know where we're going?' said Toby.

I nodded.

'And what we're going to do?'

'Sure.'

'And you're happy about it?'

'Ecstatic.'

'Good.'

'Just one thing.'

'Yes.'

'When do we collect the rest of our money?'

'In cash. On the night.'

'How come he believes us?'

He caught my drift right away. After all, nothing would be easier than to say we'd done the job, pocket the cash and vanish. 'Simple,' said Toby. 'That's one of the things I wanted to talk to you about.'

'Go ahead.'

'Schofield wears a very distinctive ring on his little finger. A cluster of rubies and diamonds. Before we get paid, Mr D'Arbley wants us to give it to him.'

'What happens if we do it from a distance?'

'Too bad. He wants at least one of us close enough to get the ring.'

'That makes it harder.'

'It's a lot of money.'

'Fair enough. What about Tyson?'

'What about him?'

'Doesn't Mr D'Arbley want his Y-fronts or something? Just to prove that we did the deed?'

'No. He'll take our word for him.'

'Magnanimous.'

'You pissed off or something, Nick?'

Pissed off? Me? No. I was fucking great, wasn't I? Halfway round the bend was all. If I hadn't been I'd've never got mixed up in this madness. 'No. It's just me,' I said. 'Ignore it.'

'OK.'

And Toby wasn't the same either. I could tell. Not that I'd known him that well. And why would he be the same? He'd lost the woman he'd loved too. We were both on a downward curve. Mad, bad and dangerous to know.

'So how do we get in?' I asked. 'This place looks pretty tough to take from the plans. Electrified fences and shit. And I imagine that Schofield has a lot of soldiers.'

'He has. Maybe ten or twelve on the night. No one said it was going to be easy.'

'I'll say yea to that. I'll need to see the place before we go.'

'You will. I already have.'

'So how?' I asked.

'I've got some ideas.'

'Like?'

'Later. How are you with automatic weapons?'

'I make out.' I thought of the Uzi I still had hidden away at home.

'Good. I've got a stash of them. I'd like you to choose what you're going to carry on the night.'

'A pleasure.'

'Right. Next week you'd better come down to where they are and choose your poison. You can see the place then.'

'I'll look forward to it.'

'So there you go, Nick. Come New Year's Day, Mr D'Arbley will be a happy man.'

'Good,' I said. I didn't mean it. Quite frankly I couldn't have cared less about D'Arbley's feelings on New Year's Day or any other. It was mine that mattered.

'And you'll've nailed the ones that murdered your wife.'

'Or die in the attempt.'

'There's always that.'

There didn't seem to be much more to say, so after one more drink, I split.

43

It was now early December, and the days were shortening fast. Toby rang again the following Wednesday. 'What are you doing at the weekend?' he asked.

'Same old thing,' I said. 'Fuck all.'

'Good. Fancy a trip to the country?'

'If you like. Where?'

'Norfolk. I've got a cottage on some land about ten miles from Schofield's place. It's very quiet. We can get into some training and take a look at the target.'

'Nothing too strenuous on the training front, I hope.'

'No. Weapons and tactics.'

'OK.'

'I'll pick you up Friday afternoon about two. If we can beat the rush out of London, we can be up there in plenty of time for dinner. There's a decent restaurant not far away.'

'Sounds like my kind of training.'

'Friday. Be ready.' And he put down the phone.

I was. Leather jacket, jeans, denim shirt, Doc Marten's. Everything the well-dressed assassin should wear. I slung some clean underwear, another shirt and toilet gear into a bag, and was waiting at the designated time when the doorbell rang. I went downstairs and Toby was standing in the porch. Outside the house was parked a dark blue Laredo jeep with wide wheels and a hard top.

'Come on,' he said. 'Let's go.'

The Laredo must've had some modifications done to the engine, as it went like hell and we were soon over the river and heading east. We took the A12 out of London, switched to the A144 and picked up the A143 at Bungay, before coming off the main highway at a place called Kirby Row, then driving down back roads until we turned off on to a rough track that took us to the cottage. By then of course it was full dark, cold, with a clear sky full of stars and a crescent moon. In the cottage, from the first-floor windows where Toby and I had our rooms, we could see no lights in any direction. We dumped our stuff, went back to the jeep and off to eat. It *was* a decent restaurant, inside a small pub and hotel about ten minutes' drive away. We saw no other traffic on the road there or back. The cottage was perfect.

On Saturday morning Toby had me up at seven. He'd rented the place for all of December and January and had obviously spent some time there previously, because of what he showed me he had hidden in the deep freeze in the cellar. Under the neatly placed food were several rolls of carpeting. Inside each roll was an armourer's dream.

Roll one: a Heckler & Koch 9 mm MP5K–PDW submachine gun, complete with silencer. Six hundred rounds per minute, thirty bullets to a magazine. In with the gun were a dozen fully loaded mags. Fold back the stock and hang it over your shoulder on its sling and it could be easily concealed under an overcoat or similar.

Roll two: a Czech V261 Scorpion in 7.65 mm fitted with suppressor so that you didn't know what had hit you until thirty rounds tore through your body. Smaller than the H & K, but pretty much as devastating. It also came complete with half a dozen full magazines.

Roll three: two Winchester 1200 Defender pump action shotguns with pistol grips. Neither gun much more than two foot long, and their blue steel barrels caught the light from the overhead fixture in the cellar.

There were four boxes of cartridges in with the guns. 'Twelve gauge,' said Toby. 'Six-shot capacity, plus one in the pipe.'

Roll four: two Colt Combat Commander semis, chambered for 9 mm Parabellum, plus a dozen full, nine-shot magazines and two leather holsters on webbing belts.

Roll five: two Colt Detective Special .38 revolvers with two-inch barrels and shoulder holsters.

'No howitzers?' I asked.

'Don't be ridiculous.'

It was just a thought.

'Choose your weapons,' said Toby. 'There's plenty of spare ammunition buried in the woods. We'll dig it up as needed.'

'Pretty risky leaving them here,' I remarked.

'What else could I do? Everything in life has a certain risk factor. Now which sub do you want?'

I took the H & K. It felt good in my hands, even if its metal was freezing. I helped myself to one each of the shotguns, the semi-automatics and the revolvers.

'Let's go outside,' said Toby. 'We can get in some practice with the carry weapons.'

I took off my leather jacket and shrugged into the shoulder holster, then put my jacket back on and strapped the webbing belt around my hips, draped the H & K from one shoulder by its sling, put on a pair of thin black leather gloves and picked up the shotgun. The spare mags and cartridges went into my pockets and we went upstairs. I clanked a little as I walked, but that could be sorted. Toby was equally festooned with ordnance and we went outside into the cold dawn and took a hike.

We walked away from the cottage, over a stile, across a field and into a copse of trees. Toby explained that all the land came with the cottage, so we shouldn't have any unwelcome visitors, and if we did, just too bad for them. As we walked through the wood I could just see tyre tracks in the muddy earth. Thin ones, nothing like the Laredo would leave, and I pointed them out.

'Nothing to worry about,' he said, and when we came to a small clearing I saw the gleaming red paintwork of a nearly new Peugeot 205 that was parked smack in the centre. It looked empty, but I grabbed Toby's arm nevertheless.

'No problem,' he said. 'I brought it here. Stole it in Norwich a week ago.'

'What for?'

'So we could get in some target practice. I'm all out of beer cans.'

'Shame,' I said. 'I could do with a lager.'

'Later. Come here.' He led me a little deeper into the wood and another clearing. Targets had been set up. The usual soldier with a tin helmet over a menacing look, a rifle and bayonet, and some advertising gimmicks featuring life-size cardboard cut-outs of grinning men and women holding their latest products, plus what I took to be the spare wheel of the Peugeot hanging from a branch of a tree by a tow rope.

'Pick your target,' he said.

I propped the Winchester next to a tree trunk and brought the H & K up into a firing position. About fifteen metres away was the representation of a pretty young model in a swimsuit holding a beach ball with the sponsor's name printed on it in red. I cocked the submachine gun and let off a burst. It was just noisy enough to frighten birds from the trees, but I doubt that anyone outside the trees would have heard a thing. The bullets chopped the model to shreds, and for a moment, in that freezing forest as the sun pushed its orangey face up over the treetops, I knew what it was going to be like to face my wife's murderers.

It was going to be good.

'Fine,' said Toby. 'Keep going.'

I reloaded the MP5K and emptied the magazine at more targets, and Toby got into the act too with his Scorpion. The clearing was full of smoke and the targets were all destroyed, before we both started blasting at the spare wheel, shredding the rubber and sending it dancing on the end of its rope.

When we were out of ammo, he said, 'Let's go and let off the really spectacular pyrotechnic display. Come on, and bring your shotgun. It'll do you good. Get some of the kinks out of your system.'

I let the H & K drop on its sling, picked up the Winchester and followed him back to the Peugeot. We stood, well out of the line of each other's fire, and he said, 'When you're ready.'

The shotgun was ready to go and I aimed at the windscreen and pulled the trigger. The glass imploded and metal was torn from the bonnet. I pumped the action and fired again at the passenger door, and Toby joined in. The Peugeot rocked on its springs as we pumped and fired, pumped and fired, and the sound of the shots was deafening. We blew out the tyres and the windows, sent the wing mirrors flying, shredded the seats inside, smashed the front and rear lights off the motor, and when we'd exhausted our cartridges we dropped our shotguns, both drew our semi-automatics from the holsters attached to the belts around our waists and kept shooting. Which one of us hit the petrol tank, Christ knows, but when I'd almost emptied the clip, it blew with a roar which almost lifted the vehicle off the ground, a gout of flame and a burst of thick black smoke. We both stopped firing and watched the car burn.

'They'll think we're burning stubble,' said Toby. 'Let's go and have some lunch. Then when it gets dark we can go and obbo the target.'

214

44

We ate at a different place. Toby didn't want to draw attention to us anywhere, as regulars in the area. Very wise, I thought, although I wouldn't've minded trying the crayfish tails in brandy sauce. Instead we opted for a restaurant on the road to Norwich. I had peppered steak. It was OK.

We dawdled over coffee and brandy, then headed back to the cottage. The guns had all been stashed away again and we checked them. All present and correct. We spent the evening cleaning them and watching TV. At eight Toby made a scratch meal from what was in the fridge, then at ten p.m. we left for our recce.

The drive to Schofield's house took less than thirty minutes. We went back on to the A143, then cut off on to B-roads and across flat marshland, until Toby swung the motor off the highway and into the pitch blackness under some trees. The weather had been kind to us. Unlike the previous evening, a low cloud cover obliterated the moon and stars and there was a hint of rain in the air.

He cut the engine and light. 'It's just down the road,' he said. 'A couple of minutes' drive away is all.'

'Right.'

'We're going to have to breach the main gate. What I've got in mind will happen so quickly, that we'll be in before anyone has any idea what's happening.'

'And that is?'

'Don't worry about that now. Trust me. The hard part will begin when we've got inside. We're going to have to get through the guards before we can reach Schofield and Tyson.

And like I said, there'll be at least ten of them, probably more.'

'Good odds.'

He ignored my remark. 'The telephone wires will be cut, but there's going to be plenty of mobile phones inside. So someone's bound to raise the alarm pretty sharpish. And we're going to make a hell of a racket, which'll bring the local cops.'

'What do we do about that?'

'Get in and out fast. Find Schofield and Tyson. Kill them, take the ring and get out in the confusion.'

'Good plan.'

'Flexibility. That's the key word, Nick. Flexibility, boldness and speed. Keep those three in mind and we'll both be a lot richer on New Year's Day.'

I really didn't give a shit about the money. 'Why don't we just wait until they open the doors for Schofield and steam in then?'

'I wish it were that simple. But he's coming in by chopper.'

I looked at him in the darkness and he sensed my look. 'Yeah, a drag, I know. But the guy's total paranoid. That's how he's stayed free for so long. He'll come in just before midnight. When the chopper dust's in, that's our signal to go.'

'Terrific,' I said. 'We could've used those howitzers after all. Can we go and look at the place now?'

'Sure.' And he started the engine again.

He backed on to the road, switched on the lights and headed across the marshes again. Suddenly from out of the blackness in front I could see a glimmer of light. Toby slowed the Laredo and Schofield's house came into sight.

It was surrounded by high walls, topped with electrified wire, and dotted with high-beam security lights. The main gate was built from thick slabs of wood studded with iron bolts and hung between two stone gatehouses, their walls blank except for narrow slits in the stonework, and I could imagine the havoc that automatic weapons poked through them could wreak on anyone foolish enough to come knocking without an invitation. All in all, the place looked to be about as tough to breach as the Tower of London.

A fucking doddle, I thought.

'How about a back way?' I asked.

'No. It's the front or nothing.'

'Terrific.'

'That's all we can see tonight,' said Toby. 'They'll be filming us now,' as he allowed the Laredo to drift down the road, then took a left off at the T-junction in front of the gate, gave the motor some gas and headed back into the night.

'Jesus,' I said. 'How the fuck do we take that place?'

I saw him grin in the glow of the dashboard. 'Easy.'

45

After that weekend, things went pretty quiet. Toby called me up every few days, but he didn't talk about anything important on the phone and I didn't see him. Like I said, I hadn't known him very well before, but he seemed like a different bloke from the one who'd saved my life. Harder, colder. But then perhaps I was harder and colder too. Circumstances alter personalities.

Christmas consisted of a warmed over pizza, a bottle of JD, half a dozen joints and James Bond on the box. It was one of the most miserable I'd ever spent. I got a few cards, but didn't send any back. I sent money to Judith to buy herself a present, and she called on Christmas afternoon after *Top of the Pops*, and we talked for half an hour or so. She didn't mention

Paula, and nor did I. She thanked me for my cheque and said that she and her mother were going to the sales to spend it. After we'd finished, Laura came on and said hello. She told me everything was fine. I wish I could've said the same.

The day after Boxing Day, Toby phoned me. 'How are you fixed?' he asked.

'Easy,' I replied.

'Good. It's starting. I need you tonight.'

'For what?'

'Not on an open line. I'll collect you about nine.'

'Suits me,' I said, and we broke the connection.

I was ready and waiting when he arrived and met him at the door. This time he was driving an anonymous-looking Ford and we got in. 'We've got to make a meet,' he said.

'Who with?'

'You'll see.' And he started the car, put it into gear and took off.

'I don't like surprises,' I said.

He grinned nastily. 'You'll like this one.'

From his manner I wasn't so sure.

We drove right across London in a westerly direction, past Shepherd's Bush and into the boonies of Acton. Toby spun round some side streets, up the back of a block of flats and shops and stopped on a corner. 'We're here,' he said.

'Everybody's got to be somewhere.'

He shook his head and got out of the car. I got out too. We walked back down the service road until we came to a ramp leading downwards. We took it and found ourselves in front of half a dozen lock-up garages. He led me towards the end one on our right and a figure materialized out of the gloom next to it. He was short and wiry, dressed in a windbreaker and old jeans. He nodded at Toby, ignored me and said, 'Round

218

here.' I thought I noticed a slight Irish inflection in his accent. I was beginning to have serious doubts about what was going on.

We followed the bloke down the gap formed by the wall of the garage and the wall of the building, and he rapped on a plain wooden, unpainted door and it was opened quickly.

I don't know what I expected, but inside, it was just a garage, heated by an electric fire to take off the chill and pretty well filled with an old Transit van with scabby, dark blue paintwork that stood in the light of an overhead fluorescent fixture. The door had been opened by another geezer, taller than the first, but just as scruffy.

'Is this it?' said Toby, nodding at the truck. Once again there had been no introductions.

The second geezer nodded back.

I was beginning to wonder what was going on and not particularly enjoying the vibrations.

'Let's have a look then.' Toby again.

The second geezer squeezed between us and the flanks of the motor and went and opened the back doors. I followed Toby round for a squint. Inside were several heavy-looking wooden boxes, with nasty water stains on the sides of them. Toby opened one. It was shadowy inside the back of the truck, but I'd recognize dynamite anywhere. It looked sweaty and unsafe and stank of chemicals.

'Fuck's sake,' I said. 'Is that what I think it is?'

The second geezer looked at me and said, 'Scared?'

'I'll say I'm fucking scared,' I said.

'Fucking English,' he said. Definitely Irish.

'These are old friends of mine from across the water,' said Toby. 'We met when I was over there, in the service of Queen and Country.'

'And MI6,' said the second geezer. 'Don't forget them.'

MI6. I fucking knew it.

Nice mates, I thought, but didn't vocalize the thought. These fuckers were probably armed and one more notch on their gun butts wasn't going to worry them.

'This is your master plan?' I said to Toby.

'Our way in,' he said.

'Terrific.' If it hadn't been for the thought of Dawn, I would've walked right then.

'Can you think of a better one?'

I couldn't, and didn't reply, just stood seething, the sweat of fear bubbling through my clothes.

'Not a falling out I hope,' said the first geezer. 'Just be cool, Toby. Let your mate drive.'

Toby looked at me. 'He is.'

'What?' I said.

Toby ignored me. 'Got the keys?' he said to the geezer.

'Got the cash?'

Toby put his hand inside his pocket and took out a wad of notes. The second geezer took them and ran a count. Once satisfied, he took two keys on a ring out of his pocket and tossed them to me. 'Have fun,' he said. 'Mind the bumps in the road.'

I looked at Toby. 'You're not fucking serious,' I said. 'That stuff's lethal.'

'Just what we need.'

'What do you expect me to do with it?'

'Park it somewhere for a couple of days.'

'Where?'

'Buckingham Palace would be good,' said the first geezer. 'Give the royals a welcome back after their Christmas holidays.'

'You realize it could go off?' I said.

'That's why we wanna get rid of it,' said the second geezer. 'It's a bit past its sell-by date and it got a bit damp where we were keeping it.'

'Jesus Christ, man,' I said to Toby. 'That stuff's suicide.'

'The best I could do under the circumstances.'

'Well do you want it or not?' said the first geezer.

'No, Toby,' I said.

'It's not stayin' here,' said the second geezer.

'Just till Saturday,' said Toby.

'There's people live upstairs,' I said. 'If it blows it'll bring the whole block down.'

'Too bad,' said Toby. 'What's a few more civilians more or less?'

Harder. Colder. I told you. I was beginning to sincerely dislike Toby Gillis.

'Not on my conscience,' I said.

The two Irishmen looked at each other and grinned. I was beginning to sincerely dislike them too.

'Where then?' said Toby.

I racked my brains. 'I'll drive it up to the farm,' I said. 'At least only a few squirrels'll cop for it, if it goes off there.'

'I knew you'd think of something, Nick.'

'Not a long drive, I hope,' said the first geezer with another grin at his mate.

'Bollocks,' was all I said.

I was furious with Toby, but I opened the truck and started it. And when the second geezer opened the main door of the garage, I reversed out, swung round into a tight two-point turn and drove the Transit up the ramp and into the service road.

I waited for Toby to follow me on foot, and when he caught up I jumped out of the truck and said, 'Are you fucking crazy?'

'We need it,' he said.

'There's got to be at least a hundred pounds of that shit in there. It's old, Toby. Old, damaged and unstable.'

'But cheap and available,' he said. 'And they threw in a radio detonator and transmitter.'

'We don't even know if it'll work.'

'It'll work OK. Just ask those people in Oxford Street.'

Things were going from bad to worse. 'And these guys are who I think they are?'

'Probably.'

'FIRE. Right? The cell that's been blowing the shit out of this town for the last month or so?'

Toby shrugged. 'What if they are? What do you care? Don't think about it, Nick. You shouldn't think so much. It'll get you into trouble.'

'Not so much trouble as being found in possession of the stuff in this truck.'

Toby shrugged again.

'And now I've got to drive it to Norfolk.'

'You don't have to drive it anywhere. Park it outside your house if you want.'

'Terrific, Toby. Got the keys to the cottage?'

He handed me a set.

'Come up tomorrow and collect me,' I said. 'If there's anything left *to* collect. I'm not hitchhiking to Norwich to catch a train in the morning.'

'Sure,' he replied. 'I had to make the journey there anyway. And Nick.'

'What?'

'I shouldn't smoke if I were you.' And he walked past me to his car.

46

That had to be one of the worst drives of my life. Every pothole and raised drain-cover was a nightmare. By the time I'd crossed London the sweat had soaked through my clothes.

I didn't know exactly how volatile the kit in the back was, and I wouldn't, until I was vaporized in the middle of a thirty-foot crater in the Commercial Road. *And* the bloody truck was a bitch. The sodding thing kept stalling and all I needed was a helpful copper asking me if he could lend a hand.

But at last I got out of town and on to the A12 heading through Essex. I was dying for a cigarette and a piss, but I didn't dare stop until I was away from civilization. Finally I pulled off the A143 into a side road and moved well away from the truck before I lit up. I was shaking like a cat in heat and could hardly fire up my Silk Cut. Jesus, I thought. What the fuck am I doing here?

Eventually I dragged myself back to the Transit for the remainder of the journey and got to the cottage about one.

I parked the truck up close to where Toby and I had destroyed the Peugeot, and there I left it before heading towards the cottage. I put on the kettle and found tea, sugar and powdered milk, plus a fresh packet of cream crackers, some butter that smelt all right and a piece of cheese with just a few green flecks on it in the fridge. From that I made my supper and it tasted as good as anything I'd ever eaten.

I went upstairs to the room I'd had last time and crawled between the freezing sheets, and was asleep in about five seconds flat.

The next morning I breakfasted on more of the same and lit a fire in the living room to warm the place up a little. Toby arrived around noon, when I was sure he wasn't going to bother. Believe me, by then I was pissed off to the max.

'Thanks for dropping by,' I said when he got out of his car.

'I had things to do. And the phone here's not working.'

'I know. I tried it,' I said, as drily as possible.

'Don't worry. I'm here now, and I take it the explosives are OK.'

223

'You'd've heard about it on the news if they weren't,' I said. 'Now. Isn't it about time you told me what's going on? I'm not some kind of mushroom punter who you keep in the dark and feed shit.'

He looked at me as if I was exactly that, and his look gave me the shivers up my back. I had the strangest feeling that if I wasn't necessary to the plan, Toby would have no compunction about killing me there and then and burying me under the Norfolk mud. 'Lock up,' he said brusquely. 'And we'll get out of here. I reckon you could do with a drink. I'll tell you on the way.'

I did as I was told and joined him inside the car. He drove off down the lanes and told me the plan.

'One of us takes the Transit, with the HE all primed and ready to go, smack up against the gate of the house, then bails out. Once clear, the other triggers the charge and hey presto! our entrance is clear.'

'Genius,' I said. 'Let me guess who the lucky chauffeur will be.'

'You know the vehicle.' He sounded dead serious. Like a WWI staff officer sending a regiment over the top at Ypres.

'For fuck's sake!' I said. It was almost funny. 'That stuff could blow at any second. And what happens if one of these guards starts popping off with a gun? If a bullet hit that lot, it would be good night nurse. And good night Nick and all.'

He glanced over at me and said, 'I thought you didn't care what happened to you any more.'

I glanced back. His face was set hard. 'OK, Toby,' I said. 'You're right. But it would be nice if you waited until I was out of the truck before you pressed the button.'

'Trust me, Nick,' he said.

Somehow, I thought, I'd heard that song before.

47

After that I didn't see Toby again until the big day. We'd arranged for him to meet me at Norwich Station at ten in the morning. New Year's Eve dawned cold and cloudy, but dry. Perfect weather, I thought. I dressed in a black denim shirt, black jeans, the good old and dependable Docs, my Schott leather jacket with myriad pockets, and black leather gloves. I didn't take any luggage. I figured it was pointless. If we made it I'd be back in the big smoke by the next morning and if I didn't . . . Well, there were plenty of clothes at home to dress the corpse. If there was any corpse left to dress, that was, considering the cargo I was transporting.

It *was* cold. Even colder in Norwich than it had been in London, but I hardly felt a thing. I waited close to the cab rank as arranged and Toby was bang on time. That day he was driving a gunmetal grey Jaguar XJ12. The wheel arches had been flared slightly and the motor squatted on fat, low-profile tyres like a frog waiting to leap. And leap it did, once we got out on to the dual carriageway.

'Nice car,' I said, as I relaxed into the Connolly hide of the front passenger seat. 'And never the same one twice.'

'I like to change cars a lot,' said Toby, as he effortlessly pushed the motor up to the ton. 'It keeps the opposition guessing. But this one's my favourite. And a real goer too. Top speed of a hundred and seventy, and nought to sixty in less than four seconds. Even through an automatic box. Christ knows what it'd do on a manual.'

I nodded, then changed the subject. 'Everything ready?'

'Sure. The guns are clean. I've dug up the ammunition, plus

a few other goodies I haven't told you about yet, and prepared the electric soup.'

'Do what?'

'The high explosive. The detonator's in place.'

'Is it stable?'

'Stable enough.'

'Every day I've expected to hear about a mysterious explosion in the Norfolk countryside.'

'It's OK. The weather's been cold and kept it safe.'

'It'll hot up tonight.'

'You bet.'

'So there's nothing left for us to do?'

'No.'

'Just wait.'

'That's it.'

'It's going to be a hell of a long day.'

'Don't you believe it. It'll fly.'

And it did.

We ate frugally at about nine. Over the meal I asked Toby what the deal was for collecting the money. Not that it was the most important aspect of the job, but if we survived, it would be a bonus.

'Simple,' he said. 'Mr D'Arbley is flying to the continent tonight from an airfield near the coast. It's not far from the mansion. Once we've done the job, we go up there and collect the cash.'

'Where exactly?'

'Don't you trust me?' That word again.

'Trust has got nothing to do with it,' I said. 'What happens if you don't make it? How am I expected to find him?'

'You're a pessimistic bastard, Nick, I must say.'

'But what happens?' I pressed.

'If I don't make it, you get your half and my half is paid

into my bank. I've made provisions. And if you don't make it, your half will be paid into your bank account and become part of your estate.'

'And if neither of us makes it?'

'The same. He won't rip us off.'

'So why are we seeing him at all tonight, then?'

'Because he wants to see that ring. He told me that it would make this the happiest New Year of his life.'

'Morbid, if you ask me.'

He shrugged.

'So tell me where we're due to meet him,' I said. 'Then we'll all be happy.'

'OK. The airfield is at a place called West Caister, near Great Yarmouth. It's just off the coast road. You can't miss it.'

'Fine,' I said.

'Satisfied?'

I nodded.

After we'd eaten, we got ready. We both put on our shoulder holsters and webbing belts, complete with guns. Then Toby brought out the extra goodies. Half a dozen L2A2 fragmentation grenades and two knives. Heavy fuckers. I removed mine from its sheath. It was made by Fairburn and Sykes, was perfectly balanced and had one razor-sharp cutting edge and one serrated. I pushed it home and hung the sheath on my webbing belt on the left-hand side.

The grenades gave me an idea. There was an old leather belt in one of the drawers in my room. I went upstairs and got it, took the knife and cut a thin strip of leather, doubled it through the ring of the pin on one of the grenades and tied it round my neck. 'What's the delay on this?' I asked Toby as I did it.

'I've set them at five seconds. You're fucking mad.'

'Fine. If the going gets really rough, I pull this off and bye bye anyone within . . . what?'

'Ten metres.'

'Excellent.'

'Suicide.'

'But with style.'

Toby took my shotgun and H & K with him in the Jag. I
didn't need anything to slow me down once I was out of the
Tranny and running. Plus he took the other five grenades in
a box and most of the ammunition. I just took spare clips for
the Commander and loose bullets for the .38 with me. The
plan was that I followed the Jag, he parked it up, we watched
for the chopper to arrive, then he'd come with me for the last
few hundred metres, I'd drop him off, let him get settled, then
do my bit.

It sounded simple, but then the best laid plans of mice and
men . . . .

48

The Transit started on the key and I gingerly eased it over
the rough grass back to the road where Toby was waiting
in the Jaguar. He took off slowly and I followed. I hadn't had
the nerve to look at the dynamite in the back. Things were
bad enough as they were. The journey took a little longer
than the last time, because I didn't let the Ford's speed get
above thirty, and we stopped where we'd stopped before at
precisely eleven p.m. I switched off the engine and lights and
went and joined Toby, who I noticed had parked his car a
good way away.

'Right,' he said when I was sitting next to him. 'We push
on from here in about twenty minutes. No lights. There's a
spot for me to leave the car down a lane. Then we move on.

You drop me off and give me a few minutes to get close and fix the phone lines. They all pass along this road on poles. It's almost prehistoric. Let the 'copter in, then do your thing.'

I knew the drill, but I imagined it reassured him to repeat it. The tension in the car was palpable and time crawled, but eventually he checked the illuminated dial of his watch and said, 'H-hour.'

'Good luck,' I said, touched him on the arm and got out of the Jag. My legs felt weak as I walked back to the Transit.

We pushed on again, until he swung the Jag into a side road. I pulled up and he came out of the entrance loaded down with guns and bags of ammo and joined me in the cab of the Tranny. I let out the clutch and the van moved off. A couple of minutes down the road we saw the lights of the house and I pulled in again, and we both got out to take a squint.

The outer walls were exactly as we'd seen them before, their dark bricks and the shiny barbed and electric wire brightly lit by security lights. And as before, there was no sign of human habitation in the gatehouses.

Suddenly, from a south-westerly direction, came the sound of an aero engine and a medium-sized helicopter appeared over the tree line and made for the house, its navigation lights blinking.

Toby grabbed my arm. 'Schofield,' he said. 'And Tyson too, I bet. We're on a runner.' The sound of the helicopter was deafening as it passed over our heads and hovered over the house, before dropping inside the walls.

'Back to the truck,' said Toby. 'I'll get settled here. As soon as I am, I'll flash my torch three times. Then go, go, go. And take care.'

As if I needed telling. I slapped a quick handshake and went back to the Transit, as Toby disappeared into the darkness to

229

fix the landlines and find a good spot to cover the main gate.

I slid in behind the wheel and waited. A long minute passed, then two, and I wanted to take a piss but didn't dare, and wanted to light a cigarette but didn't dare do that either. But most strongly I just wanted to get out of the vehicle and start walking and get as far away from where I was as possible. Then I saw three short flashes of light from Toby's torch and I knew the waiting was over.

49

It was now or never, and I twisted the key in the ignition and the engine caught, spluttered, then caught again, as I slammed my right foot down on the gas. I worked the clutch, put the stick into first and let the pedal bang out again. The worn tyres slid on the surface of the road, throwing gravel, and I was away.

I powered the old truck down the straight towards the gate and it picked up speed, ten miles per hour, up into second gear, twenty, thirty, third gear, thirty-five, forty, and I aimed straight at the door. Just before the road junction I slapped on the headlights, main beam, and they threw shadows across the walls like smoke and the van responded and seemed to jump forward eagerly. The gate loomed up ahead of me, and when it seemed that I must crash straight through it, I slammed down into second gear, dropped out the clutch with a jerk, spun the steering wheel hard right and pulled up the handbrake with all my strength. The Tranny attempted to do a three-sixty-degree turn, but instead its coachwork slammed into the wood of the door with a crash that shook it on its hinges, and before the truck had stopped vibrating from the force of the collision, I was out of the driver's door and running back towards Toby.

Forget my bad foot. Fear leant my legs wings. Fear. And the bullets from at least a pair of automatic weapons that kicked up dirt from the ground beneath my feet as I sprinted across the junction, the grenade that I'd hung around my neck banging on my chest.

Toby answered with automatic fire of his own and for a moment I was terrified I'd be caught in the cross, and I aimed myself slightly to the side of the muzzle flashes I saw coming out of the darkness. I was into the undergrowth and beside him within a few seconds, even though it felt like hours.

'Doesn't it work?' I blurted. Referring to the detonator. 'After all that.'

'I didn't want you to miss the fun,' he said calmly as bullets ripped through the leaves above our heads. 'And I didn't want to lose you either. I don't know how big a bang it's going to be. Hell of a sense of humour, those Irish.'

'Well do it then,' I said, and I saw him shrug in the faint reflection from the security lights as he thumbed the button on the transmitter that he held in his hand.

Jesus Christ! Fuck knows exactly what was in those boxes.

The charge went off with a sound like planets colliding and a flash as bright as the sun. I saw the Transit split in two as it jumped at least ten feet into the air, and both pieces were thrown bodily in our direction.

Smoke and dust rose in a mushroom cloud as rubble rained down around us.

Toby looked at me and said in a voice that I could hardly hear through the ringing in my ears, 'Nice work. Let's go.'

I slung the H & K over my shoulder by its strap, picked up the Winchester and a couple of bags of magazines and cartridges and we did just that.

We doubled over the road, keeping low, but temporarily at

least, no one was shooting at us. Close up, the gate was completely gone, blown to matchwood. The fronts of both gatehouses had been destroyed too, leaving complete rooms and staircases open. There were some bodies hanging down. Probably the people who'd been shooting at us. We ran through the gap made by the HE, guns at the ready, and crunched up the winding drive towards the house itself. It seemed much longer than on the plans I'd studied, but we made it.

Schofield's house was a bastardization of every architectural style of the last five hundred years. Tudor gables sat uneasily next to a Georgian wing and an old stablehouse had been converted into a twentieth-century swimming pool with glass all along one side.

A man in a dark suit, gun in hand, looking shocked, came out of a door in the right-hand side of the main building and Toby iced him with a burst from his Scorpion.

'Schofield will be inside,' he said. 'Come on. Quick.'

We headed towards the open door the man in the suit had come through and saw the helipad at the back of the poolhouse. The chopper sat like a giant insect on the tarmac. It was dark and empty, and Toby disabled it by shooting the shit out of the rear rotors. That was where we met our first serious resistance. Three blokes, also in dark suits, came barrelling round from behind the house, armed with handguns. With our ordnance it was like sending a trio of kids with peashooters to kill an elephant. Toby emptied his clip in their direction and I pulled the trigger of the Winchester, pumped the action and fired again. All three went down. I checked them whilst Toby changed magazines. They were out of the game. I kicked their guns off into the shadows and we made for the open door again, me in front.

Inside was a corridor, thickly carpeted and dimly lit. It was empty. But not for long. A geezer in a tracksuit carrying a big automatic appeared at the end. He fired and the bullet gouged into the plasterwork beside me. I returned fire, aiming low, and blew his legs from under him. As he went down the gun bounced on the pile of the Wilton. He lay where he fell, moaning gently. I didn't examine the wreckage of his legs, but it was for sure he wouldn't be going to any barndances in the near future.

'Is the boss in?' I asked as I picked up his pistol and stuck it in my belt.

'Bollocks.'

'Nasty,' I said and kicked him in the face.

Politeness costs nothing, my old Nan used to say.

Toby and I stepped over the injured man and headed deeper into the house. At the end of the corridor was another door. I kicked it open, waited for a reaction, got none, dropped down on to my face and peered round the doorpost. On the other side was a panelled hall. Empty. Twin staircases went up to a mezzanine floor. I looked up at Toby and he looked down at me. 'You take the right, I'll take the left,' he said.

It seemed like a fair deal, so that's what we did.

50

When we got upstairs the mezzanine was deserted. At the far end of the floor were a set of ornamental wooden doors. I tried the handles. They were locked. Toby took out his Colt Commander and fired three shots into the mechanisms. Then he kicked at them with his booted foot and they swung open. He went through first, fanning the room inside with his automatic. I was close behind, shotgun at the ready.

As we burst in, two pairs of frightened eyes turned in our direction. The eyes belonged to two women in party frocks who were huddled together by a huge fireplace where a pile of logs burned fiercely. The room was dimly lit, full of shadows that danced in time to the flames from the fire. Both women were still holding champagne flutes. 'Happy New Year,' I said. 'Where's our host?'

One of the women, a picture in pink tulle, said, 'He's upstairs. Who are you? What are you doing here?'

'Santa's little helpers, bringing the compliments of the season,' I replied, looking towards another staircase that led upwards into darkness. The bloody place was massive. At this rate we'd be here all night.

'Come on,' said Toby. 'Let's find him.' And he made for the foot of the stairs. I hung the Winchester over my shoulder, brought the Heckler & Koch into play and followed him, the barrel of my machine gun swinging in front of me. We reached the stairs and started upward, Toby slightly in the lead, when a shot rang out from above and I saw and heard the bullet hit him high on his right shoulder at the front.

He dropped his pistol, cried out at the shock and pain of the impact and fell back, grabbing at the banister for support with his good arm. I heard the explosion of another shot from the shadows above and fired a long burst at where I'd seen the muzzle flash. I heard a scream and a body fell towards us out of the dark, a large-calibre revolver bouncing down in front of it.

'You OK?' I asked Toby, as he leant against the banister. Stupid question.

'I'll survive,' he said, his face contorted with pain, as he bent down and picked up his gun. 'Go on. I'll follow.'

'You sure?'

'Piss off.'

He followed me as I climbed the stairs. At the top, I squinted round the corner and saw an ornately decorated hall with thick-pile Persian carpet underfoot. I moved round and bullets whacked off the wood panels and splinters cut at my face. I fell flat and emptied the magazine of the MP5K into the shadows at the other end, dropped it, pulled the sling of the Winchester over my head and blew several thousand pounds' worth of antique carpentry to hell and gone. I heard a cry and a body fell full length on to the floor in front of me. I reached for my machine gun, ejected the mag and reloaded, then filled the Winchester's hungry maw with cartridges, never taking my eyes off the body in front of me for a second.

From behind I heard Toby call, 'You all right?'

'Sure,' I shouted back. 'Come up and give me cover.'

He did just that, and I scuttled along the carpet and checked the body. Brown bread. The killing floor was getting bigger all the time.

The hallway stretched in both directions from where I was and I heard a movement along the right-hand leg and saw a face pop round the corner. It was Tyson, and I pulled the trigger of the H & K. He ducked back and the bullets were wasted. But I remembered what D'Arbley had said, 'Where Tyson is, Schofield is,' and I grinned to myself, turned and beckoned to Toby and set off down the hall in pursuit.

51

I chased Tyson along the corridor and up two flights of stairs. I could've shot the fucker in the back any time, but I didn't. When I killed him, I wanted to be looking at his face and him at mine.

He ran into a room, slammed the door behind him and I heard locks click shut. I shot the shit out of them with the big Winchester, buckshot ploughing into the wood of the door and frame, tearing and ripping lumps of wood away from the metal they covered, and I worked the action of the pump, once, twice, three times, before the door sagged on its hinges and I kicked it open. He was fumbling in the drawer of a bedside table and came up with a small automatic pistol. I walked through the smoke from the shotgun and slapped it out of his hands as he frantically tried to work a cartridge into the action.

'You a driver?' I demanded.

'What?'

'Driver. You drive?'

He nodded. 'What's that got to do with anything? What do you want?' he asked.

'I talk, you listen,' I said, slamming him in the mouth with the butt of my shotgun, so that teeth broke and his gums oozed blood.

'Dunstable,' I said. 'Last spring. A little Renault with two women inside. You wrecked the fucker. Killed them. You or someone else here.'

'No. No. You're wrong. I don't know what you're talking about,' he said through his damaged mouth.

'Bollocks,' I said, put the shotgun up and took the automatic pistol I'd lifted from the guard in the corridor from inside the waistband of my jeans and racked the slide. It was a Glock niner. Good gun. I shot Tyson in the kneecap. He screamed and collapsed as the bone disintegrated into a mist of blood. I kicked him in the head and I sensed someone behind me. I turned and there was a woman in a white dress standing in the doorway holding a white leather handbag. She looked kind of apologetic, like she'd walked into the men's toilet by mistake, and I gut shot her. Blood bloomed on the white material and she banged back against the doorframe and slid down into a sitting position, then keeled over on to her side. I went over and kicked her handbag down the hallway in case she was carrying. She looked up at me with a pleading expression, but I just left her where she was lying. What the fuck did I care about her? She was just another crim's whore as far as I was concerned. Good riddance. I went back to Tyson.

'Where's your boss?' I demanded.

'I don't know. Upstairs in the observatory, at the top of the house. He looks at the stars. He's never hurt anyone.'

'That's not what I heard.'

'I swear . . .'

Then Toby came into the room. His face was white and drawn with pain and I could see blood trickling off the end of the fingers of his right hand. In his left he carried his .38. 'Good, Nick. You found him,' he said, and shot Tyson in the head.

Minimum de blah, blah. Maximum de ya ya.

'Do it quickly,' he said. 'If you let them talk too much, you can get too friendly to do it at all.'

Tyson's body lay spreadeagled on the light-coloured carpet of the room, blood puddling around his head. One down, one to go.

'Who's she?' said Toby, gesturing back to the girl.

I shrugged. 'Who knows? Schofield's upstairs in some kind of observatory.'

'Let's go find him.'

52

We left Tyson where he was, ignored the wounded woman and went back into the hallway. 'There should be more stairs down at the end,' I said.

There were, and they were covered by armed men. We walked straight into them. By then we must've been getting complacent. When we got to the foot of the stairs, we were met by a hail of bullets. One went so close by my head that I felt the draught. Toby caught one in his thigh and went down. I returned fire, then dragged him back round the corner and sat him against the wall.

'Shit,' he said. 'This doesn't look like it's going to be my year.'

'I'll get you sorted,' I said. 'But we've got to clear this lot out. There's more guards here than we thought.'

'What do you suggest?' he asked.

'Easy,' I replied, reached inside my shirt, pulled the grenade off the thong that held it, felt the release lever fly off and I popped round the corner again and threw it underhand up the stairs.

There were sounds of panic from above, and then the grenade went off. The building shook and I heard screams and a cloud of smoke and dust belched down the stairwell. I ran up through it, Colt Commander at the ready. There were a couple of guys lying at the head of the stairs, bleeding profusely, and I pumped bullets into them to make sure they were dead. Another geezer was dragging himself down the hallway like an injured crab and I shot him in the back. He fell forward on to his face and lay still.

After that there was silence and I went back for Toby. He was in a bad way. He'd lost a lot of blood and he abandoned his carry weapons. I helped him up the flight of stairs to what I hoped was the top floor.

We moved cautiously along the corridor. At the end were another set of double doors. I tried the handle of one. It was unlocked. I pushed it open and found the observatory. It was dimly lit and packed with antique furniture and telescopes that ranged from what looked like the first one ever made, up to the latest hi-tech, state-of-the-art instruments. The ceiling was made of glass and obviously rolled back when the weather was more clement. Tonight it was closed. The room stank of smoke, and inside was a man I recognized as Schofield from the photograph I'd seen. His identity was confirmed by the fancy ruby and diamond ring he wore on the little finger of his left hand. He was standing by a refectory table and looked at the pair of us calmly. He too was dressed in evening clothes and was unarmed. I helped Toby inside the room, closed the door behind us and turned the key in the lock.

'So you made it,' Schofield said.

'That's right,' I replied.

'I've been expecting something like this for some time.'

'Hence your private army.'

'Exactly. You did well.'

'We had the element of surprise on our side.'

'We had the force of numbers.'

'But we were motivated.'

'By what? Money?'

'Hardly. Though there is money involved. No. It goes deeper than that.'

'Shoot him, Nick,' said Toby from where he was leaning against the wall, blood dripping from his hand and leg and forming a small pool on the floor.

'Plenty of time, Toby,' I said. 'I've been waiting for this moment for months.'

'Do it,' Toby insisted. 'Then we can get out of here. I need a doctor.'

'You'll be all right, don't worry.'

'Do you really think you'll get out of here alive?' asked Schofield.

'We got in,' I said. 'And shot your security to shit. I dare say we'll get out too. But you won't.'

'Your friend doesn't look like he's going to get very far, whatever happens,' said Schofield.

'He'll survive,' I said. 'Like I said, he's motivated by more than cash.'

'By what though?'

'By the fact that his wife is dead because of you.'

Schofield looked long and hard at Toby. 'And mine too,' I added.

Schofield's eyes came back to me. 'I very much doubt that,' he said. 'I'm just a businessman after all.'

'Dodgy business.'

'Commodities. We all have to make a living.'

'But such commodities.'

'Oil, comestibles, pharmaceuticals. What's wrong with that?'

'Pharmaceuticals. That's a good word for them.'

'What?'

'Drugs.'

He looked confused. 'Yes. Medicines. Why shouldn't I help with relieving the world's pain?'

'You certainly have a way with words,' I said. 'The world's pain. That's a nice way to put it.'

'But it's true.'

'What? Killing kids with dope?'

'No,' said Schofield. 'No. Helping them survive.'

'Do it,' hissed Toby. 'Quickly.'

'All right, Toby,' I said, then brought my gun up in Schofield's direction and said, 'You're dead, Mr Schofield.'

'What did you call me?'

'Schofield,' I replied. 'What should I call you?'

He almost laughed. 'You bloody fool,' he said. 'You should call me by my name. D'Arbley. Jason Alexander D'Arbley. Now I know *exactly* what this is all about.'

I stood stock still, the gun still aimed at his body. 'D'Arbley,' I repeated. 'No.'

'He's lying,' said Toby, pushing himself away from the wall and reaching for the .38 under his arm, his movements slow and awkward because of his injured right shoulder. 'For Christ's sake, do it. If you won't, I will.'

I turned my pistol on him. 'Leave the gun alone and stay right where you are, Toby,' I said. Then to the man I'd been told was Schofield: 'Prove it. Prove you are who you say you are.'

He walked slowly over to the desk that stood in one corner of the room and made as if to open the top drawer.

'Stand back,' I ordered.

He did as he was told, and covering both him and Toby, I opened the drawer myself. Inside was a birth certificate in D'Arbley's name, a death certificate for his wife Jennifer from 1992, and birth and death certificates for his daughter Susan. She'd been eighteen when she died, in the spring of last year as it was now. Cause of death – drug overdose. And there were hundreds of photos of him with a girl, who matured from babyhood to teenage in them. It was not the same girl as in the photographs I'd seen at the office in Bloomsbury. In the earlier ones they were with a woman I took to be his wife and the girl's mother. Exactly as the other one had told me. And I'd swallowed it whole. All lies. Bastard.

I looked at them for a minute, then let them run through my fingers back into the drawer and closed it quietly.

He said, 'Let me take something from my pocket.'

'Go on then. But slowly.'

Gingerly he extracted the clincher. A British passport in the name of D'Arbley with his photo on page three.

'Oh, Toby,' I said. 'You fucker. You conned me. Both of you.'

'No. He's lying.'

'No, man. *You're* lying.'

Toby said nothing in reply.

I took it as an affirmative. 'All along, you bastard. Why?'
I'd known there was something going on. Why didn't I do
anything about it?

'You wanted to be conned. It was easy.'

I shook my head. 'No.'

'Yes.'

'It was *all* lies.'

'That's right.'

'So that guy . . .' I felt sick. 'The one who hired us for this.
He was . . .'

'Who do you think?'

'Schofield,' interrupted D'Arbley.

'You know him?' I said.

'I should. He was my partner for years. Until I caught him
doing exactly what you've accused me of.'

'Drugs.'

'Yes.'

'Using your company.'

'*Our* company.'

'Christ.'

'That's why I have such heavy security. I had him put away.
He promised revenge.'

'You've just seen it,' I said.

'So I gathered.'

I thought of all the people we'd hurt. Killed. Mutilated.
The woman in the white dress who I'd shot down in cold
blood.

I'd wanted my pound of flesh so badly that I hadn't done
my research properly. I'd gone along with the big lie like a
kid who believed in Father Christmas. I should've asked Chas
if he knew D'Arbley himself. I should've done a lot of things.
Then it's possible none of this mess would've happened.

'Christ,' I said. 'What have we done?'

I heard Toby snicker and turned the gun back on him again.

'And there was only ever going to be one of us going to meet D'Arbley, I mean Schofield, at the airfield tonight – you.'

'You're getting it.'

'And what's the betting you even told me lies about that?'

He shrugged.

'So where *is* the meet?'

Another shrug.

'Shit.' I suddenly thought of something else. 'So what *did* happen to Jackie?' I asked.

'She killed herself, just like I said.'

'Why?'

'Remember I told you about the place we bought being a natural harbour for smuggling?'

My turn to nod.

'I *did* go along with the deal. Jackie didn't. She couldn't cope.'

'Schofield's deal?'

He nodded.

'You cunt.'

'It's no concern of yours.'

'Yes it is. She was my friend and I put you two together.'

He shrugged yet again and I shot him. I emptied the last bullets from the magazine of the Glock into his chest and he fell on to the hard floor and lay still.

I looked over at the real D'Arbley. 'Who was the young kid?' I asked.

'Who?' he said back.

'They said his name was Tyson.'

'It is. He works for me. I've got him on the trail of Schofield. He's a private detective. Works for an agency.'

'Was,' I corrected him. 'He's dead. He must've got too close. That was what was behind all this I imagine. You were after Schofield because of what happened to your daughter. Right?'

'Right.'

'He's a big-time drug importer. She died of a drug overdose. Two and two makes four. Yeah? So you were after him and he was after you too? That's why you said you'd been expecting someone. Right?'

'Right again.'

'Shit. And he needed a mug punter to do his dirty work for him. And somehow he found out about me. And that I knew him . . .' I gestured towards Toby's body. 'And that I'd trust him because of what we'd been through before. And then he tells me that you're the one behind my wife's death. Shit. Jesus, I don't believe I fell for it so easily.'

'You messed this one up, didn't you?' D'Arbley said.

'Sort of.'

From behind the double doors I heard movement, and the phone on the refectory table rang. He made a move towards it, and I dropped the empty gun I was holding and dragged the Colt Commander from the holster slung around my waist. 'Not so fucking fast,' I said. 'You're not talking to anyone.'

'It's only an internal phone,' he said. And I remembered that Toby had cut the landlines.

'Wait,' I said.

'Give up. You're finished,' said D'Arbley.

'No,' I replied. 'The real Schofield's somewhere close. I know it. Are there any small airfields round here?'

'Half a dozen or more.'

'Shit.' The phone kept ringing. It was getting on my nerves. 'Answer that for Christ's sake,' I said. 'And don't get clever.' I needed time to think.

He did as he was told. 'Everything's under control,' he said to whoever was at the other end, after a moment.

I looked at my watch. Twelve-twenty-five. It seemed like hours since the truck had blown and it had been less than thirty minutes. I wondered how long the real Schofield would wait.

'Stay where you are,' D'Arbley said into the phone. 'On no account try and get in here. I'll call you back.' And he put down the receiver.

'I've bought you some time,' he said.

'And yourself.'

'You're not going to hurt me.'

'Your people don't know that.'

'So what now?'

'Now I go and find the real Schofield.'

'How?'

'Christ knows.'

'I'll send some of my men with you.'

What's left of them, I thought. 'I'm going on my own.'

'You're going nowhere.'

'Then he gets away. If you're anything like the fake D'Arbley pretended to be, you're not into torture. So you'll never know where he is.'

'What do you want then?'

'Free passage out of here. I haven't exactly enamoured myself to what's left of your security force. They'd as soon shoot me out of hand I expect. They're not going to like me walking away, but that's how it's got to be. I'll start looking where he –' I gestured at Toby's still body again – 'told me Schofield was going to be. I'll find him somehow.'

I saw the emotions on D'Arbley's face as he thought about it.

'OK,' he said after a minute. 'You win.'

'Use the phone. Tell your people we're coming out together, and that I'm to be allowed to leave unharmed. Tell them to be cool. I'm armed, and I'll kill you if anyone tries to stop me.'

He nodded, picked up the phone and tapped out a three-digit number.

Car keys, I thought, as he did so. I needed the keys to the Jag. Still keeping my gun on him, I went over to Toby's body and went through the pockets of his leather jacket. The keys were in the right-hand one. There was a piece of paper in there too, folded into quarters. It was dog-eared and dirty and as D'Arbley spoke on the telephone I unfolded it. It was a simple map, showing A- and B-roads. At one end of the route was doodled a house like the one we were in, at the other, a crude aeroplane. That was it. That was where Schofield was waiting. 'You should've destroyed it, Toby,' I whispered.

D'Arbley put down the phone. 'Everything's OK,' he said. 'They understand.'

'Good,' I replied. 'Give me your ring.'

'What?'

'You heard. That ring you're wearing on your little finger. Give it to me.'

'Why?'

'Just do it.'

'My wife gave it to me—'

'Too bad.' I raised the Colt.

'OK, OK. Relax,' he said, and pulled the ring from his finger and laid it on the desk. I went over and got it, then went back and put it on Toby's little finger, took the heavy knife from the sheath on my belt and slammed the blade down, severing the digit from his hand. The wound didn't bleed. Dead people don't.

I picked up the ring and finger, and put them into my jacket pocket. 'That should convince him,' I said to no one in particular.

I knew then that I was going mad.

'Let's go,' I said to D'Arbley. 'And remember, this gun is loaded.'

53

I left the Winchester behind, slung the MP5K and a satchel full of magazines over my left shoulder, and holding the Colt Commander in my right hand, barrel pointing down towards the floor, I gestured for D'Arbley to unlock and open the doors. He did, and with him slightly in front of me, we left the observatory together.

There were maybe half a dozen geezers waiting for us in the hallway outside. All in suits and all carrying firearms of one kind or another. There *had* been a lot more guards than Toby had said. Christ knows how we'd got as far as we did.

'Put those down,' said D'Arbley sharply as we passed through the doorway. 'You heard my orders.'

All the guns vanished beneath dark blue and grey serge as one, and we passed through the crowd of security men who moved aside to give us free passage and me a whole bunch of dirty looks.

We walked along the hall and I saw D'Arbley wince at the damage the grenade had done. There were no signs of any bodies. He didn't know the half of it and I started to worry about the possible intervention of the emergency services. This lot was going to be a bit difficult to explain to the local coppers. We went downstairs past the room where Toby had killed Tyson and I'd shot the girl in white, and down once more to where Toby had been hit for the first time. There was no sign of the two frightened women now, or the dead gunman, apart from bloodstains on the stairs. We walked on to the mezzanine and down the last long flight of stairs to the front door. 'Open it,' I ordered. 'We're going to take a little walk, you and I. Not far. Just down to the road.'

D'Arbley did as he was told and together we went down the front steps, across the turnaround at the front of the house where I imagined I felt gunsights on my back, and down the drive to the wreckage of the gatehouses and the front wall.

'You did a lot of damage between you,' said D'Arbley.

'Two-man army,' I said. 'Not far now.'

We picked our way through the rubble and on to the public road. 'I'll leave you here,' I said. 'Don't let anyone be foolish enough to try and follow me. I'll kill them if they do.'

He nodded.

'I don't know what to say about what happened here tonight,' I said.

'There's nothing you can say.'

'But I can try and get it right when I find Schofield.'

'If you find him.'

'I will.'

'Do it then.'

'Watch the news,' I said. 'With a bit of luck it'll be on in the morning.'

'I will,' he said.

'If I come out of this alive, what happens?' I asked.

'What do you mean?'

'I've done a lot of damage. Killed a lot of your people. You're a powerful man. You've got the real Schofield running scared and he seems to have a lot of friends. I'm all on my own. What happens?'

'The people you killed were paid to take chances. Soldiers.' Like all rich men, he was ruthless.

'Not all of them,' I interrupted. 'There was a girl.' I described her and her dress.

'Tyson's assistant,' he said. 'She was sweet.'

'I'm sorry.' The words hardly rippled the surface of the way I really felt.

'Make penance,' he said. 'Nothing I could do would make you feel worse than you do already.'

He was right there.

'I'll try.'

'Good luck. Maybe we'll meet again.'

'Maybe,' I replied. And with that I left him and headed towards where Toby had parked the Jaguar.

I found it with no bother, tossed the H & K on to the back seat with the satchel, sat for a moment looking at the map I'd found in Toby's jacket in the dim glow of the courtesy light, then took off.

Trying to drive, read the hand-drawn map and work out what to do all at the same time wasn't easy. I had too many conflicting thoughts running through my head. All those people. All those innocent people.

But at least the car handled like a dream. That was a plus, and I socked it down the B1140 as fast as I dared. Which was pretty fast, let me tell you, and when I looked over at the passenger seat, Dawn was sitting there.

'*Happy New Year,*' she said.

Then I was convinced I was going Radio Rental. 'Not for some,' I replied. It was as if she'd never been away.

She shrugged. '*Got any music, Nick?*' she asked.

I put on the radio and fiddled with the dial until I pulled in some continental FM station. The DJ was jabbering away and I was just about to find something else when I heard him say 'Jim Morrison', and on came 'Riders on the Storm' by the Doors. Heavy duty spooksville. I turned up the volume and the sound of thunder and rain filled the car just as I hit the A1064. I touched a hundred and forty on the dual carriageway, almost too fast for the headlights, but traffic was non-existent and I was at the turnoff for the B1152 almost before I knew it. I had to slow on the narrow two-lane highway, and as the song finished, Dawn said, *'So what are you going to do?'*

'Fuck knows.'

'You'd better think of something.'

'I'm sick and tired of it, Dawn,' I said. 'I've had enough.'

'That's fair. It's about time you got on with your life.'

'You reckon? After all that happened tonight?'

I knew she'd know. *'Sure. Why not just take the money and get lost? Go somewhere where you can enjoy it.'*

'Sounds like a good plan. How's Daisy and Tracey?'

'Fine.'

'Good.'

'This is it, Nick,' she said. *'I'm going now, and I won't be back until we're going to be together permanently.'*

'Fair enough.'

'Thanks for thinking of me.'

'I'll never stop.'

'I know. You poor fucker.' And when I looked again the passenger seat was empty.

I almost missed the turning on to the unnumbered road that led directly to the airstrip, but caught it just in time. In front of me the countryside was pitch black and I wondered if I was on a wild goose chase.

But then, I caught the flash of a light off to my left, saw a track leading in that direction and steered the car on to it. There was an open five-bar gate in front of me and dimly through the windscreen I could see the silhouette of a low building, and next to it, the shape of a medium-sized plane.

54

The landing strip was made of crumbling tarmac and the control tower was an old Quonset hut left over from the war. But the plane looked fit, and as I bounced the motor on to the hardtop and up to the hut, the door opened and Simon, the butler/bouncer from the real Schofield's office appeared, hauling a Sig Sauer nine-millimetre semi-automatic. I got out of the motor and walked towards him, hands away from my body. I left the H & K on the back seat where I'd thrown it.

'You,' said Simon.

'In the flesh.'

'Where's Toby?'

'Dead.'

He didn't seem very perturbed. 'The boss is inside,' was all he said.

'Then let's go and see him. By the way, Happy New Year.'

He didn't echo my sentiments. Miserable son of a bitch.

We went into the hut. It was warm inside, courtesy of a Calorgas fire in one corner. The real Schofield was sitting on a straight-backed chair, sipping at a hip flask. Another bloke, one I hadn't seen before, dressed in a long cashmere-looking overcoat, sat on the edge of a scarred old desk. Another stranger, in leather jacket, jeans and boots, about my age and height, who I took to be the pilot, was pouring coffee from a thermos. They all stopped what they were doing when I walked in with Simon.

251

'Morning,' I said.

'You,' said Schofield, just like Simon.

'The one and only.'

'Where's Toby?' Just like Simon again. No 'Glad to see you' or anything like that.

I told him what I'd told his employee.

'And he told you where we were due to meet?'

'He left me a map.'

'What about Schofield?'

Things were getting confusing and I had to think carefully. 'He's dead too. And Tyson and a good percentage of the security force at the house.'

'How do I know you're telling the truth?'

'There was some talk about a ring,' I said.

'That's correct.'

'There you go,' I said, and pulled out the ring, still attached to Toby's finger, and tossed it on to Schofield's lap. He jumped about a mile, shoved it off and it lay on the floor in front of us.

'Satisfied?' I asked.

'What the fu—?' said the geezer in the cashmere nanny.

'Proof of purchase,' I interrupted. 'In exchange for the jack-pot prize.'

Schofield broke his gaze away from the finger on the floor, and looked at me. 'Take out your gun,' he said. 'And put it on the floor.' Obviously he'd got wind of my mental state too. A normal person doesn't go around with a finger in his pocket. At least not someone else's.

Simon brought the Sig round to bear on me and I did as I was told.

'Search him, Simon,' said Schofield. 'Keep him covered, Jacko.'

The bloke in the overcoat pulled out a gun of his own,

which he pointed at me, and Simon put his away, came up behind me and relieved me of my .38 and the knife.

'Check the car,' said the big boss.

Simon went outside and we waited. He came back carrying the H & K and the bag of magazines, which he added to the arsenal on the floor. 'That's it, chief,' he said. 'I looked in the boot.'

Now they were either going to kill me or pay me off. I fancied the former but I was wrong. Not that I cared much either way. Schofield got up and fetched a briefcase from where it was standing next to the desk. Just one, I noticed. And put it on the top. 'Do you want to count it?' he asked.

I walked over, thumbed the catches and opened the case. Inside were bundles of new banknotes, all neatly banded in packs of ten thousand quid.

'I trust you,' I said.

'So go,' said Schofield.

I wished then I'd had a gun, or the knife, or the hand grenade I'd hung round my neck. Then he wouldn't be able to dismiss me so easily. If I'd had a weapon, I'd've killed him there and then.

But instead I picked up the case, flipped him a carefree salute and left the hut, got into the Jag and drove away.

55

But I didn't go far. I stopped the car just beyond the gate, switched off the engine and lights and got out. I found a pack of cigarettes and a lighter in my pocket and lit one. I stood there for maybe twenty minutes, looking through the darkness, smoking and thinking about what had happened that night, before I saw the four men walk to the plane and get on board. I heard the cough of the twin starter motors and the engines roared into life.

Go home, I thought. Go home and get on with your life, and I looked through the side window of the car at the case full of money on the passenger seat.

Sod it. That was too easy.

I ran round the Jag, jumped in behind the wheel, switched on, selected reverse and put it into a screaming turn until I faced the gate once more. I drove slowly through the gap and bumped over the grass until I reached the tarmac again and was facing the plane that was just beginning to move. I put the motor into neutral, revved the engine up to the red line until the car was shaking on its wheels, then slapped the stick into 'Drive'. The rear end dropped, the bonnet reared up in front of me and with a scream from the back tyres, smoke and the acrid smell of rubber, the Jaguar took off towards the aircraft. The G-force pushed me back into the leather of the driver's seat, the needle on the speedo spun round the clock and hit fifty in the blink of an eye and I saw the plane moving at a forty-five-degree angle away from me. I pushed harder on the accelerator, twitched the steering wheel to the right and saw the white blob of the pilot's face, his eyes wide. I glanced to my left and Dawn was in the passenger seat again. She turned and winked at me, and I almost stood on the fast pedal as the shape of the plane filled the windscreen, as it struggled to take off.

So this is what it feels like, I thought.

Good job.

56

From the early editions of the *Daily Telegraph*, 2 January 1996:

FOUR DIE IN MYSTERY PLANE CRASH

At least four people were found dead in the burnt out wreckage of a car and a small passenger plane, destroyed in what would appear to be a collision between the two vehicles at a lonely airfield near Great Yarmouth in Norfolk, early on New Year's Day. A police spokesman stated that an explosion was reported by a passing motorist on the B1152 at approximately 1.30 am.

It is thought that the car was a late model Jaguar saloon, and the aircraft has been identified as a twin-engined Beechcraft of American manufacture. It is not known whether the aircraft was taking off or landing at the time of the collision, although the driver who saw the explosion, when interviewed said that he had not seen a plane coming down to land prior to it.

The Civil Aviation Authority has stated that no aircraft submitted a flight plan to or from the airstrip, which has been the subject of local speculation over the past few years that it has been used as a landing place for drug smugglers.

The body of a man was recovered from close to the scene of the incident and, as the car appears to be empty, it is surmised that he was the driver. Early indications are that he died from head injuries.

He carried no identification and is described as white, aged between 30 and 40, six feet tall, with dark hair, dressed in jeans, a leather jacket and Doctor Marten's boots.

Any information on the incident or the identity of any of the victims should be reported to Police Headquarters in Norwich, or at any local station.